What did she want fr(
He could smell her f(
femininity. Expectation l
whet his lips. His muscle

MW00625689

Stacy saw her own end in the cauterizing fire consuming his gaze. She saw her death in the abrupt angles and hollows that altered his handsome looks into something lethally gaunt and ravenous. She'd awakened the demon residing within the man, and now she would pay the price He was a dangerous animal facing the confines of an unpleasant and potentially deadly trap. Only his curiosity held him at bay. But just in case his protective instincts got the better of him, she eased the small silver cross around from where it had dangled at the back of her neck. It flashed as it caught the room's muted light.

His gaze riveted to the crucifix. His nostrils flared, and his breath exhaled in a soft hiss. He spoke with a cutting tone.

"What do you want? Money? A promotion? Your own company? Name your blackmail."

"I want your blood."

Praise for Nancy Gideon's Midnight Series

"From a unique potion of love, betrayal, witchcraft, blackmail, voodoo, passion, intrigue, chilling villains, suspense and understanding, Nancy Gideon creates a thrilling love story. Stellar! Six Stars!" —Pathways to Darkness on *Midnight Enchantment*

"Awesome! Full of action and complex character interaction. Technically brilliant! Five Stars out of five!" —Paranormal Romance Reviews on *Midnight Gamble*

"Look out, Buffy! Another wonderful treat from Nancy Gideon!" —New Age Bookshelf on *Midnight Gamble*

Other "Midnight" Books by Nancy Gideon

Available from ImaJinn Books

Midnight Enchantment
Midnight Gamble

From Pinnacle (Out of Print)

Midnight Kiss
Midnight Temptation
Midnight Surrender

MIDNIGHT REDEEMER

⫸ ❤ ⫷

Nancy Gideon

*For Dawn —
heave the
lights on !*

*Nancy
Gideon*

ImaJinn
Books

MIDNIGHT REDEEMER

Published by ImaJinn Books, a division of ImaJinn

Copyright ©2000 by Nancy Gideon

Printed and bound in the United States of America. All rights reserved. No part of this book may be reproduced in any form or by any means (electronic, mechanical, photocopying, recording, or otherwise) without prior written permission of both the copyright holder and the above publisher of this book, except by a reviewer, who may quote brief passages in a review. For information, address: ImaJinn Books, a division of ImaJinn, P.O. Box 162, Hickory Corners, MI 49060-0162; or call toll free 1-877-625-3592.

ISBN: 1-893896-17-X

10 9 8 7 6 5 4 3 2 1

PUBLISHER'S NOTE:
This book is a work of fiction. Names, characters, places and incidents are products of the author's imagination or are used fictitiously. Any resemblance to actual events or locales or persons, living or dead, is entirely coincidental.

Books are available at quantity discounts when used to promote products or services. For information please write to: Marketing Division, ImaJinn Books, P.O. Box 162, Hickory Corners, MI 49060-0162, or call toll free 1-877-625-3592.

Cover design by Patricia Lazarus

ImaJinn Books, a division of ImaJinn
P.O. Box 162, Hickory Corners, MI 49060-0162
Toll Free: 1-877-625-3592
http://www.imajinnbooks.com

ONE

What was there to live for?

She leaned over the rail, letting the cold bay breeze scour the tears from her cheeks. She'd cried enough of them over the past few days. Useless, self-deluding tears. Now it was time to take action, to strike back at the man who had broken her heart with his careless and, she had just discovered, meaningless promises.

She'd show him.

She'd make him sorry.

On an evening as depressing as her mood—gray, bleak and endlessly uninviting—she had the pier to herself. An increase in the wind swept away the fog and drizzle, leaving a night as cold and unsentimental as her lover's heart. The clarity of sight made carrying out her plan more difficult. The Sound's angry, early-spring surf seethed about the pilings below, nearly frightening her from her resolve as she dashed the moisture from her eyes. So far down. She silently cursed the nearly full moon for illuminating the restless waters, just as she'd cursed the confrontation that woke her to her true situation.

She could come back . . .

A jagged laugh spilled out. *Oh, sure. Come back later when the conditions are more favorable for suicide.* She hiccuped, on the edge of hysteria. It had taken her all afternoon in a smoky bar to find the courage to come this far.

She couldn't back down now. Such cowardice would make her deserving of her former lover's scorn even within her own broken heart. There was no going back.

To fortify herself, she recalled words that brought her to this fateful brink of self-destruction.

I never had any intention of leaving my wife. Where would you get such an idea? What we had was...recreation. Vacation's over. Time to get back to the real world, and that's my family. I never meant to hurt or mislead you...

So much for good intentions. Sobs threatened to overwhelm her again.

Fool, fool, fool.

She stretched out her arms and opened cramped fingers, releasing a spill of crumpled cash. Hush money. An indifferent wind snatched it from her palms. She watched with a sense of woeful satisfaction as the small fortune whirled crazily on the air currents, spiraling to the water below, in a path she would follow soon. How much had her hopes, her dreams—her love—been worth? She'd never counted, but they couldn't be silenced by a finite stack of guilty payoff stuffed into her purse as he'd hurried her out the door and out of his life.

She didn't want his cash. She wanted him to ache inside with remorse. She wanted him to weep when he heard the news. She wanted him to regret, as she did, the lack of integrity that had him hiding a wife and three kids from her until her emotions were too deeply ensnared to separate decency from desire.

She didn't want it to be easy for him to forget her.

She slipped one leg over the rail, then the other, struggling for a toehold on slick cement. She hadn't counted on the pull of wind being so strong. Instinctively, she clung to the rail to keep from being plucked off the narrow ledge. Then she laughed, the sound disappearing into the thinning mists. Wasn't that the idea?

Contrarily, she couldn't get her hands to let go.

What the hell was she doing?

Sanity slipped briefly through the haze of whiskey sours and self-pity.

Was she ready to die for that weasely bastard who had lied to her then cheerfully went on about his suburban life? Sobs and indecision shook through her.

But what did she have to go back to? She'd boasted of her impending marriage. She'd introduced her lover to her family, to her friends. By now, everyone knew of her humiliation. Working in the same office complex, she would be forced to see him every single day as he left the building on his way home to his unsuspecting wife and kiddies. Many had known all along that he was married and only out for some 'recreation,' but not a one of them had said a word when a word would have saved her from damnation.

How they must have laughed in the coffee room over her naivete. She choked on her mortification. Had he laughed the hardest and the loudest? No more. No more laughter at her expense.

The last laugh would be hers.

On the seat of her car she'd left a note—a wonderfully descriptive note of farewell.

Let him share the shame burning inside her. Let him squirm with the inconvenience of answering their questions when the police came to his nice suburban front door. Let him explain his involvement to his family, his friends. Let him endure their looks, their suspicions, their blame.

Let him try to go to sleep every night with her blood on his hands.

Let the conscience he didn't know he had writhe with the knowledge that he had killed her.

What a sweet revenge.

She freed one hand while closing her eyes and breathing deep to release her fears. Just then, a strong gust swept along the pier, hitting her like a propelling shove to the chest. Her feet slipped. First one arm, then both pinwheeled wildly. And she was falling.

No . . . !

Help me!

I don't want to die—

Suddenly, she found herself carried up from the salty spray of the Sound just as it reached to embrace her. Her arms, though shaking with shock, wound about her rescuer's neck as he stole her from the promise of a cold, unforgiving grave. Her nails dug deep into solid flesh.

It wasn't a dream.

How . . . ?

How had she been snatched up just shy of the last few feet in her twenty foot plunge? Her drink-soaked mind was too cloudy to grasp at the impossibility. Did it matter now that her wobbly legs were safely planted on the proper side of the rail once again?

She was alive!

"Life is too precious to waste, little one. A moment of folly leads to an eternity of regret. No fleeting pain is worth that endless agony."

Had those gently chiding words been spoken aloud or only within her mind?

Confused and frightened, she looked up and was lost within a gaze of star-like brilliance. The light pulled her in until nothing else existed except a sense of amazing awe and serenity. All her anguish fell away as unimportant. Her tears dried, forgotten, upon her uplifted face.

"It was a mistake," she murmured softly, needing to assure him that her impulsive act was not to be repeated. Pleasing him filled her with vital purpose, and the thought of his disappointment led to unbearable despair.

"I'm sure it was."

His eyes dazzled, drawing her deeper into what could only be a dream. But what a wonderful, all-absorbing fantasy.

"You will not remember whatever misery brought you to this low point. Nor will you recall coming here to do the unthinkable. You will awake in the morning a new being, filled with hope and happiness."

"Yes," she whispered as her hands moved, independent of her command, to unwind her scarf and open the top buttons of her blouse. A soft smile shaped her lips as she tipped her head back, offering her bared throat as payment for her future. Her lashes fluttered at the brief sting that followed, but a sense of euphoria quickly overwhelmed any pain of body or spirit. She drifted on a pleasant tide that all too soon left her alone upon the shore of her uncertain tomorrows. But she wasn't afraid. Not any more. Her hands clutched at his coat.

"Will I see you again?"

She felt rather than saw his smile. "You no longer need me."

And he was gone.

Glancing about the wind-washed pier, she wondered why she had come to such a desolate place on such a wretched night. If she wasn't careful, she could catch her death in the clammy mists of near midnight. She remembered leaving her car and walking but nothing more. How silly . . .

Trying to shake the fogginess from her brain, she started to turn.

Strong hands gripped her waist.

Before she could utter a startled cry, she was over the rail, plummeting like an extinguished star across the heavens, into the choppy surf below. She never heard the mocking tones of her attacker.

"Really, my dear, you should never commit without following through. It shows weakness of character."

Squinting against the harsh antiseptic light, Stacy Kimball pushed her way through double doors marked "No Exit" into "Pill Hill" hospital's basement morgue on First Hill.

"This better be good, Charlie. I left the VCR and my date on pause."

"Good to see you, too, Stace," replied Charlie Sisson. "Wouldn't have interrupted your intimate evening plans with your latest in a long line of barely legal boy-toys, but this one had your name all over it. Take a look and ask yourself, 'Who loves ya, baby?'"

Her irritation was forgotten along with the last name of her distraction-of-the-moment. She'd abandoned him at his apartment with scarcely a word, and now she banished him just as easily from memory.

"What do you have?"

She'd spent almost a year working next to Charlie, listening to his ribald jokes and learning how to develop the rhinoceros hide necessary to do the job no matter what mess came in each night. He was nearly as thin as one of the corner skeletons he enjoyed dressing in honor of the seasons, the way suburban housewives garbed their cement porch geese. His sense of humor was often more stomach turning than the work they did, but that seemed to make the latter easier to handle. Not surprisingly, he was twice divorced, a man of bad taste and worse luck, a lonely soul who lived for the night shift. In that, they were alike. Perhaps that's why they'd developed their odd bond of kinship that remained even after they went their separate ways.

He was fond of saying that he was always dead serious when it came to his profession. Despite the bad pun, she found that to be true. So when he called, she came without question.

What goodies had he found for her this time?

Curiosity piqued, Stacy approached the drawer he pulled out from the floor-to-ceiling bank of stainless steel vaults. She leaned in close as Charlie placed his half-eaten tuna sandwich atop the covering sheet in order to peel the drape back from the top. Stacy examined the gray and bloated features of what once had been an attractive blonde woman and gave a sound of dismay.

"What a smell!" She glanced at the offending sandwich. "How can you eat that?"

"Such is the lonely state of my life. You want a bite?"

"Ugh. No thank you." She took the Latex gloves he extended, blew into the cuffs to inflate them slightly so she could slip her hands inside without sticking. "You pulled me away from Bruce Willis to look at a jumper?"

Charlie's smug and secretive smile was the only reason she didn't turn and walk righteously away. "Not a simple jumper. That's what I thought at first. Especially when they found a 'good-bye cruel world' lover's lament in her abandoned car. But that was before I saw the marks on her throat."

"Marks?" Intrigued, Stacy leaned in again.

"Yeah, right there at the jugular. Not self-inflicted and not from the fall. I'd guess it was some kind of bite right before she bit the big one."

Stacy glanced up. "The cause of death?"

"No. That was definitely the 50-degree water I drew out of her. She drowned."

"So?" she asked him, straightening and peeling off the gloves. "What does the one have to do with the other?"

"It just changes my conclusions from suicide to murder. She was attacked before she went over. There were the marks on her neck, and I found traces of blood under her nails. She didn't go of her own free will."

Stacy sighed. "Okay, this is all very interesting, but—"

"What makes it better than Bruce Willis?" He grinned at her, letting the suspense build.

"Come on, Charlie, spill it. You can be such a pain in the butt, which is why we don't go out any more."

"We don't go out any more because I'm not a steroid-popping teenager who goes all night like the Energizer bunny."

She made a kissy noise. "You never were, doll. You were saying . . .?"

Charlie Sisson restored the sheet, covering the young woman's unseeing eyes that had trapped the image of her killer within them, then he gestured toward a tabletop crowded with lab equipment. "It's not the girl, it's the sample I took."

"The blood sample?" Now, Stacy was all ears. "Show me."

"Take a gander, and tell me that's not the freakiest thing you've ever seen."

She bent to peer through the microscope eye piece, studying the smear he'd made. After blinking and rubbing at her eyes in disbelief, she looked again, adjusting the focus and light, then finally just staring in amazement.

"Didn't I tell you?" her former partner crowed. "Is that going to get me a yes answer when I ask you out again?"

"Charlie, who else knows about this?"

Alerted by the sudden hush of her tone, he was all serious business. "No one, Stace. You were the first one I called in. There's more."

"Tell me."

"Our chart for the lady's blood type is B+. But that's not what the current test shows. There's been a change in her typing. Those same strange cell patterns that are under the nails are in her own blood chemistry." He waited for Stacy's reaction. When there wasn't one, he prompted, "Is it something important?"

"It's something, all right," she whispered. "This is between you and me for right now, okay? Until I can run some more sophisticated tests." It was all she could do to lift away from the fascinating slide. She'd never felt such a fire of excitement and intensity.

"Well, I haven't finished a complete autopsy yet. They'll ask for one once they get the word she's not a simple splasher. I can keep it under my hat until then."

"You are a stud, Charlie."

He grinned. Picking up his sandwich, he took a bite and mused thoughtfully, "So tell me, what do you think we've got? A Nobel Prize?"

He was kidding. He didn't realize.

Her hands shaking, her insides quaking in seismic tremors of anticipation, Stacy smiled with a fierce, ambitious pleasure. "If what I think proves to be true, what we've got here is the secret of life."

He stopped mid-chew to give her a blank stare.

"Charlie," she explained breathlessly, "I think we're about to unlock the door to immortality."

He laughed nervously. "Right."

"More than right. Righteous. No one, Charlie, no one sees this slide." Her mind whirling like a centrifuge trying to separate the data, she tried to slow down her galloping thought process to grasp the next logical step. "Who is she?"

"The jumper?" He checked his chart. "Wanda Cummings. It wasn't a robbery. She had her ID, credit cards and about thirty in cash on her when they fished her out this morning. It wasn't the married boyfriend. He was chaperoning his eight-year-old son's birthday party." He made a disgruntled face. Though a double divorcé, he had strong opinions about the sanctity of wedlock. Unfortunately, his two wives hadn't shared those opinions.

"Anything special about her?"

"Other than the fact that she's dead?"

"Why is she dead? Does it have something to do with where she worked, who she knew, the place it happened—what?"

"That's what the police are asking. It's what they get paid to do. Rhetorical questions aren't in my job description. I deal with the plain and simple."

"Okay, here's plain and simple: Where was she found?"

Realizing how far in over his head he was getting, Charlie began to hedge. "I don't know, Stace. This is an ongoing investigation—"

"Cut the crap, Charlie. I can get the same info from Burke in Homicide. Would you rather I go out with him?"

That took care of his career-minded scruples. He handed her a slightly soiled sheet of paper, a copy of a copy of the police report that had come in pinned to the young woman's body bag.

"You didn't get that from me."

The warning wasn't necessary. Stacy had already forgotten about him as her gaze swept over the significant details that told her maddeningly little.

"This tells me exactly jack." Still, she folded it carefully and slipped it into the huge, ugly shoulder bag she carried as if she were a hobo with a train to catch. "I need something more to go on, Charlie. Whose blood is under her nails? I need that someone."

Charlie glanced about uneasily as if he feared one of his overnight guests might be eavesdropping. "I probably shouldn't say anything, but one of the cops that brought her down, some kid who doesn't know enough to keep his mouth shut, he told me our Ms. Cummings isn't the first they've seen with those odd marks on her neck."

"And?"

"And that's more than I should tell you."

"Except the kid's name."

When she saw his conscience bob annoyingly to the surface once more, she moved quickly to push it under again. Scruples were for the unambitious.

Charlie had taught her that, too, so he had only himself to blame.

"I've got tickets to see Payton and the SuperSonics next Friday. Any idea on who I could give them to?"

"Friday's good for me. Ken Fitzhugh, fresh-faced, right out of the Academy." He scowled sourly. "Just your type. Those tickets have my name on them."

"And this case has got *my* name on it. No one else's, Charlie. Right?"

"Right."

She unclipped the slide, and after protecting the evidence, it, too, found its way into her purse. "Could you get me samples from around that neck wound and of the victim's blood?"

Charlie threw up his hands. "Sure. Hell, they can only fire me once, right?"

Stacy grinned. "Right. Who loves ya?"

"You'd better," he grumbled. After passing over the samples, he made a shooing gesture. "Now, get outta here and make mischief elsewhere, so I can do my job."

"Call me if you get anything else of interest."

"Yeah, yeah." But he smiled on the receiving end of her quick kiss. "Next Friday night," he reminded her. "You and me?"

"If I'm not swamped with work, you got it."

But what exactly did she have tucked away in her bag? Stacy wondered as she hurried out of the building. The possibilities were thrilling. And dangerous. Very dangerous if word leaked out to the wrong parties.

To her thinking, there were certain parties who should never be trusted with the safety and security of the America people. The government was on the top of her list.

She didn't draw a deep breath until her apartment door was deadbolted behind her. Then the shaking set in—deep, bone rattling, teeth chattering tremors of delayed shock and adrenaline overload.

Feeling suddenly as if she were one of the Rosenberg's with a bag full of atomic secrets, she wobbled across the dark room to collapse upon her favorite rocker/recliner. Kicking up the footrest, she lay back, ugly purse clutched to her chest. Long moments passed as she stared up at the shadowed ceiling in frantic uncertainty.

If even a sliver of what she supposed was true, think of the possibilities.

She was thinking, hadn't been able to stop thinking since that smear had come into focus. Slowly, everything else tuned in with equal clarity.

She was wasting time.

Slamming the footrest down, she snapped on the pole lamp beside her chair and fished in her bag for the report and the samples. With both on the coffee table before her, she began to narrow that focus into a feasible plan.

The shrill of the phone had her clearing the chair cushion by a good four inches. When her heart left her throat, she picked up the receiver. The petulant demand from the other end left her mind in a total blank.

"What the hell are you doing home?"

"Who is this?"

"Lance."

"Lance?" The word might have well been Swahili for all the connections it made.

"I had my hand up your shirt an hour ago, and you've forgotten me already?"

Oh, that Lance.

"I thought you were coming right back," he grumbled.

Returning to the studio apartment with its stale smell of athletic socks and raging hormones held the appeal of a root canal. Suddenly, she couldn't recall what the appeal had been in the first place. Tousled blond hair, one-hundred-watt grin, washboard abs . . . oh, yeah. Now she remembered.

But, too bad for Lance, the hot-blooded attraction had been replaced by a cold-blooded slide.

"I had an emergency at work. I'm sorry I didn't call." She added that last to be kind. She wasn't sorry, not really.

"An emergency? For God's sake, you're a geneticist. What kind of emergency could you people possibly have? A new chromosome split, or something equally earth-shattering?"

How unattractive he was in his nasty ignorance. Funny, she couldn't remember why Lance had ever remotely interested her.

"Nothing a single-celled organism could be expected to understand." Her tone burned like dry ice.

Frustrated, but too vain to get the big picture, Lance tried to pour on the silky charm. "I deserved that, I know. Let's forget about it and get back to you and me."

"I've got a better idea, Lance. Let's just forget about you and me."

She replaced the receiver gently on the cradle.

When the phone rang again, the sound angry in the silence, she didn't pick it up. Instead, she held up the first sample, studying the blotch ineffectually with the naked eye, her naked anticipation surging like the tide that had gotten the best of the unfortunate Wanda Cummings.

"What secrets are you hiding, my friend? Don't be shy. You can tell me."

The stain gleamed bright and beckoning as she turned it before the light.

She pursed her lips thoughtfully, then murmured, "You'll tell me everything . . . eventually. Including where you came from. Especially where you came from."

TWO

Officer Ken Fitzhugh stared across the busy waterfront café, unable to believe his luck. Stacy Kimball. Her name sighed through him in shy, boyish reverie. In person, she was more stunning than rumor led him to hope.

In person, she made it hard for a man to breathe.

Kimball was legend around the station house—the Goddess of Gore, the Queen of Cadavers, the Mistress of the Morgue, Elvira of the Eleven-to-Seven Shift. She'd done her interning in forensic medicine before his time, but the mark she'd made upon the wet dreams of the precinct house lingered on.

It was easy to see why.

She may not have had the prettiest face he'd ever seen. The angles were too strong, her jaw too mannish, her mouth too big, but the sheer ooze of sensuality from those wide red lips and the invitation simmering in direct gray eyes obliterated that fact. She was sex incarnate, the stuff of adolescent longing hidden under teenage mattresses in glossy, airbrushed perfection, waiting all bed-rumpled and willing to go again to the limit of a horny boy's fantasies.

So what did she want with him?

He didn't exactly project the kind of Casanova image that assertive women noticed.

Her call had come out of the blue. An invitation to meet her for coffee during a break in his evening shift, her treat. Wrong there. The treat was all his the minute she stepped over the threshold atop Needle-high heels that left an amazing acre-length of legs bare before the hem of her hip-glazing blue leather skirt. Her aggressive, more-woman-than-you-could-possibly-handle walk strained the neck of every male in the room as heads swivelled her way. And to think that dynamite package was coming *his* way. He shot up out of the booth, menu held at belt level as a precautionary measure.

"Officer Fitzhugh?"

Her voice had the low rumble of fast water over rough rocks. Fitzhugh was swept away without the slightest desire to save himself.

"Yes, ma'am."

"Call me Stacy, please."

Her smile delivered a Stone Cold Stunner to the brain. He stood, just staring open-mouthed, for a long, dazed moment.

Wow, didn't even come close.

She was like no scientist he'd ever seen.

"May I sit down?"

Shaking his head slightly to jar his eyeballs back into place, Fitzhugh gestured to the opposite seat then went to help her peel down her short-waisted suede jacket. She wore a snug sweater any self-respecting ram would have gladly surrendered his fleece for in hopes that it would grace her dramatic curves. Fitzhugh swallowed anxiously as those long, long legs tucked under the table. Left standing with her coat in his hand like a witless hat tree, he hung it on the booth hook and quickly assumed his own seat. He ordered two coffees, anxious to be rid of the waitress and end the suspense.

"You said you wanted to talk to me, Miss . . . Stacy? What about?"

Again, came that killer smile meant to send the testosterone level into outer space.

"This is strictly off the record, Ken. Do you have a problem with that?"

At that moment, he wouldn't have had a problem with anything, illegal or otherwise. "No. I mean, I guess it depends on what you ask."

"Of course it does, and I wouldn't want to get you into any kind of trouble."

If he had any sense, he'd realize he was already hip deep in it.

Stacy played out her wet-lipped smile to dazzle the boy into compliance. It was so easy, she felt ashamed of herself . . . almost.

"I heard through the grapevine that you have a theory about these attacks that left victims with strange marks on their necks."

All the gosh-golly blushes were gone in an instant. His features firmed into hard, angry lines as he demanded, "Who put you up to this?"

"No one, I just—"

"Just thought you'd have a laugh at my expense. Well, ha ha. Thanks but no thanks, Miss Kimball. I may be green, but I'm not an idiot."

As he surged out of his seat, Stacy stilled him with the press of her hand over his. She glanced about uncomfortably, aware of the attention they were getting. This wasn't something she wanted broadcast for the six o'clock news. To calm the situation, she spoke softly, soothingly, as if to an upset child about to throw a tantrum in the candy aisle.

"Officer Fitzhugh, believe me, I'm not here to embarrass you, so please, don't embarrass me." She pointed to his seat, and reluctantly he sat. "I assure you, no one put me up to anything."

If she found out that Charlie was pulling her chain, she'd strangle him with it.

"Really?" He still looked suspicious but was willing to be convinced by the continued rub of her fingertips along his knuckles. "Sorry, if I snapped at you. I've been taking a lot of ribbing from the guys...well, you know how it is."

"Indeed I do. Please, tell me your theory. I promise I won't react like your Neanderthal squad members."

Encouraged, he leaned forward. "There've been five of them."

"Five of what?"

"Victims. You know, all with those same puncture wounds and . . . "

"And what?"

His voice lowered. "Blood loss. Dramatic blood loss, as if someone or something had tapped a vein and bled them nearly dry. Something like—like—"

"Like?"

"Like a vampire."

He cringed, waiting for her to laugh, but she didn't. She repeated the word in a whisper, mulling over its meaning.

Vampire.

"Not the actual creature from myth, of course," he went on to say in his own defense. "Probably some wacko with a Bram Stoker fetish who gets off on playing the role. I heard of a group of kids that pay over $3,000 apiece to be fitted with a pair of porcelain canine teeth that resemble fangs. Nothing that goes on in this city surprises me."

But Stacy wasn't listening. She wasn't contemplating a crazy cadre of pseudo-blood suckers stalking the night for kicks. She was wracking her brain for folklore facts.

"Vampires. They're supposed to be immortal, right? They drink the blood of human beings in order to survive, and they come out only after dark."

"And turn into bats and sleep in coffins." Fitzhugh grimaced. "If I had a dollar for every rubber bat that's turned up on my desk since I first expressed my opinion, I could retire."

"And only sunlight, silver and a stake through the heart can harm them," Stacy mused, combing through her midnight movies repertoire.

"And plastic fangs—I've got a drawer full of them. Everybody's a comedian."

Stacy fixed him with a steady stare. "And no one took you seriously enough to check out the obvious?"

"Oh, sure, after nicknaming me Fitz the Freak." He waved a dismissing hand. "We've run computer checks on the known weirdos and kinky sex shops but so far, nothing." He studied her soberly. "You think I'm nuts, too, don't you?"

"No. I think you still have enough imagination left to look beyond the obvious. So, what aren't they seeing?"

Again, the conspiratorial attitude. "I don't think this is your run-of-the-mill nutball."

"And why not?"

"There's never any physical evidence. The cult crowd isn't that careful. This guy is smart." His tone was almost admiring. "These attacks are planned out. Isolated spots, women alone, no witnesses—not even the victims themselves. No tie in between them."

"They were all killed? Why haven't I heard any of this on the news?"

"Not killed. Well, only this last one, that is. The others were found wandering around, weak from blood loss, with no memory of the attack itself. The details were held from the press out of respect for the victims and to keep a lid on possible hysteria and copycat crimes. One of them was the wife of a judge, the other the girlfriend of some rock star."

"Blackmail, you think?"

"Not that I'm aware of. Just the wrong place at the wrong time."

She pursed her lips, focusing on the useful tidbits of what he was saying as if they were presented on a slide before her. The picture forming wasn't clear. And she liked clarity.

When she didn't speak right away, the young officer rushed to fill the silence. "So tell me, Stacy, what's your interest in this case? You're not with the Force any more."

"I still do some trace evidence and DNA charting for them on occasion." She made her answer purposefully vague.

"And is this one of those occasions?"

"My interest is purely unofficial."

He made a disgruntled sound, a sound of injured ego. "I didn't think they'd be clever enough to call in a professional at my suggestion. I'm the new kid on the block. I transferred in eight months ago, so I don't have any clout."

"Clout or not, I think you might have hit on something important."

He straightened immediately, hungry for affirmation. "You think so?"

"They'll catch on, eventually, but until they do, maybe we can help each other."

His eyes narrowed slightly. "How's that?"

"You could keep me informed of any new developments in the case, and I could let you know if I can put any of the genetic puzzle together."

"I don't know—"

"As long as you're not breaking any rules, that is. I wouldn't want you to risk your career."

He supplied a sudden, grim smile. "Are you kidding? If I could make this case, it would make my career. You've got a deal."

Before he could think better of it, she asked, "Could you get me the names and addresses of the other victims? Just for some behind the scene digging. Discretely, of course. We wouldn't want to ruffle any feathers."

"I guess I could do that." He checked his watch. "I've got to get back out on patrol. Where can I send the information?"

She handed him a card with her e-mail address, then delayed him with one last question.

"Has anyone been brought in for formal questioning on the case?"

Fitzhugh paused, cocking his head to one side. He was a handsome boy, she decided, in a casually rumpled, innocent sort of way, with his fair hair and mild blue eyes. The innocence wouldn't last long, not in his profession. Too bad.

"Just one that I'm aware of and that was just routine. Nothing came of it."

"Who?"

"Louis Redman, the importer. Ever heard of him?"

The answer surprised her. He was talking top of the food chain. "Who in Seattle hasn't? He's kind of the Pacific Northwest's answer to Howard Hughes. How did they manage to coax him out of his hotel to come to the station house?"

"By asking, I guess. I didn't get a look at him. He was in and out slick as you please before the press ever got wind of it. Guess nobody wanted to cheese him off, seeing as how he funds half the city's charity efforts. Apparently, he knew several of the victims, and one of them was coming from one of his fund raisers when she was attacked. You don't think this has anything to do with Redman, do you?"

"I don't know enough about the man to form an opinion. I don't think anyone really does. And I think he prefers it that way."

Fitzhugh checked his watch again. "I gotta get back on patrol. I'll see you later?"

Such hope and anticipation in that simple phrase. Another conquest to discourage. She made her reply carefully impersonal, but knew he wouldn't be put off. They never were.

"As soon as something develops."

She could have—should have told him that nothing intimate was going to develop between them, but she needed him on the string to feed her information. This was too important to worry about a young man's heart. Just a twinge of guilt, uncomfortably pushed aside for the sake of expediency.

Stacy sat back, barely aware that he'd left the diner with a slightly breathless "good night."

If he only knew how close to the right track he was on, he would be more than a little agitated.

That meant she was on the right track, too.

Stacy ordered up a huge breakfast special, suddenly starving. And as she ravenously put the meal away, her analytical mind was spinning in concise circles.

Vampire.

Nonsense.

Then, she made herself look beyond the logical. In this case, the impossible could be the only possible answer.

But that led to another question.

How did one go about tracking down a supposed vampire to ask for a sample of *his* blood?

She had a name. Louis Redman. Okay, it wasn't an easy place to start. Redman's influence on the powers that be was like a seducing drug. No one wanted to risk alienating his affection. Well, she wasn't interested in his affection. She was interested in his blood chemistry.

And she wasn't without some influence, herself.

While her fresh cup of coffee cooled, Stacy flipped open her cell phone and punched in a number. After being rerouted through several departments, she finally was rewarded with a rather curt greeting.

"Alex Andrews."

"Catch you at a bad time?"

His tone warmed immediately. "Hey, Stace. It's never a bad time, if you're involved. What can I do for you?"

"Could you put that sexy, inquisitive brain to work on something for me?"

"Oh, you sweet talker, you."

"I need you to dig up all you can find on Louis Redman."

"The zillionaire hermit?" He whistled. "You don't call in any small favors, do you, babe?"

"Good things come in big packages, Alex," she cooed. "Let me know what you find out."

His chuckle made her smile. "It'll cost you dinner."

"You pick the place."

"My place?"

"We'll discuss that when we see what you come up with."

"Oh, baby, I'm coming up with something right now."

Shaking her head, she ended the connection. Alex Andrews was a regular gopher when it came to digging up dirt. That's why he made such good money working for a scandal rag. The best outrageous tale was based upon truth. All she'd have to do was strip away the exaggerations. If there was anything to find, Alex would come through for her. She'd worry about the dinner later.

Right now, she was worrying about how she was going to get next to Louis Redman.

And then inspiration struck in the guise of a quickly discarded memo and invitation.

If it wasn't already too late to R.S.V.P.

Snatching her coat, she flung a wad of bills onto the table top and ran out to hail a cab, indifferent to the degree of whiplash she caused amongst the diner's clientele.

***

After twenty minutes of mining through her personal and business correspondence that left an avalanche from cluttered desktop to equally paper-strewn carpet, Stacy seized upon the prize she was looking for.

"Yes."

Dumping a stack of unread periodicals off the seat of her chair, she plopped down with a buoyant sense of victory. She'd received the cordial note a month ago, tossing it aside as unimportant. She wasn't much for glitz and glitter affairs. She preferred her affairs to be of the one-on-one variety. She brushed her thumb over the elegant embossing.

Harper Research and the Western Division of the National Leukemia Foundation invite you to an "Evening of Note" with Special Guest, Louis Redman.

Tonight.

Responses were due back two weeks ago, but she could finagle her way around the deadline. Now all she had to do was finagle an introduction and a way to circumvent the odd stipulation at the bottom of the invitation.

No cameras.

The whim of a publicity-shy recluse or something a bit more sinister?

It would be difficult for the victims to recognize their attacker if there were no known photos of him on file. She recalled that piece of trivia because it had intrigued her when skimming an article on the mysterious benefactor who had opened his checkbook for Harper Research, otherwise known as her employer. How odd that such a well-known philanthropist had managed to slip the limelight for so long.

Some rare condition that made him light sensitive, according to rumor. She wondered. Maybe his obsession with privacy came from another, less sympathetic cause. Like the fear of being identified.

She sighed as she studied the invitation. Maybe she was reading too much intrigue into the whole matter. Maybe Redman was just some harmless, quirky old duck who was camera shy and had more money than God.

But she'd find out.

"I thought you said you weren't interested, Stacy."

Phyllis Starke, the director of Stacy's department, had never gotten over the fact that someone had dropped a house on her sister. At least, that was Stacy's rationale for why the woman was so relentlessly sour. More likely, it was the resentment of the older model being outshone by something sleeker, faster, younger and with more under the hood. If she was a threat to her supervisor, it was only on the business front. But Starke would never believe that.

Just because Phyllis believed in cooing her way to the top, she'd no reason to inflict her questionable morals upon every other female on staff. She'd never been discrete about her objection to bringing Stacy on board and had never gone out of her way to make the newcomer feel welcome.

At least she wasn't a hypocrite.

Just a bitch.

"I had a last minute cancellation on my schedule, and I'd really like to go." No, no. No matter how desperate, don't beg. Stacy altered her approach. "Greg suggested I make contacts in the area to further our research. Otherwise, you know I'd never break protocol and call you at home to ask such a favor."

Touche.

She imaged Phyllis's wince as the well-placed thrust took her in the inflated ego. She might run roughshod over the lab as if it were her own private playground where she was queen bully on the jungle gym, but Greg Forrester held the purse strings to all their individual projects, and his word might well have come chiseled on tablets of stone. If Greg wanted Stacy there, Phyllis would move continents to accommodate her.

"I suppose we could juggle the seating chart one last time," she grumbled, not hiding her irritation. "Nothing like waiting until the last possible minute."

Stacy knew her well enough to realize there would be some small payback to come when she least expected it. This was one more brick in the wall of the older woman's envious illusions. Phyllis had once been the one Greg Forrester sent out as his envoy. Now it was Stacy. And that had to gall Starke something fierce. But Stacy would grin and bear the unpleasantness to come to earn this particular victory.

"I appreciate all your trouble, Phyl. I really do. And so does Greg."

Okay, so she felt a little ashamed of herself for that mildly spiteful needling. Just a little.

Stacy could picture the cream-clotting smile as Phyllis pooh-poohed her shallow thanks. She was quick to end the undesired contact.

She had what she wanted.

Now, to find just the right dress and make the most of it.

THREE

The company's "Evening of Note" was one of notable boredom to Stacy. Her feet hurt within her new strappy sandals, and someone had spilled a cocktail on her favorite evening gown. Hardly the start of the adventure she desired.

After spending the first hour milling about the crowded lobby to the mediocre strains of a three piece string ensemble, they'd been herded into the dinning room where she'd found herself wedged in as an uncomfortable ninth with eight of the most uninteresting people in the world. She could almost hear Phyllis Starke laughing a good one at her expense. After rubbery chicken, dry couscous and rich coffee that was the meal's only saving grace, Stacy was grateful to be back on her feet for post-Pepcid cocktails. There, her temper fraying, she endured the sloppy gropings of several inebriated salesmen who would apologize tomorrow and still snicker in the lounge.

And still no sign of Redman.

She had shrugged out from under the too friendly arm of Harper's PR front man swallowing down her retort of "when hell freezes over" in answer to the married fellow's invitation, when a commotion from the raised dais caught her relieved attention.

Finally.

She applauded gratefully as Greg Forrester and his anorexic wife, who compensated in millions for her lack of looks, made their way toward the microphone. She listened with fading patience to his political blather about charity beginning at home, when a less likely spot couldn't be imagined, and clapped again as the Foundation's fund-raising chairperson was coaxed up to join them. A heartfelt speech of thanks followed with missionary zeal.

And then the atmosphere in the room changed.

It was a palpable shift as excitement stirred, a feeling as though the air conditioning had just kicked up an extra notch to create shivers of anticipation. Though many in the room would have attended just to be polite and to be seen, the real draw for all of them was the rare chance to glimpse an enigma in the flesh.

When Louis Redman was announced, the room seemed to stretch a head taller as everyone craned for a look at the notorious recluse. Silence quivered like a suspended breath. Then a ripple of surprised exhalation, begun in front, swept back like a tidal wave.

Stacy's gasp blended in with the rest. Louis Redman wasn't at all what she'd expected.

From his rumored isolationism, she'd pictured some bizarre figure with long stringy hair and uncut fingernails, someone old and bent, cinched into his cummerbund like a girdle and shuffling like the dirty little old man she remembered from *Laugh-In* reruns. The Louis Redman who strode across the stage was . . . a hunk.

Young, virile, handsome as sin itself, he looked comfortable in the elegant evening wear as few men ever did, yet powerful at the same time. He wasn't a big man but the impression he made as he crossed the stage in strong, graceful strides was that of a giant. Perhaps it was the mystery added to the money, or perhaps the way his gaze scanned the sea of expectant faces as if he recognized each and every one of them. He was a man who knew how to work a room.

And he was working on her, big time.

Her mouth was dry by the time she remembered to close it and force a swallow.

Remember the mission, Stacy.

As he shook hands and took his place before the microphone, Stacy lifted the palm-sized camera she'd snuck into the event and snapped off a half dozen shots in rapid secession. It wouldn't hurt to give Alex something concrete to go by, or the victims a face to possibly link to the horror they had suffered.

As she stared through the viewfinder to take the final candid, she froze in dismay. Louis Redman, though half a room away, was staring straight at her, his dark brows pulled together in a mild scowl of displeasure. The connection startled her, as if she'd received a mild electric shock. She lowered the forbidden camera and secreted it quickly within her evening bag. When she looked up again, Redman's attention was on the trio who shared the stage. He hadn't called security. She wiped damp palms upon her designer gown. He hadn't seen her. Surely she'd imagined him picking her out in the tightly packed room for that brief, chastening glower.

But could she have imagined the galvanizing effect it still had on her nervous system? She tingled.

He'd begun his speech, presenting Forrester and the Leukemia representative with a beyond generous check to further their research. In spite of herself, Stacy lost herself in the listening.

His voice was nearly as seductive as his good looks—soft, exotically accented and strangely mesmerizing. Not even ice cubes dared clink in interruption of the room's almost hypnotic silence as he concluded his oration. Then the applause was deafening.

And Redman was gone.

Blinking as if she'd woken from some strange stupor, Stacy scanned the stage and the edges of the platform. Where had he disappeared to so quickly? She'd been staring right at him, yet he was gone in an instant. Had she seen him leave the dais? She couldn't remember.

Obviously, he not only knew how to make an entrance, he knew how to exit, as well.

Not so fast my wily friend.

Pushing her way through the crowd, she slipped out into the cool of the lobby, giving it a cursory search. Not there. What was the guy? Part magician?

Then she caught a glimpse of a elderly Asian man holding open the rear door of a black limousine at the curb out front. Something about the sleek vehicle's smoky windows alerted her. They screamed privacy. She began hurrying toward the double glass doors just as an unescorted figure started down an adjacent walk toward the car.

Damn, she wasn't going to be in time to catch him.

She stepped out into the crisp night air, her attention on the glossy luxury car and the man about to get inside. There was a flash of movement off to her right, but she was too focused on her target to realize that she was one, herself.

They struck silently, without warning.

The unexpected shock of being splashed with the liquid contents of a bucket startled a cry from her. She stopped in shock as if mortally wounded. Clearing the dampness from her eyes, she stared at her hands in dismay. Blood. Her hands were covered in blood.

The ugly protest chants rang in her ears as pamphlets scattered about her feet. Those opposed to the genetic work Harper Research was doing were quick to run away, leaving her standing in dripping distress in the middle of the walk.

Stacy took a ragged breath, and time started up again. Her hair, her face, her gown, were all drenched in sticky gore. A sick sense of violation stained equally well. Shock gave way to an anger that couldn't quite overcome an awful swell of anguish. If they'd had guns...

She'd been alone, vulnerable. A victim.

Her shoulders began to quake. Helplessness shuddered its way through the clog in her throat to burn her eyes, obscuring her awareness of the man who approached. Until his words caressed gently, for her benefit alone.

"Such fools to fear what they don't understand. Let me help you."

Before she could protest, the protective folds of a man's overcoat engulfed her. Equally gentle strokes of a linen square wiped the goo from her brows and cheeks, clearing her vision for a much greater surprise.

Up close, Louis Redman dazzled the beholder.

He was, in a word, gorgeous. Foreign, fascinating and utterly fabulous. Short-cropped dark hair gleamed with auburn highlights beneath the artificial light. Heavy, slashing brows offset the dramatically cut angles of his face. Eyes of an incredible emerald color and the sweeping contours of his mouth were softened with concern . . . for her.

If she hadn't been shaken by the abrupt assault, she felt traumatized by the rescue.

"Are you all right, Miss Kimball?"

That he knew her name provided the spark to jumpstart her brain.

"Yes, of course. Just startled is all. And mad as hell."

She raked the now-vacant area with a furious glare. Where was the security team Harper provided for such events? It was just the two of them on the blood-splattered walk that looked like the center of a crime scene. It could have been, had the science militants decided on less environmentally-friendly weapons of choice. The shivers started through her again. She fought them off with the strength of her outrage.

"I should be used to those damned vultures by now."

"It's the coward's way to choose concealment over honorable confrontation. Are you sure you haven't been harmed?"

"Just wounded in the ego." She managed a faint smile and was rewarded by the sight of his in brilliant full bloom.

Be still my heart, she cautioned in a sudden panic of attraction.

"Allow me to provide you escort home. I fear you might have difficulty hailing a cab in your present state."

The reminder brought a horrified flush to her cheeks. "Good grief, I'm a mess. And I've ruined your coat."

"Don't give it a thought, Miss Kimball." He'd taken her by the elbow and was steering her toward his elegant ride. The Oriental at the door regarded her with unblinking inscrutability, as if she didn't represent a bio-hazard.

"I can't possibly get in," she argued against the relentless pull of his kindness. "Look at me."

He did look and, surprisingly, that scan revealed no hint of disgust. Instead, it smoldered with an odd inner fire. As a woman, she reacted to his intimate study with a quiver of heat and excitement, but another, deeper part of her responded unexpectedly. The hairs at her nape rose with a tingle that spread across the surface of her skin in tight, prickly gooseflesh. A strange reaction to the attention of an attractive man, yet too powerful and visceral to ignore.

Something was not right about the hungry intensity of his stare.

"You look fine to me, Ms. Kimball."

Even his low tone woke contrasting results, the sound both gruffly tender and faintly predatory. What was there about this handsome stranger? Earlier suspicions had her balking at the idea of being alone with him. But her analytical mind argued that there was no chance of discovery without risk. This was the moment she'd hoped for, yet confused signals of alarm and anticipation forced a stalemate, arrested her decision until he made it for her.

"After you, Ms. Kimball."

She stepped into the gleaming black vehicle. The sensation was like being swallowed up in a deceivingly comfortable void . . . a trap. Why that connotation came to mind, she didn't know. Still, she couldn't shake the uneasiness that came in from the cold with the elegant Louis Redman.

He sat opposite her on the supple leather seats. Once the door was closed, the interior was devoid of light save the startling flicker of his eyes, like sudden shocks of flame from flint on steel. Then there was darkness from out of which came his quiet request to know her destination.

Did she really want him to know where she lived?

What was she inviting home with her, a naive fly to the spider? A hungry spider.

It was too late to escape now. The web had already tightened around her. What explanation could she give for the panic she felt inside? What reason for her rejection of his generous offer?

Excuse me, but my mama taught me not to accept rides from suspected serial killers.

She sat back on the seat and tried to relax. A futile effort. Anxiety closed about her chest in a constricting fist as she gave her address. He repeated it to the unseen driver. The car started forward, the movement so smooth, it was like floating. Everything about the moment conjured a discomforting air of unreality.

Then she remembered all of Fitzhugh's insinuations about Redman.

Was this man, incredibly, impossibly, the stuff of legendary nightmare? A vampire?

Oh, please.

Her cynicism should have easily conquered her worries. She didn't believe in superstition. Her scientific mind had no tolerance for things absent of logic. She operated upon tangibles, not fancies. Yet how to explain the tremors of intuition whispering for her to have a care? What was intuition if not a protective sort of sixth sense warning of danger? Probability, she answered within her own clinical frame of reference. Instinct was merely the ratios of chance intruding upon the subconscious.

So why didn't the smug cocoon of her convictions make her ride more comfortable?

Perhaps it would have been easier to relax if she hadn't felt Redman's eyes upon her. His stare was intense, invasive, almost as unsettling as the attack on the walk. Both left her with a lack of equilibrium.

Putting her queasiness aside, Stacy focused on her immediate goal. A chance like this might never come again, her chance to converse one-on-one with the noted recluse.

"How did you know my name?"

His answer was slick and without hesitation. "I asked your employer. I make it a point to know the people I'm dealing with."

"And are we going to be dealing with one another, Mr. Redman?"

His chuckle was warm and somehow, still slightly sinister because of the impenetrable darkness.

"That depends, Ms. Kimball."

"On what?"

"On you."

Before she could pursue that amazingly vague reply, he surprised her with another observation.

"I've been following your work with interest. Combating disease on a genetic level. It's no wonder you incite the ignorant to such extremes of alarm."

She was alarmed, by his awareness of her while he was still an unknown to her. By his calm assertions that their futures would be linked if his will won out. Why it should feel as though their wills were already engaged when the rules of combat had not yet been defined, left her at a loss and oddly defensive. She responded with a bristle.

"It's not as though I'm doing cloning experiments in some Aryan attempt to purify the race. I'm doing disease research. Blood diseases, in particular."

Did she just imagine the almost visible sharpening of his interest? His stare felt as if he were directing the concentrated beam from a magnifying glass on a rare sunny Seattle day into her brain. She stammered on with her rationalization.

"These zealots show up every time our clinic is mentioned by the media. They target us as a whole, not by the individual researcher. I doubt that they know me by name, as you seem to."

"Yet their attack was very personal. You became the brunt of their fear and rage. For that, I apologize."

"You have nothing to apologize for."

She could feel his smile at her sincerity.

"If my name had not been linked to this affair, it would not have piqued the press's curiosity."

"But the attention brought a huge influx of much-needed funding to our projects. The rather unexceptional dinner went for $200 a plate. So I guess my own small sacrifice was well worth the outcome."

"I admire your thinking, Ms. Kimball, and your graciousness. Please, send me the bill for the cleaning of your gown or for its replacement."

Startled by the offer, she blurted, "That's hardly necessary."

"But it would give me great pleasure. Few things do these days."

The faint tug of poignancy played bittersweet upon her soul. Loneliness from one who had every advantage seemed all the more ripe for her usual cynicism instead of her sympathy. Why should she feel sorry for this man of privilege who chose by his own eccentricity to be alone?

Perhaps because her life was equally empty.

Aware that the car had stopped, she gave a slight jump when the door was opened. The decorative flood lights at the front of her building muscled into the interior blackness of the limo like a bullying intruder, too stark and all revealing for the mood of quiet comradery that had settled over them. In the wash of clarity, Stacy once again saw the redness staining her hands. As she examined them in renewed dismay, she glanced up at her companion to find his attention there as well. Not just an idle glance but riveted with fierce and unrelenting fascination.

She would liked to have flattered herself into thinking he was searching to see if she wore the claim of another man's ring. But it was the blood that drew him. She knew it with a cold, clear shiver of certainty.

Vampire.

Killer.

Was he one or the other? Or both? Suddenly, she couldn't wait to escape the all too intimate interior.

Scrambling out onto the front walk in a graceless hurry, she was calmed by the firm yet gentle claim of the driver's hand upon her elbow. He didn't speak, but his dark gaze bid her to be careful.

Careful. Yes, she must be careful. She must remember the dangerous circumstances and forget the odd electricity generated by the man in the car.

"Would you like me to escort you up?"

Redman's request appeared motivated by concern for her safety. So why did Stacy's denial spring so vehemently to her lips? It was more than her almost phobic reluctance to open her home to strangers.

"No, I'm fine."

Hearing the near hysteria in her own reply, Stacy tempered it with a grateful smile and a soft, "Thank you for your kindness. Mr. Redman."

"Again, my pleasure."

She was about to turn away when he called to her again.

"Ms. Kimball, your bag."

She glanced down at her empty hands then at the evening purse Redman possessed. His hands rested upon the beaded satin as if he could feel the imprint of her forbidden camera within. She hadn't imagined his stare earlier. Would he take it from her now, to her shame and embarrassment? He had every right considering her blatant invasion of his privacy.

She hesitated then bent with hand outstretched. He placed the bag within it without pause.

"Can't have a lady going without her necessities," he murmured, betraying no hint of suspicion or accusation.

Stacy smiled, guilt frozen upon her face as she straightened.

He knew, yet he chose not to act upon the knowledge.

A strange man.

A dangerously compelling man.

She turned away from him, hearing the car door close quietly upon their unsettling encounter. As she made her way down the walk, she never heard the vehicle pull away from the curb, but when she reached the outer door and glanced back, it was gone. Something about that silent vanishing disturbed the rash of creeping skin once more.

Shivering, she clutched the coat tighter about her shoulders, remembering for the first time that his expensive garment was still draped about her.

Either she could return it, cleaned, by courier . . . or she could hand deliver it herself.

She now had her excuse for seeing him again.

***

A lovely and intelligent lady.

Louis Redman responded to his driver's sentiments even though they weren't spoken aloud.

"Yes, she is, Takeo."

An intriguing and potentially dangerous combination. Be careful that you don't confuse your celibate condition with your cause.

Louis chuckled softly. "Are you chastising me, old friend? If so, you needn't worry. I've no interest in Ms. Kimball other than the services she can provide."

From the front seat, the Asian made a grunting sound of disbelief.

Louis sat back and smiled to himself. Another time, he might have enjoyed arguing the fine points of his determined avoidance of humankind, especially the female of the species, but tonight, he wasn't in the mood for dialogue. He was busy replaying over in his mind the discourse he'd had with the charming Stacy Kimball.

Takeo was right. She was delightfully witty and sharp as a sword edge. And beautiful in a bold, voluptuous fashion. Her gold lamé gown had been designed to attack the fragile male libido with its daring curves and alluring plunges. But Louis found none of those obvious enticements half as endearing as the brief vulnerability he'd seen as she stared down at her hands, or half as appealing as the flash of spirit he'd witnessed a moment later.

He inhaled, sampling her scent. Spicy, bold, not the floral foolishness so many women wore to disguise their female sexuality. Her perfume was unapologetic, unafraid. Direct, like the lady. He liked it. It told him more about her than their all too brief words had conveyed.

Her heat, her very humanity added to the allure of subtle fragrances. But there was more, something not of her, that lingered in the rear of the plush vehicle. An aroma that wasn't subtle, but strong, vital, overwhelming all but his most basic instincts. Instincts that responded not to a seduction of the senses but to a deeper, darker appetite for survival.

Blood.

The air was thick with it. Animal, not human, but still potent and difficult to ignore.

Had he been a less noble creature, he would have caved in to the temptation presented to him so deliciously. But he'd learned control, and he'd learned patience. And he'd learned to deny needs both mortal and unnatural. That was all that kept the pretty doctor safe in his company. At least for the moment.

He was honorable, but he wasn't a saint. And Stacy Kimball was fashioned for sinning. Everything about her appealed to a different facet of desire. Intentional or not, she stirred him in ways he could not risk, agitating restraint and resolve, but so far, not resilience.

He would resist.

Geneticist Stacy Kimball was a challenge he could not afford to meet except on the professional level. He'd sworn off all other entanglements with women as too brief, too unsatisfying. He would have to be careful that, while she teased his intellect, she wasn't also provoking his purposefully dormant emotions.

His hands fisted where they rested upon his knees. In the darkness, his eyes gleamed like quicksilver, a reflection of what he was and what else she'd almost awakened.

He would not lower his guard again. He would not be vulnerable to his longing for human contact.

And he would not love again.

FOUR

"What do you mean, he doesn't exist?"

"Just that. His background is as shallow as a Presidential promise. He set himself up in Seattle about seven years ago and before that, nothing. No record of a Louis Redman having lived anywhere in the U.S."

She didn't need this now. She was already running late to work, her last pair of pantyhose had a racing stripe streaking up her left leg, and she was out of coffee. Not a good time to throw another obstacle in her path. Fumbling on her dressing table for the mate to the jade stud already fixed in her other ear, Stacy vented at the closest source.

"Come on, Alex. Guys like Redman just don't show up out of nowhere with enough money to balance the national debt. If you don't want to do this favor for me—"

"Now, now. No need to get your estrogen in an uproar. I didn't say I was finished looking, did I? A guy with this many secrets gets my journalistic juices flowing."

Unable to find the second earring, Stacy pulled out the first. *Someday I have to clean up this place.* She stalked into the living room on a caffeine-free rampage.

She couldn't go up against a man of Redman's social stature without some hefty ammunition. If the police hadn't found enough to hold him on Wanda Cummings' murder, why was she so determined to find him innocent or guilty? She'd wanted Alex to tell her that either he was Snow White with a flawless IRS record or that he had some Hannibal Lector-like secret tucked away in an East Coast sanatorium. Not an unsatisfying mystery.

Because Redman had gotten to her.

It was more than the prickles of her rarely heeded intuition whispering that there was something wrong with Redman. It went beyond her desperation for the solution he might represent.

Redman intrigued her. Personally and professionally. And that made him dangerous.

She couldn't afford a distraction in her life, not now that she had it running on an effortless autopilot.

"Where are you going to start looking, Alex?"

"He's supposed to have some link to a newspaper in New York, but unless he was married to a Hearst or a Pulitzer in a past life, I can't see any big bucks there. Maybe he has Mob connections. That would explain his underground tendencies."

"Go ahead and check that out." Though she gave the nod to Alex, she couldn't quite see the dapper Louis Redman hanging out with wiseguys. If he was into something illegal, she'd bet it was something with a little more style. Or a lot more bizarre.

Then she remembered his accented voice. "Have you got any international pull?"

"I used to bang a diplomat's secretary before she was sent home because of his unsavory conduct with a thirteen-year-old. She had to leave the country with him."

Stacy's laugh was as tacky as the wad of gum she found on the heel of her best black flats. One of those days, she grumbled to herself.

"Did you talk to those women on the list I gave you?"

"Oh, you mean the Stepford Wives? I have never seen a collection of ladies with fewer things to hide. Or blanker memories. None of them could tell me a thing, and all of them were particularly anxious for me to let the matter drop. You'd think they didn't care to find out who attacked them."

"Or they already know and for some reason have repressed the information."

"Brain washing? Doesn't have the right feel. These women weren't afraid to tell me. They just plain didn't want to. It was like they were protecting whoever jumped them. Maybe this Redman is some sort of hypnotist."

Stacy didn't think that was the answer, either. Whatever Louis Redman was, it wasn't something so simply explained away.

"I'm picking up a roll of film on my way to work. I should have some good shots of Redman for you to flash around. Maybe that will jog their recall."

Alex whistled his admiration. "How did you manage that when *Newsweek* couldn't get him to pose for a cover issue?"

"Feminine wiles, Alex. Feminine wiles. Now hit the streets and put that famous nose for news to the ground."

"Yes, ma'am."

She hung up, giving up on the sticky pair of flats and opting for running shoes. The whole scene was getting curiouser and curiouser. What was Redman hiding that made secrecy so imperative? Some past indiscretion, either financial or personal? Though it rained everything else in Seattle, she couldn't recall tycoons falling from the slated skies. And what made victims band together to shield the identity of an attacker if it wasn't fear or a threat of some kind? She may not have been a reporter, but she had an investigative itch just out of reach and driving her crazy.

Just as Redman was driving her crazy.

She didn't like men who stayed on her mind. She liked them to be like Lance What's-His-Name: great sex, untaxing conversation, and totally forgettable once they were gone. Redman, on the other hand, lingered like the scent of a fine cigar—rich, aromatic, and out of place in her sterile lifestyle. She preferred to study her specimens under a microscope not from a too-close-for-comfort distance. Impersonal and purely objective, that was her jaded view on work and men. Well, maybe just on men.

Keeping a close eye on her dash clock, that annually seemed to lose fifteen minutes into the accurate time Twilight Zone, Stacy broke some of the more annoying moving violation laws in her rush to get to work. She'd been chomping to get into the lab all weekend, to verify suspicions blossoming like a new species in the morgue's Petrie dish. Making an impatient drive-through at the Photo Mat, she tossed the developed pictures onto the seat beside her, not quite enough of an Indy 500 wheel to manage the traffic while thumbing through her prints. They, like the slide in her handbag, would have to wait for the office.

She made better time once she left the city limits behind and sped out into corporate suburbia where Boeing, Microsoft and Nintendo held court, and 140 other bio and medical companies competed to pump $2 billion into the state's economy from the private sector.

Harper Research nestled into a grassy hillside, its rock and natural wood facade designed to meld into the environment while the work that went on inside was designed to alter it. Everything about it, from the smooth green lawn to the meticulously groomed landscaping, was meant to put the eye and mind at ease. And the high surrounding fence was meant to keep the increasingly vocal protesters at bay.

Slowing her vehicle so as not to graze any of the questionably employed sign carriers who shouted and pounded on the hood of her car, Stacy rolled down her window only as far as necessary to fit her ID badge into the scanning unit by the gate. A click, a hum, and the gate rolled back to admit her. She drove forward through the crowd, who despite their angry gestures, wouldn't pursue her inside. It was a daily routine. They wanted to make their presence known but had no desire to be carted off to jail where their opinions would cool while awaiting bail. A stalemate. A balance of wills. A game, Stacy thought to herself as she followed the winding road to a cleverly environment-friendly stone opening that led into the underground parking structure.

Ducking out of sight like she had something to hide.

That was the government for you—tell the people they had nothing to worry about, then start sneaking around as if they did.

The unfortunate fact of life was that Harper couldn't survive without the government contract grants. She didn't like the covert, hush-hush aspect of the job and the doors that weren't open to her because of 'National Security,' but she lived with it because it provided her with a darned good living and the chance to do the work she had to do, not out of love but from necessity.

Pulling into her assigned parking space, Stacy cut the engine and tucked the packet of photos into her briefcase. Even at the early hour, the level was almost filled with the sleek, expensive cars status demanded. Her own oil-burning tank stood out in wincing contrast. She could afford better. She could afford luxury. But there was something comforting about the all-metal macho of the Delta 88 that she couldn't bear to part with. She'd bought it used with her first big paycheck and kept it as a symbol of her independence. That was nothing she'd surrender easily.

Even in broad daylight, the parking structure was dark as a tomb. She hated it. The low, claustrophobic ceilings had sparse flourescent lights dangling down on chains to threaten the roof of vehicles passing beneath them. And there was the echo, each footstep seeming to reproduce itself in ever weakening repetitions. She always walked a little faster. Her gaze always moved a little quicker in its scan of the shadows. Not that any undesirables could penetrate their working fortress. Still, she didn't release her breath until the elevator doors shushed efficiently behind her.

The interior of Harper was a catacomb of cubicles and glass offices, at least on the floor where Stacy had clearance.

Pinning her photo ID tag to her lapel, she ducked into the break room to put her coat and purse into her locker. No personal effects were allowed in the labs. After slipping into her bleach-stiffened smock, she made a stop at the coffee machine then went on to her lab where the three walls of windows made her feel as though she worked inside an aquarium. Flipping on her computer, she got right to work. First the required research, then she could slip in the slide she had smuggled in her lab coat pocket.

"Hey, Kimball, how was life amongst the elite?"

She glanced up at Herb Watson who occupied the next bell jar. Her confusion must have been stamped in big letters because Herb wasn't a real bright bulb when it came to interpersonal communications.

"The party?" he prompted.

"Oh. Fine. Loud, bad food and tight shoes."

"Geez, you make me glad I stayed home with a rerun of *The Boys from Brazil*."

An insider joke amongst geneticists. Stacy laughed to fulfill her obligation then went back to work. But Herb lingered at her doorway, forcing her, after a long moment of studious indifference, to look up again. Would the guy never go away and let her get on with her work? Anticipation was making her patience wear thin.

"Was there something else?"

His features puckered into an unattractive collage of curiosity and envy. Like Phyllis Starke, he'd been at Harper for most of his employment history. When Stacy came on board, some of his better projects had ended up under her care. Sleeker, faster, newer, with more under the brain pan. Though he never exactly made his jealousy of her known, it simmered beneath the surface, coming to a head like an unattractive boil on occasions such as these.

"Forrester wants to see you. Something going on?"

At first, she frowned, thinking he meant some sexual innuendo, but no, Herb Watson was as asexual as the samples in her freezer.

"If there is, no one told me."

"If it's a promotion, don't forget to mention that I'm the one who taught you everything you know."

"And if it's a pink slip, I'll be sure to add that bit of information, too."

Herb scowled, his tiny sense of humor sorely strained in its deciphering of her meaning. Finally, he managed a wan smile and disappeared back into his own sterile space.

What would Greg Forrester be calling her upstairs for? She checked her hair in the green glow of her computer monitor then squared up her shoulders. Promotion or pink slip, six of one, half a dozen of the other odds. A number of familiar faces had vanished over the course of the past months, since the government's influence had taken hold of the budget like an encroaching infection. Was she to become the latest of the missing in action?

If she was, the timing couldn't be worse.

If her job was on the line, would she be forced to reveal her unofficial project in order to save it? She hoped it wouldn't come down to that unpleasant choice. This was something she didn't want Harper's government-washing hands in.

Stacy stepped out of the elevator. The labs were below ground, with the security floor burrowed in one deeper. She blinked like a mole at the brightness of the day, a rarity in Seattle in the early months of the new year. The CEO offices and meeting rooms were blessed with windows to the outside world where natural light flooded in to warm decorator shades of coral, taupe and cream into an almost welcoming atmosphere. Unless one took into account the interior designer's fondness for calla lilies. The sleek, funnel-shaped flowers were a part of every floral arrangement, reminding Stacy, not of elegance and Art Deco style, but of death. A harbinger of bad news to come? Again, she hoped not.

Forrester's office commandeered a corner space. Situated in the center of a green plant jungle was his horseshoe-shaped desk. Stacy swallowed down a bad feeling when she saw that Phyllis Starke already occupied one of the chairs around it. The woman's look held the gleam of a suspended guillotine blade. Forrester's smile of greeting did little to dissuade her sense of foreboding as she took a seat on the other side of the bend, placing a sizable distance between herself and her immediate supervisor.

What was Starke's beef now?

"Congratulations, Ms. Kimball. I don't know how you managed to pull it off, but we are in your debt."

Stacy blinked owlishly at the CEO, not sure how to respond to what she didn't understand. Her gaze followed the piece of paper he slid across the marble surface toward her.

"What's this?"

"It's a name-your-own-study grant, and might I say, a damned generous one."

She glanced up at him nervously. "But Mr. Forrester, you know I prefer not to do government work."

"I know. That's why I know you'll be thrilled with this offer from Louis Redman to head up your own team in the field of your choice."

It was a joke. It had to be. But one glimpse of Starke's foul countenance decided it. If she was that annoyed, it was for real.

"I don't know what to say."

"Say yes to cocktails this evening at the Needle with Mr. Redman. He wants to go over the details with you in person at seven. His car will pick you up."

Stacy found it hard to draw a breath. A research carte blanche just dropped in her lap. The chance to study, to develop, to cure. Without interference, without red tape, without having to clear each nitpicking step with Starke.

"But why me? Herb has more hours—"

Forrester put it bluntly. "Redman asked for you. Specifically. And we won't disappoint him, will we?"

Stacy shook her head, the daze of disbelief yet clinging to her thought processes. He'd asked for her. He'd entrusted her with a grant of incredible heft on the basis of one ride in his car. The man had either done his homework on her, or he was foolishly fickle.

Either way, she had a program to put together.

"All the department heads will assemble their wish list of projects for you to evaluate," Starke was saying as if something bitter clung to each word.

"But it's my choice?" Stacy needed that clarified, right up front, right in front of the head honcho.

"Yes, Ms. Kimball," she annunciated with surgical precision. "It is your choice."

***

Stacy had no memory of her journey back to her lab. Her mind was spinning like a child's top, bouncing off countless ideas before careening each time in a new direction.

She had nothing suitable to wear for a meeting with a millionaire.

Once she stood in the center of her work space, the solid familiarity of sight and antiseptic smell coaxed her from Cinderella panic back to the real world.

She had a million things to do. Facts to gather. Figures to find. Then, as she brushed damp palms over the sides of her lab coat, she felt the outline of the slide in her pocket. The sample and the photos. She'd totally forgotten her intentions in the rush of excitement.

Was that Redman's intention?

To lull her curiosity with a fat research grant that would allow no time for poking around in his private business?

She reached for her briefcase and pulled out the pack of pictures. Slowly, she dealt through them. The lighting and composition was good though sometimes the angle was a bit askew. All and all, she had good shots of the dais with the Forresters and the Foundation rep.

And none of Louis Redman.

She shuffled through the pictures once again, her breath quickening with agitation.

How had she managed to miss getting him in any of the shots?

She hadn't. She knew she hadn't. But the space beside the hosts and other guests was strangely and inexplicably vacant. Where Redman had been standing, refusing to appear on her pictures as if he'd developed a personal stealth technology. Was that why he'd handed over her purse, camera inside, without a twitch of hesitation? Because he knew she had nothing?

With shaking hands and backbone as supportive as one of Seattle's infamous six inch slugs, she drew out the negatives. In each numbered square, one figure was conspicuously missing.

Louis Redman didn't like to have his picture taken, not because he wasn't photogenic. It was because he didn't show up on film.

"Sensitivity to light, my hind leg," she muttered, studying the oddly empty photos. Her stomach tightened with alarm and more strongly, with excitement.

Piece by piece, she was gathering evidence that Louis Redman was . . . what? A creature of the night? The undead? Her scientific mind rebelled against those superstitious labels as the toothsome image of Nosferatu played against more basic reason. But he was something, all right. Something not quite natural. Something that presented both threat and promise tied up in a mysterious and attractive package.

She would start unwrapping those layers tonight.

Until then, she would learn all she could about the sample from the dead girl. The results were startling. And exciting. And unbelievable.

The moment the cells from the killer's blood encountered cells from another sample, they became aggressive and dominant, completely surrounding and ultimately altering the cell structure of the second sample to match its own.

She ran the test again, using another specimen. The same metamorphosis occurred.

Finally, her hands unsteady, she took a dot of her own blood and applied it to the slide. Almost afraid to hope, she adjusted the focus and waited for what might be a miracle.

Slowly, the weakness in her own chemistry was absorbed by the stronger, healthy cells of the other sample until no sign remained of them at all.

She whispered a soft oath, not daring to speak her amazement aloud.

For on the slide, from a yet unnamed donor, was the secret of cell repair. The answer to needless death and disease.

The answer to her prayers.

Now, all she had to do was beat the authorities to the man whose system produced the miracle she needed.

FIVE

The Space Needle's revolving restaurant was an elegant, expensive setting Stacy usually reserved for special business lunches. But exiting the elevator on Louis Redman's arm gave the experience a fairytale quality she wasn't sure how to handle within an impersonal realm.

The lights of the Sound and the Emerald City of Seattle dazzled beyond the 360 degree vista of glass. It was like being amongst the stars. Beautifully dressed tables gleamed in welcome, all but a few occupied by equally well-dressed diners. Beside her Louis Redman, in his exquisitely tailored suit, with his exquisitely European flare, dazzled far brighter than the lights or the constellations. The perfect prince for her Cinderella. His effect upon her was as unsettling as it was scintillating.

"This way to your table, Mr. Redman," the sleek host murmured.

As they followed between the tables, Stacy glanced toward the windows. Against the dark view of the Sound, their reflection became more prominent. She looked like a glamorous film star in her shift of ivory silk and beads with her hair dramatically swept up atop her head. At least a B-movie, she thought upon a more wry examination of her statuesque build and spiky heels that brought her eye to eye with Redman.

But where was her elegant escort?

Not in the reflection beside her.

Startled, she studied the mirroring surface, seeing herself, the maitre d' but not her dark companion. As she stared, perplexed, they took a turn, and the lights of the city obscured their reflection.

"How is this, sir?"

Distracted from her alarmed musings, Stacy glanced at the inside table then toward an empty setting by the windows.

"Might we have that one?" she asked even as her escort frowned slightly. It wasn't an impulsive request. Nor was she interested in the scenery. She wanted to see if Redman's image would appear once the tower made its return revolution toward the dark waters of the bay again. Once mistaken, perhaps, but not twice.

The tone of their meeting had definitely taken an eerie turn.

When she was seated next to the glass, Stacy concealed her nervousness by mulling over the wine list, finally agreeing to a full-bodied red that her companion suggested. Then they were alone and she had no excuse not to give him her complete attention.

He mesmerized. She'd never seen eyes so green, set jewel-like in a surround of thick black lashes. Looking into them, she felt a mild disorientation, as if she'd already consumed more than her allotted single glass of wine. Blinking, she shook off the strange light-headedness, deciding there was only one way to combat Redman's charm—business.

"Why me?"

"Excuse me?"

But he didn't look surprised by her blunt question.

"Why did you choose me for your grant? There are many at Harper who are far more qualified to—"

"You don't want to head the project for me?"

Taken aback, she could only sputter the truth. "No. I mean, yes, of course I do. It's an incredible opportunity for both me and the Center. I was just wondering about your selection—"

"Do you feel unable to handle the challenge?"

This time, she let a slight flare of ego strengthen her reply. "No. I'm looking forward to it."

"And as to why you, of course I studied your credentials. Impressive and impeccable, but as you said, not outstanding amongst your peers."

Her cheeks warmed at his candid assessment. Why did it feel so necessary to shine in Louis Redman's eyes? She'd never cared for accolades, either professional or personal, before.

"But you were not chosen," he continued smoothly, "because of your academic abilities."

Warning bells jangled. Stacy straightened in her seat, narrowing her gaze into defensive slits. Here it comes. The not so subtle suggestion that their business and pleasure combine in a mutually satisfying arrangement. Damn, she'd hoped . . . What? That Louis Redman would be above such sleazy manipulations? She knew her choice of attire was rather—suggestive. She had a great figure and enjoyed clothing that made the most of it. She enjoyed causing a stir, but in her professional field, she adhered strictly to a look-but-don't-touch policy. Sure, those like Phyllis and even Herb assumed that she'd peddled her looks to get ahead. She'd never cared enough about their opinion to correct that misconception. But she wasn't a user. She wasn't a tease. And she wouldn't be blackmailed into trading favors, no matter what this project meant to her.

She'd wanted to think better of a man of Redman's obvious breeding.

But the bottom denominator was, he was a man. And men tended to see what they wanted to see.

Her fingers tightened on the fragile stem of her wine glass, imagining the satisfying stain the dark red would make upon his stark white shirt front. Already, regret weighed upon her as she thought of the stellar opportunity plunging to Earth, a satellite knocked from its comfortable orbit.

"And just what was your criteria for making your choice, Mr. Redman?" Her tone shivered like a crack spreading across safety glass. Let him make his nasty proposal. She was ready for him. Even though it hurt and disappointed her.

He leaned back in his chair, daring to smile, to appear amused by the situation even though her voice was sharp enough to slash his sophisticated air to humbled pieces.

"From what I've observed, both at the gala and so far this evening, you have attributes that far surpass mere intelligence. Intelligence does not always imply common sense or courage, and those are the qualities I need if one is to work for me."

Stacy blinked.

When he'd said attributes, the hair bristled on the back of her neck. All her indignant rhetoric rose up in a tidal wave of insult and superiority, ready to sweep him and his smug confidence into the cold water of the Sound. But his next words sapped the power from her affront. All she could do was scramble to recover her balance as her cheeks brightened with the horror of misunderstanding, and her mouth drooped slightly in her loss for appropriate comment.

"You have, if I may be so bold, guts, Ms. Kimball. I admire that. You were not intimidated by my reputation or by your company's rules. You proved yourself quick to rebound from distress after those militants assaulted you. Resilience is another requisite. And I like you. That's a bonus."

He smiled, this time the gesture heating his jeweled stare until it glittered—hot, green fire. That flame consumed her awkwardness, her embarrassment, her shame. And she smiled back, sharing the amusement at her own expense.

"Ahhh," he added appreciatively. "And there is the other thing."

"What's that?"

"You don't take everything too seriously. The scientific community has a decided lack of humor that makes me . . . weary. You and I shall get along splendidly, I think."

"I hope so, Mr. Redman."

"Louis. If we are to be friends, it must be Louis."

"And are we to be friends?"

"That would also be a bonus. A man in my position has few acquaintances with whom he can relax."

She should have said she had enough friends, thank you. She should have curtly advised that their relationship was to be strictly professional. But again, she caught that vulnerable note in what he wasn't saying, and it played havoc upon her usually reliable logic.

And what better way to discover his secrets than to establish a non-threatening guise of camaraderie? She regrouped and formed a new, more direct attack upon the mystery of her benefactor.

"In order for strangers to become friends, they should get to know one another better, don't you think?"

A subtle hint of wariness slipped into his easy smile. "And what do you wish to know?"

"What's your interest in genetics? What kind of work is it that you want me to do?"

He wagged a finger at her. "Ah-ah. That is not personal. Let's agree to leave business behind for the next hour or so. Let us be ourselves instead of our public relations department."

If he wanted personal, she could get personal.

"Are you married?" She refused to blush as he regarded her with some surprise.

"No. I have been."

"Divorced?"

"No. I have . . . outlived both my wives."

"Is that where you got your money?"

He put up his hands and chuckled. "You are too good at this game. No, I did not do away with my wives to inherit their fortunes. They were both worth more than any wealth could measure. And you? Why aren't you wed?"

She couldn't help feeling it was more an evasive maneuver than a need to know that had him deftly flipping the topic to put her on the hot seat. The intimate glimpse he had given her into his love life made her uncomfortably aware of the barrenness of her own. At least, he had loved and lost. That was a risk she could never afford to take.

"I've never met a man who could match my exacting specifications."

He saw right through her forced gaiety to the ache she attempted to hide. Pity wasn't something she wanted from him. But, before she could bristle up on the defensive, he gentled the subject with a soft chiding. "You have a check list, then? And how have I fared so far?"

She released her breath and laughed. "You scored high on the financial end. The rest, I've yet to tabulate."

"You will let me know how I score?"

"If you do, I'm sure you'll be the first to know."

Was that a flush upon his lean face? Did modern bachelors—even widowed ones—blush when confronted with sexual innuendo? Not to Stacy's experience. She found his modesty oddly appealing in an old-fashioned sort of way. In fact, she found way too much appealing about her dinner date.

Not a date, she reminded herself sternly. No matter how relaxed and even flirtatious, it was business between her and Redman. She couldn't let it become more.

"Do you have family, Ms. Kimball?" he asked as a means to recover himself. When she hesitated, he simply met her gaze, and the reluctance went away. Just like that.

"Family? No, not any more. My mother died. She was a nurse. She contracted AIDs through a needle stick at the hospital where she worked. A poor reward for all her service to mankind. I've lost contact with my father over the years. Her death hit him hard." How easily he pulled the painful facts from her usually well-guarded personal resumé. To distract

him from more questions, she used his own methods against
him. "And you? A family?"

"A daughter, her husband and a grandchild I love dearly.
They do not live nearby and I miss them dreadfully. I find
family anchors one in reality. There are few things that matter
in comparison."

"Yes," she murmured into her nearly empty wine glass.
"On that, we agree."

"More wine?"

Uncomfortable with the direction of their conversation, she
nodded, eager to mute the sense of emptiness and loss any way
possible. To date, she'd found nothing that worked.

Restlessly, she glanced out the window. During their
conversation, the restaurant had made an entire revolution. The
brightness of the Seattle cityscape became the opaqueness of
the bay, and against that flat black mat, the restaurant's interior
shown clearly upon the glass.

All, that is, except for Louis Redman.

His chair was empty even though he occupied it. The glass
of wine lifted as if by its own accord, though she could glance
at him and see he clearly held it in his hand.

The shock startled all else from her mind.

This was no casual date, and she wasn't certain Redman
was even a man.

There was a sudden flicker of light as Louis lit the candle
centerpiece on their table. Even the small flame obscured the
reflective quality of the windows. But Stacy could not forget
what she'd seen...or what she had not seen.

He didn't photograph, and he had no reflection.

What the hell was he?

She had to know.

As their elegant waiter began to pour her a second glass of
wine, she made an abrupt movement, knocking the glass off the
table before the liquid had a chance to reach it. When the
delicate crystal bowl shattered, she made a sound of dismay and
bent as if to retrieve the pieces. At the same time, Louis

reached down, and with one quick gesture, she nicked the side of his thumb with a shard she held firmly in her hand. She heard his hiss of breath and exclaimed, "Oh, dear, have you cut yourself?" as she straightened.

"It's nothing," he assured her as the waiter efficiently retrieved the broken glass in a heavy linen napkin. But as Louis sat back and looked at his hand, the bright line of blood trickling down toward his sleeve contradicted his claim. He stared at it for a long moment, seeming not to breathe.

"Louis, are you all right?"

His gaze flickered up, and for a brief, alarming second, it was ablaze with strange, almost phosphorescent fire. A reflection of candlelight. It must have been. For what else could make his eyes glitter so unnaturally.

Her reaction must have shown, for he blinked and was himself again. He pressed his table linen to the tiny cut as if the sight of it a moment before hadn't shaken him from his composure. "I'm fine. Forgive me." Then to the waiter, he said, "Another glass for the lady, please."

But everything wasn't fine, and Stacy's eyes hadn't deceived her. And though he might pretend otherwise, Louis wasn't fine, either. His voice was suddenly thready, as if labored by some supreme strain. His breathing had deepened into a slow, rumbling cadence. Almost a growl. His elegant manner and poise suffered a sudden loss of control. A struggle raged within him. And seeing it frightened her.

She remembered then his strangeness, and the threat she'd felt when they'd been in the car together after the benefit, when he'd seemed oddly preoccupied by the sight of blood on her hands. It wasn't an aversion. It was a fierce, fixed attraction. One word fit what shone briefly in his expression.

Hunger.

"Could you excuse me for a moment?"

Mumbling that hurried apology, Stacy grabbed her purse and headed for the restroom. There, in the safe, clean glow of the makeup lights, she carefully made a smear on the empty slide she carried and sealed it and the stained sliver in a case for later study. There. She had her sample to compare to the DNA found under the would-be jumper's fingernails. Now all she had to do was return to the table as if nothing had happened and act normal.

Normal.

Nothing about the man or the evening fit that definition. Nor did her own agenda. For God's sake, she had cut the man to get a sample of his blood to see if he was a murderer.

No, not for that reason. She had taken it to see if he was her potential savior.

Her hands shook as she washed them under a stream of steaming water. Glancing up into the oval mirror, her own pallor shocked her. She looked as if she'd seen a ghost. Her lips thinned and curved wryly.

Not a ghost. What else Redman might be, she wasn't quite sure.

What Redman was, she discovered upon returning to their table, was gone.

"Miss Kimball," their waiter murmured sympathetically. "Mr. Redman was taken suddenly ill. He begs you to forgive his departure and encourages you to enjoy your meal."

Staring at the abandoned table and the reflection beyond, she reached for her coat. "I find I have no appetite. Thank you."

As she was helped on with her long coat, the waiter advised that Louis's driver waited below to see her home, but the minute she emerged at the Needle's base, she knew she wasn't ready to face the stoic Oriental or the reality of what this night revealed. For the moment, an irrational panic reigned.

Pretending not to see Redman's sleek limousine, she took an abrupt turn and began walking briskly down the wide concrete walk that had been made to accommodate the 1962 World's Fair crowds. Now the tourists used it to flock to where Paul Allen, Bill Gates' other billionaire half, recently opened his EMP museum at the Seattle Center. She was quickly enveloped in the leisurely mill of tourists and left to the confusion of her thoughts. Ahead, the Seattle Center monorail offered a ready solution. She quickly bought a pass and found herself an isolated seat, trying to appear inconspicuous in her glittery evening wear. Only after the cars jerked into motion did she exhale in shaky relief.

Had she expected Redman's man to pursue her? Had she thought he'd had some sinister alternative in mind other than a polite ride home at the end of an awkward evening? She scrubbed her palms over her face, wondering how to find any sense of sanity in what she'd just gone through.

Then, she went completely still.

Someone was watching her.

A creepy sensation brushed over the delicate hairs on her arms. A tingling feeling of impending danger woke an instinctive response. Her attention sharpened. Her focus turned to those around her. The car was sparsely occupied. Several cuddling couples, an exhausted shopper with two young children, a panhandler, all on their way downtown. No threat to her surfaced from any of them. Yet the feeling persisted, growing stronger, not placated by the lack of likely suspects.

Stacy clutched her coat about her as a chill shook her to the bone. Her teeth began to chatter, and her breath plumed as if she'd just stepped into a freezer.

What was it? What enveloped her with an icy touch like death?

Then, just as abruptly, the cold was gone and with it the queer sense of being followed.

She looked about to see if any of the others had noticed anything unusual. Apparently, the arctic blast phenomenon was localized to her alone.

Nerves. That was it.

But coming to that conclusion gave no comfort as they continued along the line, away from her strange meeting with Redman and the oddities she didn't want to recognize as truths.

Later as she sat huddled in the darkness of her apartment listening to the low croon of her favorite R&B collection, she considered all that had happened.

What was Louis Redman? More than a man, surely. Or was he a man at all? Scientific reason failed when applied to him, and that left her adrift in a realm of unknown possibility. What was it about him that mesmerized her into lowering her guard when they were together? Into forgetting her purpose, her resolve. She'd talked about her family. She never did that, not even with those who worked beside her every day. Yet something in Redman's hypnotic green eyes had made her feel safe enough to reveal a sliver of her past.

She liked him, and that seemed more dangerous than the fact that he might be a killer.

Tomorrow she would check the slide against the sample Charlie had given her. The comparison would prove or disprove the elegant recluse's involvement in the young woman's death.

Irrationally, she knew she didn't want it to be Louis. It was more than her desire for the grant money and the research opportunities it would bring. It was more than the status she would achieve in her field if her work knew fruition.

She liked Louis Redman. She liked his humor, his cleverness, his modesty, his looks. She liked the fact that he treated her as a person instead of an object. And she didn't want to cast him in the role of killer.

And if he was convicted, she wouldn't have the chance to investigate the strange properties she'd found in his blood, if indeed, it was his.

The shrill intrusion of her telephone interrupted Sam Cooke's soulful serenade. Could it be Louis calling to apologize for his abrupt disappearance? Anticipation leapt, unbidden, within her as she picked up the phone.

"Stace?"

Charlie Sisson.

"I just got another one."

"Another what?" Her thoughts were slow to assemble after her initial disappointment. Why had it become so important to hear Redman's voice?

"Another body with those same strange bite marks on the throat."

From the shadows, he watched her leave her apartment.

Good. Everything was going better than he could have planned himself. Her curiosity, her tenacity would all play right into his hands.

He was satisfied to stay out of sight now that the unfortunate young woman's vitality warmed through him. He'd almost let his hunger get the best of him earlier, and that would not do.

He was a schemer, and to know success he would have to practice patience, the reward of which would be well worth the wait.

In his hand, he weighed the token taken from the dead girl, smiling as he imagined the surprises to come.

Let the game begin.

SIX

"Liver, normal color, no outward signs of trauma or disease." A wet splut and a creak of the scale. "Weight . . . oh, there you are, Stace. Hope I didn't pull you away from something too important."

"You know me, Charlie. Always on call. I have no life." Stacy snapped on the Latex gloves and moved up beside her former partner.

"Unfortunately, neither does this young lady. Hey, that's confidential."

Stacy evaded his retrieval grab for the chart. "If you didn't want me to know everything, you wouldn't have called. Massive blood loss. Significant crushing trauma to the neck." She frowned. "Who the hell is this guy?"

"Or what is he?"

She scowled at Charlie's Bella Lugosi impersonation. "Any leads, witnesses?"

"Zip. Some schmo delivering the catch of the day found her near Pike Place."

Stacy lifted the corpse's hand.

"Way ahead of you," Charlie interrupted. "No trace evidence this time. Our boy was careful."

"Who was she?" Stacy asked, trying not to see beyond the bluish skin of the girl's face to the vibrant blush of a future cut short. One of the tricks of the trade: never imagine them alive. "College student. She'd been partying with some friends. The last time they saw her was when they got off the monorail around eight-twenty."

"What?" Stacy's head snapped up.

"They rode into the downtown area on the tram. Lisa, that's her name, said she wanted to pick up some fresh lox, and that was the last they saw of her."

Stacy stared at the still features, breaking a cardinal rule to mentally infuse warmth back into the marble-white cheeks. A pretty girl, young, blonde . . . and with a handsome college boy and another couple, laughing over some joke on the same rail car she'd rode in on.

She'd seen this girl alive only hours ago.

The sudden chill of coincidence reminded her of the odd breath of cold she'd felt during that ride downtown. A chill of death hovering over an unsuspecting victim?

Stacy shook her head. This was too weird, her thoughts too Twilight Zone.

"Where are her effects?"

Charlie gestured toward another steel tabletop where a large plastic bag stored all that was left of the vivacious young woman Stacy had so briefly encountered. Stacy pulled it open and poked through the separately bagged items, knowing better than to risk contamination by handling the belongings.

"There's only one shoe here, Charlie. Was the other at the scene?"

"You know, I thought that was strange, too. Not as strange as her taste in footwear, though." He returned his attention to the liver, noting the dimension before dropping it back into a basin. "I asked. No second shoe."

"The killer took it? Why?"

"Took it or tossed it. Maybe he has some kind of fetish. Who knows."

Stacy studied the single shoe, a platformed canvas tennie covered with red glitter and blue and white sequined stars, size seven, narrow. A touch of frivolity doomed to plastic imprisonment, never to dance the night away again in careless abandon. Sadness winced through her.

"What story are they giving the media, Charlie?"

"Heads will roll if one whiff of the word serial killer gets out. With all the strange-o's in this city, think of the copycat activity."

"Then what story are they telling each other?"

Charlie gave her a long, solemn look. "This one's got them nervous, Stace. No one's saying much of anything. If anyone's got an opinion, other than the obvious Anne Rice correlation, they're keeping it to themselves. They're spooked. And if the news grabs a hold of it, the whole city's going to be spooked. They better catch this guy and fast. He's leaving corpses now. Could be he likes the fantasy a little too much."

"I need a sample of her blood."

"Way ahead of you. I looked. The same weird distortion of her blood type. What's going on, Stace? Some kind of drug cult, you think?"

Stacy said nothing as she carefully resealed the personal effects bag.

Fantasy or fact?

Was she getting too close to the truth to tell the difference?

***

The image blurred then sharpened into focus with a twist of a knob. Stacy studied the slide she'd made from Redman's blood, frowning as she found the same abnormality as the earlier sample. Only a complete DNA test would show a match, but if she were to hazard a guess, she knew she was looking at the same animal.

And what kind of animal did that make Louis Redman?

An animal who killed.

Rubbing her eyes, she leaned back from the microscope. What she had should go to the police. By concealing potential evidence, she could be shielding a murderer. But, could their understaffed and overworked labs get the information back any faster than hers? A weak argument but a placating one. She'd already begun testing the original sample and now would send off the new one for a comparison, and therefore would have the results back sooner. Once she knew for sure, she would give them what she had. Until then, she could study the strains of unusual blood chemistry without interference.

She didn't consider her motives, whether they be humanitarian ambition, selfish need or just morbid curiosity. The thrill of investigation groomed by her years in forensics created a determination to solve a puzzle once presented. All these strange pieces seemed to fit around Louis Redman, making a picture too bizarre to be believed. Until she had a clearer whole, she would keep the bits and pieces to herself.

But first, she had to protect the next victim from Redman's dangerous proclivities.

Perhaps it was the paranoia that came with working in a partially funded government installation, but Stacy never completely trusted the lab phone lines. On her break time, she sought the small concrete patio that in the summer would house cheery café tables to give employees relief from the sterile environment within. With the threat of more wintery weather still hovering, it was now an empty slab swept by blustery wind, but it was private, and that's what Stacy counted on.

Officer Fitzhugh couldn't be reached until his evening shift started. Controlling her impatience, she left a message for him to call her cell phone number. She would start with the eager young policeman and build a net around Redman so that he couldn't leave his posh hotel building without his every movement being monitored. Yes, it was police work, but for now, she preferred it be undercover work. Strictly off the record. A man's reputation was at stake, a very wealthy man who was contributing a heap of funding money to her and the Center. If it was discovered that she had launched her own witch hunt against an innocent philanthropist, her job credibility and longevity would both be zero.

When she reentered the building with a swipe of her security card, the chill of the morning still clinging to her hair along with her rapidly puffed cigarette's smoke, the greeting was immediate from one of the quickly passing staff members.

"There you are, Kimball. Forrester wants to see you."

Making a quick trip to drop off her coat, she stepped into the private elevator to go 'topside.' Why the meeting? Had Redman expressed some dissatisfaction with her? Was that why their benefactor had disappeared so unexpectedly? A sinking sensation splashed down in her belly, churning stomach acid on its unrestrained plummet to the bottom. Her opportunity could well be ended before its official start.

But Forrester welcomed her with a smile, no Starke on hand to sour the moment. Just Stacy and the boss. He came out from behind his desk to clasp her hand in his smooth ones.

"Ms. Kimball, delightful to see you again. I hope I'm not interrupting your project selection process, but I wanted to take a moment to see if you have everything you need and to tell you how happy we are with you here at Harper."

Overwhelmed, Stacy collapsed into the chair she was offered. "Thank you, Mr. Forrester. I enjoy my work."

"Good, good." He went back to assume his own seat, the mein of a benign yet powerful despot settling upon his expression. Those trusty warning bells jangled along Stacy's nerve endings again. He was up to something. And that something, she wasn't going to like.

"A lot of pressure is going to be put on you until your project gets under way," he continued, his slow smile supplying all the leeway of thumbscrews. "I want you to know, there will be no interference from me in that decision." His smile tightened, letting her know that it wasn't his generosity, but the terms of Redman's grant, that kept him from interfering.

"I appreciate that."

"To free you up for the additional administrative work you'll be doing, I've assigned you an assistant. We can't have you burning the candle at both ends, now can we?"

An assistant? She straightened in her chair, wary and not exactly overjoyed by the offer until she discovered what puppeteer's strings were attached.

Forrester tapped a button on his massive intercom system. "I'd like you to meet Frank Cobb. He'll be your new right hand on this project."

She never heard him enter the room, but there he was at her elbow. She nearly jumped out of her pantyhose. One quick overview told her everything: high and tight cropped hair, granite jaw, shirt collar a size too small, which made him look as though he was strangling in his own properly knotted tie, cheap, sensible shoes. A government stooge sent to spy on her.

Damn!

"Mr. Cobb, welcome aboard." She extended her hand and his engulfed it for a no-nonsense press. The fact that he didn't react to her sultry delivery and ambiguous words by lowering his gaze to her bustline clinched her suspicions. Fed. No sense of humor and no sex drive—at least while on duty.

And it was obvious to her that Mr. Cobb's duty was to watch her every move.

"I'm looking forward to working with you, Ms. Kimball."

"Dr. Kimball," she corrected with a frosty smile.

His hazel eyes crinkled at the corners in acknowledgment of her ire. Good. They understood each other.

Smugly certain that his plan had gone off without a hitch, Forrester sat back with a magnanimous wave. "I think you'll find Mr. Cobb most useful, Stacy. So, when do you think you'll have your decision on the project made?"

The use of her first name wasn't lost on Stacy. The implied intimacy meant she was now a team player. She smiled wryly. "I'd like to touch base with Mr. Redman one more time. I should have everything in place by the first of the week, providing Redman is agreeable."

"Where you are concerned, he seems to be. Keep up the good relations. Redman could be a valuable resource."

Forrester thought she was sleeping with him.

Her initial outrage tempered with cunning, Stacy saw the advantage of her boss's misconception. Besides being insulting, it also gave her leverage as Redman's supposed lover. Let him think what he liked as long as it didn't interfere with her work. Now, that just left the problem of her watchdog who followed her dutifully to her lab.

"What can I do for you, Dr. Kimball?"

She turned to face him, blocking the entrance to her domain. "You can stay the hell out of my way, Cobb. If I catch you snooping through my papers or messing with my research, you'll be out of here so fast, you'll have to overnight express yourself to catch up with the butt I'm going to kick through this door. Got it?"

"Yes, ma'am." Again, the rather attractive crinkles of the smile he wouldn't release appeared at the corners of his eyes. "But what can I do in the meantime?"

"Coffee. Black. And fresh brewed. Can you handle that, Rambo?"

"I think so."

"Good. Then maybe we'll get along after all."

When he went to see to the task, she entered her lab, pausing to assess the huge bouquet of Calla lilies situated on her desktop. A gift of appreciation and welcome to their exclusive upstairs club.

Carefully, she picked up the granite bowl and set the flowers aside, hoping the choice wasn't prophetic, that this project wouldn't be the death of her.

And as she worked for the remainder of the afternoon, sipping from cups of excellent coffee, Cobb stayed outside her area, watchful but not intrusive. Best of all, he kept others away who would have bombarded her with their own ideas and plans for the grant money. She pretended not to see her co-workers' confused entreaties as she poured over her notes and texts, assembling an outline to present to Redman. A project that would be mutually beneficial.

"Doc, I hate to interrupt you, but you've got a special delivery here."

She glanced up from the computer screen, pleased to note that Cobb hadn't stepped inside her boundaries. He was in the doorway, a plain parcel in hand.

"Who's it from?" Her voice sounded cranky. Weariness, stress, anxiety. Face it, she wasn't Cinderella on the best of days.

He studied the box. "There isn't a return. Maybe I should open it for you."

His caution got the better of her bad mood. Stretching to relieve the past few hour's accumulation of kinks, she then stood and went to take the package from him. "I appreciate your paranoia, Mr. Cobb, but I don't normally receive letter bombs at work."

His smile was thin and humorless—Fed-like. "There's always that first time that blows you away."

"Stand down, soldier. I'll take my chances."

She carried the box to her immaculate work station, a startling contrast to her home spaces. Who could have sent her a gift? Then she remembered Louis's promise of a gown to replace the one the protesters had ruined. Was this that replacement? The thought pleased her inordinately. After giving the small rectangle a curious assessment—must be a very tiny dress, indeed—she tore into the unmarked paper. A shoe box? Someone was sending her footwear?

Pulling off the lid, she stared inside the container, dismay tightening her features.

"What is it, Doc?"

She didn't respond—couldn't respond through the wad of horror and bile thickening in her throat. Then Cobb was there beside her, not awaiting her invitation.

"It's a shoe," he stated in flat bewilderment.

Stacy slapped the lid down before Cobb had a chance to reach inside. "Yeah, someone's idea of a joke."

A sick, sick joke. Her stomach jumped, ping ponging off all the caffeine and threatening to reject the turkey sandwich she'd had for lunch.

What she had in the box was evidence. But why send it to her? For what purpose? A warning? A challenge? Who knew she'd been to see Charlie, or that she'd be aware of the shoe's significance? Well, just maybe she wasn't up to playing someone's decidedly unfunny game.

The sight of the sparkling, sequined tennis shoe sent a shaft of mortality stabbing right to her core.

"Are you all right, Doc? Do you want me to get you some water or something?"

Or something. She wanted him to take the box from her sight so she might pretend she never saw the contents and thus now was faced with what to do about it.

"I'm fine, Cobb. Just tired. I'm going to knock off. You go . . . do whatever it is that you do."

"I'll see you in the morning, then."

"I'll be looking forward to it."

Her pale attempt at expected sarcasm alarmed more than it reassured. Cobb paused, obviously in a quandary.

"Good night, Mr. Cobb," she said with more authority, finally convincing him that she wasn't going to fly into hysterics or do something worth reporting to his superiors. He left as silently as he'd arrived.

Her first impulse was to shove the box and its damning contents down the hazardous waste chute. Rational thought stopped her. It was evidence from a crime scene. It might contain fingerprints from the killer or other trace evidence. It needed to go to the police.

And the minute she handed it over, there would be questions. And she would have to come up with answers. About her involvement in the case, unofficial as it was. And she would have to implicate both Charlie and the young police officer. And reveal her suspicions about Redman. She surrendered to a moment of awful projected consequence. The situation wasn't acceptable.

Carefully, she picked up both box and wrapping and placed them inside the tote bag she sometimes used to carry extra files home in. She might be breaking the law, but she would do everything possible to keep from destroying any potential clues. Carrying it and her briefcase, she left the building, riding the elevator alone into the parking structure.

She started walking, keeping out in the center of the lane. Her footsteps cast a single pattern of sound. Then, from someplace in the cavernous garage, metal danced off concrete, setting her nerves up on toe shoes. Glancing about in a rapid sweep, she quickened her pace, nearly jogging by the time she reached her car. Keys jangled in her trembling fingers. The door flew open, banging her hip with a protrusion of chrome. Her curse echoed colorfully as she tossed her belongings into the passenger seat, slid beneath the wheel and locked the door. She exhaled in shaky relief as the big V-8 growled to life.

Snapping on her seat belt, she shifted into reverse, glanced into the rear view and then turned toward her side door. The sight of a man standing close enough to block her vision brought an involuntary scream she quickly bit back as Frank Cobb stooped down to peer in, his face inscrutable. Repressing the urge to flail him alive with the sharp edges of her fear, Stacy rolled down the window. Before she could accuse him of trying to scare the liver out of her, he pointed to the garage floor.

"You're leaking antifreeze. You might want to get that looked at when you have time."

She could only stare at him, the word antifreeze as foreign in her panicked mind as some Federal cryptographer's code.

Then without an apology for nearly bringing on heart failure, he straightened and was gone before she had a chance to run him down in retribution for the fright he'd given her.

"Damn, sneaky Feds," she muttered as she rolled up the window. For the longest moment she sat frozen behind the wheel, listening to the hum of the heater and the static crackling from her underpowered radio. Slowly, she forced a swallow and made her hand reach for the shift again.

Her heart rhythm didn't return to normal until she'd reached her apartment complex.

***

From the shadowed niche of the elevator bank, Frank Cobb lit a cigarette and watched her drive away. He drew a long drag then said, "She's a pistol, all right."

"And a damned fine geneticist," Forrester added.

"So why the cloak and dagger? You suspect her of smuggling secrets or something?"

Forrester gave him a chilling stare. "It's not your job to ask questions, Cobb. All I want from you is what you see and hear."

"Yes, sir. That's what I do best. Seems odd to waste the taxpayers' money on a damned fine employee if you trust them."

"Trust is a subjective word, Mr. Cobb. Dr. Kimball has recently been awarded a very lucrative grant from a very secretive man. Louis Redman is someone Harper has wanted in their pocket for a long time. Any information you can get linking the two of them together for whatever purpose can only be beneficial."

"You want me to peek in the windows and take dirty pictures?" He was careful not to betray his disgust.

"I want to know why Redman picked her out of all our other 'damned fine' scientists. If there's nothing to find, there's nothing to find. But if something's up, I want to know about it. Got it, Mr. Cobb?"

Cobb snubbed out his half-smoked cigarette beneath the toe of his shoe, having lost the taste for it and the conversation.

"Crystal clear, Mr. Forrester."

***

As Stacy juggled her purse, package and briefcase, her cell phone began to ring. Pushing inside her apartment, she dropped her parcels and locked the door, deadbolt and all, behind her before flipping her phone open.

It was Fitzhugh returning her call.

His youthful voice was a refreshing dash of reality. Just what the doctor ordered.

Before she could stop herself, she broke another of her cardinal rules by asking in a breathless voice, "Could you come over?"

***

Ken Fitzhugh stood in the doorway of Stacy Kimball's apartment, overwhelmed by one observation.

What a pig sty!

For a woman as together as the gorgeous Ms. Kimball, the home she lived in was little better than a hovel. There was probably furniture under the mountainous heaps of magazines and junk mail. A rug was most certainly beneath the overflow of paper and pools of abandoned outerwear and empty boxes but not enough of it was available to discern pattern or color through the mess and dust.

"Come on in," she called, disappearing through the maze of teetering periodicals into what was supposed to serve as a dining area. A computer and scattered files covered the small table, and more paperwork occupied the cheaply covered café chairs. The countertop beyond was a jumble of empty snack cracker and cereal boxes, more mail, unopened, and a jungle assortment of dead houseplants whose mummified leaves littered the kitchen-area floor. Dirty glasses and coffee cups made pyramids in the double sink. A coffee maker with a permanent eight cup stain line displayed a half inch of questionably aged fur-topped liquid. He didn't want to see what the refrigerator held. Probably mold and spore samples not of scientific origin.

"Forgive the mess," she muttered in an absent aside. "I'd offer you a seat, but there probably isn't one."

He waited while she lit another cigarette from the stub still clenched between trembling lips. It flared and caught and quickly replaced the end she smashed out in an overflowing ash tray. With cigarette in one hand and a glass of something on the rocks in the other, she gestured for him to follow into her living room. There was one empty chair and she dropped into it without apology, stretching long legs out in front of her at odd angles, like a discarded marionette.

"Bad day?" he ventured, wresting his gaze from those sleek calves and firm, rounded thighs. She was either into jogging, had a gym membership or a treadmill hidden beneath some of the junk in the living room. She had an athlete's legs. Strong, very nice.

"A strange day," she corrected, dragging herself up into a sitting position as she dragged deeply on the Kool filtertip. Her manicured fingers played with the sides of a box that rested on a pizza carton on the table in front of her. Finally, she pushed it toward him. "I got this at work today. Be careful of prints."

Curiously, he used the tip of his ballpoint to nudge up the lid. He blinked at the gaudy shoe inside. "And this means, what?"

"The other shoe was on an unfortunate new resident of the morgue. A guest with marks on the side of her neck."

He blinked again, considering her take on the relevance. "Why do you think someone sent this to you? Do you have some kind of link to this case other than what we talked about earlier?"

She shook her head, but deception clouded the gaze she wouldn't lift to meet his.

"Did you ask me here just to show me this?"

She pulled on the cigarette, exhaling a thick stream of smoke to momentarily mask her expression. When it cleared, he saw concern and fear there in those lovely contours.

"It might contain evidence you can use to find the killer. For my own reasons, I don't want to be the one to surrender it over to the investigators in charge. Could you say someone left it in your patrol car? That way it could get to the lab without a link back to me."

She must have seen the reluctance in his face, for she heaved a weary sigh and covered her eyes with her free hand. "I know it's too much to ask. I knew before I called you."

"All right."

She peeked cautiously between her fingers. "What?"

"All right. I'll say it was left anonymously. If the lab boys come up with something, we'll go from there."

Her smile was shaky, bordering on sloppy drunk, but the alcohol didn't affect the graceful way she unwound from the chair to approach him. Her lips pressed warm and all too brief against his cheek, giving him the fleeting impression of perfume, scotch, Kools and desirable woman.

"Fitz, you are a prince among men."

He felt himself stiffen. "Hardly."

While she bundled the box up in some sort of plastic grocery bag to protect against outside contamination—though just exposure to her apartment would be enough to rate a toxic hazard—she passed him the parcel as if it contained dangerous bio-material. And that anxious movement prompted him to ask, "Are you all right, Ms. Kimball?"

"Better now," she confided as he took the sack. "But there is one more thing, one more favor you could do for me."

Why did he just know it would be another impossible request?

"Louis Redman."

"What about him?"

"I need someone to watch him, to chart his comings and goings."

"You think he's the killer?"

"Let's just say I think he warrants a good hard look, but it's too early to call it full-blown suspicion. I'll pay for the surveillance. I just didn't know who to ask."

"I know a couple of guys drawing disability that could use the extra cash. I'll set something up."

"Ken."

Her hand touched his arm, arresting movement and even thought.

"I don't have to remind you that this is all confidential."

He smiled reassuringly. "Mum's the word."

Anything for the lovely Ms. Kimball.

***

After Fitzhugh had gone, relieving the majority of her anxieties, Stacy poured another glass of Dewers and gave a jump as the phone rang. It was late, approaching ten. As she reached for the receiver, she knew from the square knots forming in her belly who was on the other end.

"Ms. Kimball . . . Stacy? It's Louis Redman. We need to talk."

SEVEN

The old brick and classic cornices of the Easton Hotel sat nestled between the glazed glass and soaring steel of modern Seattle, appearing as innocuous as a rotary dial on a fax machine. Once the residence of the lumber tycoons, it now housed the city's wealthy eccentrics who preferred not to move on with the times. A uniformed guard at the door kept the unwanted away. Visitors were screened and directed to an elevator that only opened upon a particular guest's floor. A top level mobster now retired, a former senator's mistress, and Louis Redman were said to be inhabitants, but no names were listed on mail boxes or call phones. A bastion of security where one paid the high price for privacy.

Stacy paused, prepared to show ID to the guard but obviously he was waiting for her, for he waved her right in and pressed six for the building's top floor. The doors to the elevator sighed shut, and on the smooth ride up, Stacy had plenty of time to rethink her visit.

Was she nuts?

She was on her way, alone, to pay a near midnight call upon a suspected killer.

Or worse.

What could be worse, she wondered, watching the old-fashioned arrow tick off the floor numbers.

She should have turned everything over to Fitzhugh when she had the chance—her empty photographs, the slides, and her suspicions—as well as the single sneaker. She had no business risking her life following the bizarre turns of this acquaintance with a possible madman.

He cast no reflection, for God's sake! What kind of logic could explain that away? Iron poor blood? A poor self-image?

Or was he an honest to goodness, bite 'em and suck 'em dry vampire?

Her well-trained capacity for reason denied that suggestion. There must be some rational . . .

Right. Isn't that what they all said as they stepped into the fiend's parlor on the late show?

She fingered the small silver cross she hadn't worn since she'd laid her mother to rest. Religion had died in her that day, along with the notion that there was any sense of fairness in the world. Necessity had her unearthing the relic of childhood catechisms. Just in case. She kept it inside her snug sweater, slightly embarrassed by the sign of what she considered ritual weakness and by the ecclesiastical direction of her superstitious folly. Her colleagues would laugh themselves silly if they saw her going to battle against age-old evil waving a cross as her only defense.

But her colleagues weren't riding with her in the elevator, were they?

Better safe than sorry, wasn't that what her mother always told her father when she reminded him to wear his bullet-proof vest even on the most mundane calls? And he was still alive, thanks to her advice. If only there had been some charm Stacy could have given her mother to keep her safe as well. Science hadn't saved her. Faith hadn't rescued her.

But perhaps, with Louis Redman's help, Stacy could save others.

If she could save herself.

If Redman could be trusted not to turn on her.

What game was he orchestrating? If he was the guilty party, why send her the victim's shoe? Was there a reason, or just the skewed machinations of a mind gone mad? Was she playing right into his hands by coming here alone?

Questions begot more questions, and by the time the doors opened on six, her mind was circling with them like a SeaTac approach on a holiday weekend. She stepped out onto the plush black-and-gold-diamond patterned carpet. The door shushed closed behind her, sealing off her options. All that remained were the double doors at the end of the corridor leading to Louis Redman's lair.

Lair.

She laughed at herself, the sound bolstering her quavering courage. For the love of Mike, she was a scientist not a sci-fi groupie. She was going to meet a benefactor not a monstrous serial murderer from the Late Night Creature Feature.

But there were worse things than make believe.

There were real monsters in the world. And no tiny silver cross would save her from one of their legion.

Pushing her wild misgivings into a closely relegated corner of her consciousness, Stacy strode down the hall, aware of the camera that tracked her movements. A perk of living at the Easton, or a product of Redman's paranoia? One thing for sure, her Louis certainly didn't want anyone getting the drop on him.

Her Louis?

Before she had the uncomfortable opportunity to puzzle over that Freudian *faux pas*, she reached out to tap on the door only to have it swing soundlessly open. Her heart leapt until she saw the Asian manservant bowing her way inside.

Get a grip, Stace.

"Good evening. I'm here to see Mr. Redman."

Silently, the servant took her coat and directed her with a gesture into the living room where the word 'posh' took on a tangible presence.

All in dark green, gilt and old wood, the setting was a page out of *Architectural Digest*. The only evidence of the Twentieth Century were the electric lights and the Levelor blinds closing out the cityscape beyond. The furnishings were an antique dealer's dream, displayed with showroom precision to the soft accompaniment of an Italian aria. Any moment, she expected some ad company to arrive for a photo shoot to peddle exotic vacations or Orson Wellsian aged liquor.

And on the center of one of the low tables lay a folder which accidentally spilled out several documents, or perhaps artfully revealed them. She caught a glimpse of her own black and white photo and was about to see what other goodies the cautious Mr. Redman had collected, when his exquisitely accented voice interrupted.

"Ms. Kimball . . . Stacy. How good of you to come on such short notice."

He was just there, standing practically at her elbow. She hadn't heard him or seen him enter the room, nor had she noticed exactly when the ancient manservant disappeared. She hid her startlement behind a tart reply.

"Most people use more conventional hours for their business meetings."

"I am not most people." His bland smile underlined that tremendous understatement. "And your portfolio stated you are—how do you say?—a night owl."

He didn't even try to deny that he'd had her investigated. Her resume didn't contain her sleep patterns, or for that matter, her sleep partners. She wondered if his portfolio did. Her chin came up a notch.

"I wanted to beg your forgiveness for the other night," he continued as if he hadn't announced a personal invasion into her private history. "I felt unwell and was forced to exit the restaurant rather hurriedly. I trust you found your way home without any difficulty. Takeo waited as per my instruction, but he did not see you leave."

But had Louis? Had he been watching? Had he seen her take the monorail and noted her youthful co-travelers? Had he chosen the pretty co-ed just to let her know how vulnerable she'd been outside the realm of his protection? Just to let her know he wasn't a man to be toyed with?

Well, he'd find that she didn't scare easily or respond well to threats, veiled or otherwise.

"I can always find my own way home, Mr. Redman. My mother taught me to always carry money for a cab when going out with a strange gentleman."

And gentlemen didn't get much stranger.

"Ah, a resourceful woman, your mother, and quite sound advice."

He moved into the room, his graceful step taking him to the bank of windows where he stood, staring at the shades as if he could see right through them to the night beyond. Had he planned for her gaze to follow him there in her helpless fascination with his dark looks and elegant manner?

Wryly, she thought, yes. How well he could read her weaknesses. But that didn't mean he could use them to manipulate her.

"Here I am. What was it you wanted? Just to make an apology? You could have done that on the phone."

He didn't turn in reaction to her crisp tone. Instead, his hands laced behind his back in a pose of extreme ease. Her own posture was threaded with taut rods of tension.

"I prefer to do my business face to face. Deceptive tool, the telephone. It's hard to read intention in a far distant voice."

"You think I have something to hide from you?" Did he know it was true?

"No, of course not. Do you?" He turned then and confronted her with a cool emerald stare and a mild, chiding smile.

"I am an open book. Or should I say," she amended, gesturing to the coffee table, "an open file."

He chuckled at her claim. "Please sit down, Stacy. We have much to discuss."

Noting her choice of solitary armchair over the more intimate spaciousness of one of the sofas, Louis perched on the edge of the large table. He nudged her offensive dossier with his fingertip and began his smooth interrogation.

"You began your career in a rather odd circumstance. Perhaps to serve your night owl propensities."

"Not so odd. My father was a policeman, my mother was a nurse. Their occupations brought them together, and I became a blend of their interests."

"The morgue?"

"Forensic medicine seemed a likely avenue for my leanings. I enjoyed the work. The night shift let me continue my education in medicine while I interned. A perfect match for a night owl. I dislike a lot of supervision. And there were no complaints from the customers."

He smiled faintly at her autopsy humor.

"Why did you go into genetics and blood diseases? Is that also because of your family history?"

His right-between-the-eyes assault upon the most private of her emotions brought an unexpected prick of tears to glimmer along her lashes. She blinked them away in irritation. She'd cried a river and where had it gotten her? The plain, bold truth was what would gain her what she needed.

"Yes. Purely selfish, granted, but highly motivating."

His voice softened like a caress. "There is nothing selfish about wishing to protect those you love."

"But I couldn't, could I? With all my knowledge, with all my skill, with all my education and influence, I couldn't protect them."

Then came his silken trap woven of seemingly innocuous words.

"And if you could have, what would you have been willing to do?"

"Anything. Everything. I would have made a deal with the Devil himself if it would have meant giving them even a few more years of life together."

"You are a romantic, Doctor Kimball." It was a statement of neither admiration nor accusation, just fact. "I wonder how many others realize that about you?"

Not many, she could have told him. After dashing a trembling hand across her traitorous eyes, she glared at the perversely calm Louis Redman. "Is that what you wanted to know?"

"It is what I knew the first moment I saw you. We understand each other, Stacy Kimball. We both know the pain of having power within our reach thwarted by the frustration of being helpless to bend it to our will."

And she felt that connection, suddenly, inexplicably, and soul-deep as his mesmerizing gaze consumed her pain with an empathy born of experience. She remembered then that he had buried two wives. How woeful that their kinship should arise from such unhappy circumstance. Yes, in that, they understood each other perfectly.

For a moment, Louis allowed himself to become lost in her sorrow. Waves of it radiated from her like heat from the sun he never saw. Tragedy was a powerful force, he knew, shaping strong character or unhealthy bitterness. Which prompted the lovely Ms. Kimball, determination or anger? The first he could utilize, but the second was dangerous and destructive.

"Now," she said, "it's your turn to tell me what prompted your interest in those same areas. Why put so much money into Harper and into this project? How do you benefit from it?"

"Must one benefit from having compassion for his fellow man?"

Her delicately arched brow called him on his evasion, but he couldn't tell her the truth. Not yet. So he continued with banal generalities.

"I fund many projects, Doctor, not just those at Harper. I donate to the environment, to the poor, to political campaigns if they sway my interest. I've helped build libraries as well as hospital wings. I am blessed with more fortune than I can spend. I have the luxury of holding many interests."

He could sense her dissatisfaction with his reply. She'd wanted him to reveal something more personal though her motives remained clouded. Like the rites of courtship, their conversation danced around the real issue.

What did they want from one anther?

For a human female, Stacy was difficult to read. She seemed to have mastered the usually easy-to-read mask of emotions that mortals wore so sloppily. She was stingy with her feelings, keeping them zealously close and out of his reach. A good thing, for he found himself all too vulnerable to her rare displays of heartache.

Though she didn't weep over this mother she had lost, the tears hovered near the surface, glimmering as her gaze shifted uncomfortably away, hanging heavy in the rough clearing of her throat that would deny sentiment's grip upon her. Such strength of purpose and compassion—an intriguing combination. He found he liked Stacy Kimball, the quixotic scientist with the brilliant mind made for discovery and a lush body fashioned for pleasure. A pleasure he could not afford to enjoy.

He got up suddenly. She jumped back, alarm stamped upon her expression like a passport destination.

"I beg your pardon. I didn't mean to startle you."

But he had.

Why did she fear him? Had she guessed the truth? Would her analytical mind let her investigate possibilities beyond the realm of reason? He didn't know whether to hope or worry. It had been so long, so very long since he'd shared his secret with someone of the regular world. The weight of it had grown so burdensome of late. What a relief it would be to release some of its crushing consequence. He sensed the strength to bear such a terrible knowledge in the graceful slope of Stacy's shoulders. But strength was not enough. Trust was tantamount.

Could he trust her with the truth? Could she help him without knowing the entire sordid tale?

Would her love of facts versus fiction keep her from fleeing him in terror? Would her rational intelligence allow her to accept without judgement? Could she be tempted with what he offered without being frightened away by what he was?

Would she work with him toward a common goal if she got a glimpse of what he was?

He wished he knew. But such certainty could not be rushed no matter how desperate he was to confide all and go from there. Patience. Let her come to terms with the truth at her own pace. He knew she had suspicions and yet, still, she was here. She was no coward. And he found himself anxious to discover what else she was.

But not tonight.

Not tonight, when he was looking at her as something other than a practical scientist.

"It is late," he announced abruptly. "You should go now."

It was already too late to contain the attraction. He should have known better than to arrange this intimate face-to-face. Across the phone lines, the temptation would not be so great. Through the receiver he could not sense her heat or scent her very humanity. With such impersonal distance between them, he wouldn't be thinking of how alone he'd been these last decades, of how fine it would feel to hold a woman in his arms again for a purpose other than that of sating his nightly hunger. He had other appetites, other cravings that suddenly stirred and demanded satisfaction. A yearning for the taste of a sweet kiss, the sound of a soulful sigh, the quickening of passion within a lover's embrace. He'd denied these things as dangerous but never deceived himself into believing them unimportant. He'd been human once, and a trace of that frailty yet lingered to eternally torment him. Though he chose a solitary life, it wasn't his preference. It was for his protection—protection of his way of life, of his sanity, of his heart. Of the three, his treacherous, once-human heart offered the most challenge and put up the greatest resistence to his plans.

He wouldn't care for Stacy Kimball. He could work with her, he could like her, but he could never, ever let himself get close to her. That would spell disaster for both of them.

She rose from the over-stuffed chair, leaning forward as she did to unconsciously present him with a glimpse of delightful bounty as the low, rounded neck of her sweater gapped away from her breasts. Warmth teased through him, through his belly, through his loins, exciting twin hungers both best ignored. Stacy was not here to fulfill fantasy or necessity. She was here to grant him a rare glimpse of hope, for that was all that kept him going in this newest, most optimistic millennia.

The hope of finding happiness and his lost humanity once again.

"Before I forget, this is yours."

He stared curiously at the wrapped parcel she'd carried in with her.

"Your coat," she explained. "I had it cleaned."

He smiled, surprised by the gesture. "That was hardly necessary."

"A small repayment for your gallantry."

Their gazes met and held for a long beat.

"Good night, Mr. Redman—Louis."

She extended her hand professionally, but he captured it with a courtly purpose that brought a flush of embarrassed pleasure to her face.

He touched his lips to the taut skin of her knuckles—sweet, soft and salty.

Delicious.

Some of that appreciation must have shown in his gaze because her expression hardened, and her hand was quickly pulled away. Ms. Stacy Kimball was not interested in attachments any more than he himself was. Or so they both believed in order to make the idea of working together more palatable.

"I'll have an outline of my project study for your approval in the next day or so." Her crisp tone was all business. Her body language was all beckoning femininity. The confusion of messages held him at bay.

"I shall look forward to seeing it. You can fax it to me at your convenience."

There it was, the flash of disappointment that both gratified and warned him. She didn't want a machine to be their go-between.

"If that's your preference."

How stiff, how displeased she sounded. How frustrated by her failure to conceal her true feelings.

"No," he told her quietly, holding her gaze, her attention, her very breath hostage with that simple, single word. "But perhaps it would be for the best. My hours are so . . . irregular."

"I'm a night owl, remember?"

He couldn't find it within himself to extinguish the tender bud of expectation unfurling with her soft smile.

"Leave a message for me then, and we will arrange a meeting."

She hesitated for a moment. He could see her mentally weighing the consequence of what she'd just done. He saw a woman who hated to act out of foolishness, out of impulse. But he also recognized a loneliness akin to his own, a desire to quench the thirst for companionship, if only along the line of business. And that, he could not resist, either.

"I shall look forward to hearing from you."

Too much so.

***

The spell Louis Redman cast over her sensibilities finally waned as she rode down in the elevator.

Stacy sagged back against the polished paneled wall and sighed in exasperation. She'd let opportunity slip away. She'd let him coax memories and motivations from her without revealing any of his own. She knew nothing more about him than she had while taking the ride up a scant hour ago. He'd never really answered any of her questions. How had she so completely lost control of her situation? Was it Redman and the lure of his masculine magnetism? Or was it her own sad state of affairs, or rather the lack thereof? If she couldn't rein in her raging hormones when around the man, how could she ever expect to learn anything?

He might well be a killer.

And it scared her to death when that sentiment failed to stir the proper amount of caution.

She would see him again. Not because she needed to know more but because she didn't want to stay away.

What was wrong with her? Was she so desperate for a relationship that she would grab at an attraction to a man who may not have been a man at all?

Or did the attraction stem from that fact itself?

Was her interest in Redman all the more intense because of its very impossibility?

She rubbed her eyes and castigated herself for her lack of judgement, for her lack of reason, for her lack of alarm.

Even if Louis Redman proved himself innocent of her darkest suspicions, he still wasn't going to be more than a business partner.

Not a bed partner. Not a life partner.

She'd just have to get over the disappointment.

EIGHT

They were the same.

Stacy stared at the DNA results, a sick sensation seeping through her stomach. There could be no mistake. The multilocus DNA fingerprinting tests she'd run were accurate within 1/135,000,000. Not a lot of wiggle room for even a wannabe skeptic.

Louis Redman's blood had been found under the floater's fingernails. He had attacked her, viciously, then thrown her off the pier to perish in the icy waters below. He wasn't the sad, benevolent patron whose melancholy struck a kindred chord within her.

He was killer.

And now, he was taunting her with that knowledge. By teasing her ambitions with the temptation of a grant. By goading her with her own mortality, sending her a shoe that could have been from her own foot instead of a passing stranger. To keep her silent or to merely torment her? Whichever it was, Stacy didn't like the circumstances. She was a cop's daughter. Her dad may not have been the best father, but he'd been a great cop. He'd always had unswerving integrity. He never compromised right with wrong. He never saw shades of gray. And neither should she. Science didn't recognize gray, only the degree of black or white.

It was time to go to the police.

She had enough evidence—if not to convict, then at least to warrant an investigation of Louis Redman. Could she weigh the death of the next innocent victim against the payment the Center had received?

She sighed and returned her study to the probes of DNA. Such an odd and interesting formation. The potential residing in those combinations may have held the secrets of immunity, of immortality.

She would never know, if this chance to study Redman escaped her.

A soft whisper twined around the firm pillars of her conscience.

What were a few lives compared to the thousands her research might save if her suspicions were correct? What were they when balanced against her own future?

She pushed out of her chair, the violence of the movement alerting her ever-vigilant watchdog in his seat by the door. Ignoring his questioning stare, she massaged at the tension knotting in the back of her neck.

Such God-like decisions weren't hers to make. Harper Research wasn't an extension of Nazi Germany, no matter what the protesters might claim on their hand-lettered signs. Maybe they dabbled in genetic engineering, but not in genocide.

She glanced at Frank Cobb, noting the chill of his hazel-green eyes. He wouldn't have any difficulty making a choice. It probably came with his on-the-job training. Whatever suited government interests. If she presented him with the details, she wondered what he would do. What would he consider the right thing?

Not that she planned to give him the information.

But would turning it over to the authorities place it in any better hands? Were they better suited, better trained to make decisions involving the future of mankind?

The shrill of her cell phone startled her from her troubled musings.

"Hey, Stacy, it's Alex. And you're not going to believe what I uncovered."

"Try me, Alex. I'm rather open-minded these days." She purposefully turned her back to Cobb so he wasn't privy to her expression.

"I kept digging. Louis Redman's trail might end here in Seattle about seven years ago, but Luigino Rodmini's goes back to fifteen century Florence."

"What?"

"I mean to tell you the guy is good. If I wasn't such a wiz on the Internet, and of course there's Claudia and her overseas connections, I wouldn't have gotten beyond his first few road blocks. He's careful, and he's smart. And if my research can be believed, he's over five hundred years old."

Shielding the receiver with a cupped hand, she whispered shakily, "You have proof of this?"

"Oh, baby, all the proof you'll ever need. You don't sound surprised."

Why wasn't she?

True, Fitzhugh had prepared her with old folktales and wild suppositions, but had she really, *really* ever given them any credence? So why was it so easy to take Alex at his word? To believe that Louis Redman's lifespan was almost five times greater than the average madman's?

"I'm not saying that I do, yet," she countered cautiously. "Let me see what you have before I make up my mind. I'm a firm believer in logical explanations."

He laughed. "If you can find one in this case, I'll be your slave for life. Just promise that I get this story. I'll be doing front page features for the rest of my life once I break this one."

"Alex, you can't go public with this. Not yet. When it's ready, it's all yours. Okay?"

"Don't make me wait too long, Stace. You know I don't have a lot of restraint."

Lowering her voice into a sultry rumble, she cooed, "That's not the way I remember it."

His laugh was all prideful male. "Yeah, well, what can I say? I'll wait. For you, babe."

"Can you get everything you have to me this evening?"

"On a silver platter. I've got to go out of town, but I'll get a courier to run it to your apartment. That work?"

"That's great. I owe you, Alex."

"And I'll collect. Count on it."

She stared at the severed connection for a long, pensive moment.

It was a whole new ball game now.

***

Carrying the bulky parcel from the private courier into her living room, Stacy shoved aside the cartons of Chinese take out and ripped into the mailer envelop. Pouring the contents onto the newly cleared coffee table, she poked through the papers between mouthfuls of Moo Goo Gai Pan. Very quickly, the food was forgotten all together as she stared at the delicious blend of history before her.

Almost six centuries of documentation. The life of Florentine noble, Luigino Rodmini, a life that instead of ending after an expected number of years, continued with a new name, in a new city. In the early 1800's he surfaced in London, wedding Arabella Howland, the daughter of an acclaimed physician. He was then Louis Radman. As his surname changed to Radouix and his residence to France, Arabella bore him a daughter, Nicole. As Louis Radcliffe, he had appeared in New York near the turn of the century, living with his grandmother, Bella, who was most likely his wheelchair-bound and aged wife. After her death, he married Cassandra Alexander, heiress to a newspaper empire. They disappeared in Europe, their businesses handled by proxy. His daughter, Nicole wed a French expatriate and lived with their daughter, Frederica, on the island of Martinique. Then, more silence as the family seemed to vanish, from print at least, until the wealthy eccentric, Louis Redman set himself up in Seattle.

How could Rodmini and Redman be one in the same?

How could they not be, given all the evidence before her? She believed in what she could see, touch and prove. All of that was spread out on her coffee table. She'd been in the medical field long enough to have seen quirks of nature and the unthinkable become truth. Somehow Louis Redman had managed to transcend the effects of time. Whether that made him an undead creature of folklore or the victim of a rare blood disorder, she could not deny who he was. He was almost six hundred years her senior and looked to be her peer.

Was he a fiend who needed to feed upon human vitality in order to survive? A killer who disguised the evil of what he was behind a suave demeanor and generous checkbook?

If he had the option and she, the talent, would he willingly offer his unique properties in study for the benefit of mankind? Or was his benevolence just a ruse to hide the darkness of his soul?

Did he have a soul?

Nudging the papers back into a single pile, Stacy leaned back in her chair, lost to swirling thought. A sudden bang against her door had her leaping in involuntary alarm. Then, laughing softly at her own jumpiness, she went to the door and peered through the peephole. The hall was empty.

Frowning slightly, she thought about returning to her chair when a quiet ripple of intuition had her turning the knob instead.

A small, brown-paper-wrapped box lay on her doorstep.

She stared at it for a long moment as if it were a cobra basket with the lid askew. Any minute, something lethal would lunge out at her. She stood, sweat gathering on her brow, welling in her palm, itching at her scalp. There were no outward marks on the package but she knew, *she knew* what it contained.

It contained evidence of another death.

Wishing she could close the door and shut out the awful responsibility placed unwanted upon her doormat, she cursed softly and toed the box inside her apartment. As perversely fascinated as that snake charmer defying death by looking inside the basket, Stacy used a thin-bladed knife to slit the packing tape, careful not to get her fingerprints on the wrapping or smudge any that might be there.

She thought at first that she was looking at someone's pet, a hamster or perhaps a bunny. But as she peered more closely at the soft tangle of gold, she saw it was a length of human hair, a ponytail still bound in a hot pink scrunchie. Her vision blurred. Nausea sank sharp talons into her middle and twisted hard. She felt the hard whack of her unvacuumed rug beneath her fanny as she sat down abruptly, shivers dissolving the strength from her legs like an acid bath reaction.

It wasn't someone's deceased pet. She was looking at the mocking evidence of another dead girl.

Hours seemed to pass instead of minutes until her wits gathered enough for her to dial the phone.

"Charlie?"

"Stacy? Is that you? What the hell's wrong?"

The bass boom of his concern helped fortify her.

"Charlie, has another of those bite victims come in tonight?"

Good, she sounded better, stronger, almost nonchalant. The phone receiver played an erratic tympani against her ear and jaw as her hand shook fitfully in protest of her pseudo-calm.

"Let's see. All I have on my agenda for the evening is a gunshot victim from a drug deal gone south, and a hit and run. Were you just curious, or is there something else going on that you're not telling me?"

Giddy with what would most likely be a short-lived relief, she said, "I just can't get this whole thing out of my mind, I guess. Silly and unprofessional, I know. I was hoping you'd have some more information for me."

"Nothing yet. The lid's clamped down on this one like a pressure cooker steaming vegetables. Just steam so far. Nothing edible."

"Thanks, Charlie. Don't forget to call me."

"Stace, some advice?"

"Sure, Dad."

"Get some sleep. Alone, preferably."

Charlie couldn't see her wry smile or know that her own bed was always solitary when it came to sleep. "Good night, Charlie."

"Sweet dreams, doll."

She doubted it. Not while she was waiting for some poor girl to show up somewhere with her hair cropped crudely and her life cut short.

***

Stacy was spitting her toothpaste in the sink when she heard it.

She always listened to the news as she readied for work, the voice from her clock radio her only morning companion. She was only half paying attention when the solemn story hit her in the solar plexus.

"The body of seventeen-year-old Brianna Kerschner was found by a jogger in Pioneer Square this morning, the victim of an apparent attack. At this time, robbery does not appear to be a motive. Authorities say she was not sexually assaulted."

The rest of the report details were drowned out by Stacy's retching.

She made it to the bed, collapsing there in just her slip and heels with a cold washcloth covering her eyes. Her head and her conscience pounded miserably. There was nothing she could have done to prevent the crime. It had already happened by the time the package was delivered to her door.

It wasn't her fault.

But then again, it was.

If she'd turned the earlier evidence in sooner, if she'd made a full statement to the police, perhaps Charlie wouldn't be calling her even now.

"You heard?" His voice was strangely sympathetic.

"Yeah. On the radio just a minute ago. Have you seen her yet?"

"Right here in front of me. Marks on her throat, signs of strangulation, blood loss. And, get this, her hair was chopped off at the scene. There were strands of it all over her coat, like somebody used a knife. Stace? Are you there?"

"Yeah, Charlie. What was the cause of death?"

"I'd say, and this is preliminary, that it was massive blood depletion. Another sidebar. I heard there was next to none found at the scene."

"Thanks, Charlie. I've got to get to work. I'll talk to you later."

"Yeah. See you on the six o'clock news. I don't think they're going to keep this under wraps much longer."

After hanging up, Stacy tottered on ridiculously weak legs back into the bathroom to rinse her mouth a second time. The taste of horror still lingered, sour and filled with regret.

She couldn't help Brianna Kerschner, and she could only hope there'd be time before the next victim was found for her to stop Louis Redman.

***

"You look like hell."

On a better day, her glare would have cut Frank Cobb in half. Today, it sparked and fizzled, her battery too weak to sustain the energy.

"Coffee?"

The thought of caffeine chafing on her raw stomach lining made her grimace. "Tea with lots of creamer."

Cobb raised a single brow into a high arch of wonder, but he said nothing. Wise man.

Sinking into her computer chair, Stacy slid her briefcase under the desk where it rested against the side of her shoe. In it were the papers from Alex Andrews and a bagged sample of Brianna Kerschner's fair hair. The first, she didn't dare leave unguarded. Perhaps some of Cobb's raging paranoia was rubbing off on her. The hair sample she would test to compare to Charlie's most recent guest.

Before her courage failed or her shadow returned, she snapped open her cell phone for a quick call.

"This is Stacy Kimball. I need to see you this evening. I'll be there at seven. There are some things we need to go over regarding the project."

She rang off, not leaving him any options.

But she had a feeling that Louis would see her. He was expecting her.

"Tea with creamer."

She jumped as Cobb reached in front of her to set the cup on the desk. For a long two minutes, her heart beat wildly in her throat. Cobb was too well trained not to notice and too smart to comment on it. He went to assume his seat by the door, giving Stacy her space as per their agreement.

Her fate had been set in motion. By calling Redman, or whatever his name was, she'd left herself no alternative. She would meet with him then confront him with what she'd learned. And then, they would either strike a bargain, or he would kill her, too.

How valuable would one researcher be to a man whose lifetime spanned centuries?

"Are you all right, Doc?"

She glanced at Cobb and could only guess at how she looked with her eyes wide, wild and rimmed with red from her earlier worship of the porcelain god. She tried to smile, but her lips began to quiver. She pinched them together and offered a pale facsimile. And to her surprise, her G-man lost his composure watching her trying to cling to her own.

"None of your bullshit now. I'm not stupid, and I'm not your enemy, either. Whether you believe it or not, it's my job to help you. Maybe not behind the computer or with whatever bugs you're working with under the microscope, but if something's spooked you, I'm a helluva handy guy to have around."

And he looked it, too, with his hazel green eyes narrowed and dangerous and his scowl full of woe to whomever might get in her way. Even unarmed, his body was built to be a compact weapon, lean, taut and tempered steel. A handy guy, to be sure, but could she trust him?

How wonderful it would be to brace Redman with Frank Cobb beside her for support. How gratifying to spill the horrifying events of the past few days and turn their resolution over into his capable hands. He wasn't Ken Fitzhugh. He wouldn't have to concern himself with the law. He was most likely above it. And he would protect her with his life. She knew it. But could she trust him with her secrets, knowing who employed him?

No. Regretfully, no.

She smiled in genuine thanks. "It's just some personal stuff, Frank. Nothing anyone can help me with, but I appreciate the offer."

If she expected him to melt before the bestowal of her charm, she could save her energy. He stared at her unblinkingly, disbelievingly. But he didn't challenge her words.

"Just remember the offer," he said at last.

***

She wished she'd taken him up on it as she stepped from a cab and through the first set of doors to the Easton. To the polite inquiry of the doorman, she replied, "Mr. Redman is expecting me."

She waited, breath compressed within her lungs like a deep sea diver's . Her chest ached with anxiety. Her palms were damp. But her gait was all aggressive certainty as she crossed into the elevator at the doorman's affirming gesture.

Time to brace the beast in his den.

The ride up seemed interminable. She kept her mind focused on what she would say and away from what he might do. That's the only way she could convince herself to continue. She'd come to terms with the information Alex had sent her.

Logic insisted she accept what the facts told her. Science urged her to find out how those facts were possible. And her own situation prompted her to ignore physical danger in order to satisfy both.

Those were the external claims working upon her. But inside, where she pretended they had no pull, were two very different reasons for her to go to Redman.

Anger and disappointment.

She'd believed him, wanted to believe in what she thought she saw in him. Decency. Honor. Concern.

Lies. All lies.

She didn't know what Louis cared about, but it wasn't the fate of humankind.

He'd led her to think he would help her. That with his money and his charm and his interest in her work, she could break through the barriers of time and red tape to complete the study. Another cruel lie.

The truth was destroying her every hope. And she resented the hell out of it and out of him.

Why couldn't things just go her way a little while longer? Just until she found the cure? She'd come so close. She'd seen the possibilities there in her microscope. Now, that hope was fading, slipping farther and farther from her grasp as the illusion Louis Redman hid behind began to unravel.

She couldn't partner herself with a killer. She couldn't align herself with a devil. And she wanted him to know that. She wanted to tell him to his face—no insincere telephone call—how much his deception had hurt her.

Then they would come to terms.

If she lived that long.

It was possibly the only purely irrational moment of her life.

She was met at the door by Redman's manservant. He scanned her apparel without obvious disapproval but she guessed at it in his slight hesitation before he waved her inside. Her footsteps were swallowed up by the thick plush of the carpet. As frantically as it was beating, she was surprised the pulse of her heart wasn't audible. Or would it be to one of Redman's dark heritage?

"Stacy, your call was a pleasant interruption."

Gasping because she had neither heard nor felt his approach, Stacy turned to face the enigma of Louis Redman. His single statement managed to artfully convey his tolerance for what was nonetheless an intrusion.

"Good evening. Thank's for seeing me."

She felt his gaze skim her appearance and wondered if she'd chosen her attire wisely when he crooned, "It is always a pleasure to see you. What business have you to discuss? Your message sounded urgent."

Might as well get right to the point before her courage failed her.

"I've discovered some interesting things today and would like your input on them."

His brows arched elegantly. "Oh? Something to do with your project?"

"Indirectly. No, that's not true. It has everything to do with my research."

At her hesitation, he prompted, "Yes?"

How on Earth to broach the unbelievable? By just plunging in the way one would acclimate to the chill waters of a swimming pool. Once you were up to your neck and beyond to the point of no return, the adjustment was quick albeit not quite painless.

She took a breath.

"Mr. Redman."

"Louis," he corrected smoothly. "I thought you'd agreed to call me by my name."

"What name would that be, Louis?"

He froze in anticipation of her summary.

"Redman or Rodmini?"

NINE

Louis had no idea why she'd called to request a meeting, but the urgency in her voice made him wary. And the anticipation in his mood made him equally concerned.

Just a tool, he continued to remind himself. That's all Stacy Kimball could be to him. Her intelligence, her talent were meant for him to take advantage of, not admire. Experience had taught him to keep his distance. Set her on the path and let her own curiosity lead the way. A woman of her clever initiative couldn't resist the journey. His hope was that it would end where it would do him the most good.

But then Stacy Kimball arrived, and as she skimmed off her coat, he was staggered by what she revealed. A dull ache began, an impatient throb below his belt. A twin rumble of need and want growled to be recognized and appeased. He would do neither. He could do neither without compromising all.

But whatever else he was, he was still a man.

And she was a scientist. What kind of scientist looked like a Venus and dressed like a harlot? It was his experience that one didn't advertise what wasn't for sale. And Stacy Kimball looked like a red light special in the seduction aisle.

A thick French braid captured most of her honey-gold hair. Wisps escaped to frame her face with flirty softness. Blue gray eyes were kohled to the envy of a Middle Eastern concubine, the defining smudges lending a smoky sensuality to even the most innocent stare. Her mouth, so wide and lush and tempting, appeared just kissed by glossy color. And her high, glamorous cheekbones displayed the tint of a maiden's blush.

And blush, she should have, when observing herself in the mirror. The sleek inviting line of her long neck led to a seemingly endless downward visual plunge where skillfully undone buttons directed the eye into an amazing curve of cleavage. Fragrant shadows beckoned between gorgeously soft contours. Drowning there would be a man's sweetest fantasy. Until his gaze dropped to the tight skin of her black vinyl skirt. It barely topped her thighs then tormented the imagination with a zipper sketching up one sleek hip. In his raging imagination, he could feel the metal tab between his fingers, hear the rasp of paradise opening, revealing inch after inch of firm, nylon-clad leg.

He locked his hands behind his back, laced fingers going pale with tension.

What could the woman be thinking to present herself in such a fashion? Was it her purpose to distract him? If so, she'd succeeded brilliantly. Did she want him to forget that a razor-sharp mind lay beneath the tousled hair? That within her gloriously ripe breasts beat a blind ambition? He'd read her dossier. He knew she hadn't slept her way up through the scientific community. Her affairs were outside the field, brief, puzzlingly inappropriate, and severed with clinical precision. She never looked back.

What made a beautiful, passionate creature like Stacy Kimball settle for cheap, screw-top wine when she should have been bathing in champagne?

It wasn't his business to wonder. But he had to wonder what business brought her.

Then she hit him between the eyes with it.

Rodmini.

Protective instincts that had kept him alive for centuries surged to the forefront, demanding that he take swift, unwaveringly brutal action to guard his secret from further exposure. Exquisite agony pierced through his gums as necessity and need combined. He'd been hungry for her from the very first, and now he had an excuse to lose control.

He could smell her fear entwined intoxicatingly with her femininity. Expectation brought the anticipated taste of her to whet his lips. His muscles coiled with predatory intention, until logic slapped the urges from him.

If she knew who and what he was, why was she here?

Curiosity reined in his hunger and quieted his defensive panic. Why place her life in peril unless the risk was worth the potential gain?

What did she want from him?

Stacy saw her own end in the cauterizing fire consuming his gaze. She saw her death in the abrupt angles and hollows that altered his handsome looks into something lethally gaunt and ravenous. She'd awakened the demon residing within the man, and now she would pay the price.

Suddenly, even as she struggled to hold her ground against the expected attack, the danger lessened. The phosphorescent gleam extinguished. The sharp bones of his face softened. And he looked at her with a suspicious intensity while she shivered in realization of how close she'd come to death.

"Where did you hear that name?"

Relief made her cocky once more.

"My sources prefer to remain anonymous. I'm sure you can understand why."

Out of respect for her intelligence, he didn't try to spin some reasonable explanation as either a lie or a mistake to wave away the information she possessed. Instead, he studied her, gaze piercing and penetrating, in search of a different sort of truth.

"What do you plan to do with what you know?"

"That depends upon you. May I still call you Louis?"

His mouth tightened into a fierce smile as he made an affirming gesture with his hand. "Why not?"

Stacy wasn't fooled by his almost cavalier manner. He was a dangerous animal facing the confines of an unpleasant and potentially deadly trap. Only his curiosity held him at bay. But just in case his protective instincts got the better of him, she eased the small silver cross around from where it had dangled at the back of her neck. It flashed as it caught the room's muted light.

His gaze riveted to the crucifix that had more significance to him than to her. The sight of it took a huge bite out of his good will as his stare winced away. His nostrils flared, and his breath exhaled in a soft hiss. He spoke with a cutting tone. "What do you want? Money? A promotion? Your own company? Name your blackmail."

"I want your blood."

He blinked, then issued a genuine laugh. There were few things she could have said at that point to so neatly defuse the danger from the situation. "What an ironic reversal. Sit down, Ms. Kimball. Tell me more."

Cautiously, she eased into one of the over-stuffed chairs. Her attention followed Louis as he began to roam the room, his restlessness a sign of his dissatisfaction with the corner she'd maneuvered him into.

"I don't know what you are," she began tersely. "I hadn't thought such a thing possible. But here you are, and so I must believe. No matter how much I despise the deceptions you hide behind, I cannot ignore your importance to my work. You have certain properties in your blood that make your rather unique existence possible. They keep you alive. They extend your life expectancy well beyond the normal range, perhaps even indefinitely. Unfortunately, they seem to break down quickly and completely when exposed to sunlight."

"How did you get a sample . . . ah, yes. At the restaurant. How resourceful of you."

It didn't quite sound like a compliment. For a moment, Stacy experienced an odd twinge of shame, as if she'd violated his privacy in some unacceptable fashion. The moment quickly disappeared.

What did she have to apologize for?

"It was the only way I could think of. You weren't likely to volunteer."

"But why did you suspect me?" Louis wanted to know. "Was it the photographs you took? In this modern age, one doesn't leap so quickly to cry 'vampire' just because of certain eccentricities."

Vampire.

Stacy shuddered involuntarily then grabbed onto the saving strength of her profession. Approach him calmly, step by step, braced behind the power of logic.

"The girl on the pier. She had trace amounts of your blood under her fingernails. You were the only one the police questioned in earlier attacks, even though they had no proof to hold you. I just put the two together."

"The young woman on the pier? She volunteered this information?" He seemed surprised, as if it meant some sort of personal betrayal.

"In a way. I took the sample from her in the morgue. She didn't object."

Louis winced at her harsh tone. He turned away for a moment, and Stacy thought she heard him murmur, "So she jumped, after all. A pity."

How dare he? His inappropriate regret fired Stacy's outrage, making her forget her immediate situation in favor of Wanda Cummings's brutal end. "Are you asking so you can cover your tracks more carefully next time?"

He glanced back at her. His slight smile said 'touche.' "My tracks, as you call them, are extremely well covered. It would take a very determined and very clever individual to expose them for what they are."

"And you for what you are," she added, hoping to attain a bit more leverage so she could put her fears to rest. And to needle his own in payment for what the poor Wanda must have felt. And Lisa. And Brianna after her. But Louis would not be so easily frightened.

He pinned her with a sudden, white-hot glare. "Is that what you mean to do? Expose me? To what? Sunlight? Publicity? The police?"

"No. At least not for the time being."

"I will not be threatened, Ms. Kimball."

She wasn't deceived by the purr of his voice. Threat vibrated through it. He was a panther about to strike unless she could convince him not to spring. Difficult to achieve when she was a potential meal poking him with a stick.

"And neither will I. I wanted to tell you that myself so there would be no misunderstanding. I didn't come here to threaten. I came to propose a truce."

Again, she had caught him off guard. Bemusement plain on his darkly handsome face, he asked, "And what is the nature of this arrangement?"

"I want to study you. When you . . . feed, something in your blood chemistry alters any other blood type it contacts into a compatible arrangement so it can be absorbed to sustain you. Do you understand what that might mean? The end of transplant rejection. A universal supply of blood. And there's another benefit that could eventually wipe out disease by eliminating weaker strains. An end to AIDs, leukemia."

"Ah, the crusader, not the capitalist."

"What if I am? That changes nothing."

His soft response was mild and mysterious. "Perhaps it does."

"I'm interested in curing diseases that kill more in a moment than you have in a lifetime. That makes me willing to bargain."

"And there's this," he added softly, a whisper that should have prepared her.

He extended his forearm and pushed up his sleeve to bare his inner arm. Deliberately, he drew his thumbnail from elbow to wrist, inhaling sharply as blood welled up from the gash he opened. Stacy gasped in shock, but her alarm quieted into amazement as, before her eyes, the wound closed and faded until no seam remained. She seized his arm, checking the validity of what she'd seen by rubbing her fingertips across what should have been, but wasn't, torn flesh.

"Instantaneous cell regeneration," she breathed in astonishment, not noticing the chill of his undamaged skin.

"Not always immediate," he corrected, calmly covering the unblemished area with his shirt sleeve once again and in the process, brushing off her touch. "But always complete. The time frame depends upon the degree of injury."

"Then it's true." Her hushed words were almost inaudible. "Immortality." Her gaze flashed up to his, her enthusiasm firing her eyes and quivering in her voice. "You must let me study you. I guarantee completely secrecy. I'll do all the research on my own time, so my findings will be strictly confidential."

"So, any moral objection you might have to what I am is easily overcome by my scientific significance, is that it, Doctor Kimball?"

"Not easily," she replied in response to his acidic tone rather than his pointed words. "But one endures what one must for the greater good."

"The greater good." He chuckled, taunting her with her own self-righteous stand. "When one has led a selfish life, thinking only to preserve that which should never have survived, you play the wrong tune to win my compliance."

"It's the only tune I know."

"And what do I get for my cooperation?"

"What do you want? Why did you fund my work and the projects at the center? Is it for greater power or to gain Harper's protection—"

"I seek a cure."

Now, she was surprised. That, she hadn't expected. "A cure?"

Watching him speak of it, she couldn't doubt his sincerity. The mere prospect animated his features, firing the green of his eyes like heat purifying a rare jewel.

"Is it possible? I must know. I followed your work, the direction of your studies. That's why I chose you, Stacy. With what you now know, can you create a cure? Do not lie to me or lead me on if you know there is no chance of success. I guarantee you, you'd do well not to disappoint me."

As he had disappointed her? His bullying only strengthened her resolve instead of intimidating. Her clinical cool would have frost-bitten an ordinary man.

But nothing about Redman was ordinary.

"There is every chance of success. While I separate out the special aspects of your condition to benefit my cause, I'll also work on a way to reverse it."

"To make me mortal?" He asked as if he were requesting an impossible dream become reality. Stacy shrugged.

"Yes."

The breath left him in a rush. His eyes closed tight and his body swayed. Stacy reached for him, steadying him with her grip on his elbows. She was about to ask if he was all right when quiet laughter escaped him.

"You make it sound possible."

"It is," she assured him.

He looked at her then, a bittersweet joy lending his features a youthful innocence. She had no immunity to that unexpected glimpse of vulnerability. Quickly, she released him and stepped back, but it was too late to distance herself from the way his poignant melancholy moved upon her heart.

She must be very, very careful not to come to care for Louis Redman.

"Why are you smiling?" she asked him.

"You remind me of someone, the way you hold your chin with such bold certainty." Then he seemed to shake himself to scatter tender thoughts, and he was the one to turn away. "How long will it take? When can I expect to be human again?"

His sudden brusqueness shattered the mood of companionable intimacy, changing it to one of impersonal business again. She reined in foolish sentiments that threatened to run away with her against her staunchly held will and noble agenda. He was an object of study, a research specimen, nothing more.

Anything more would be too dangerous.

"I'll start by getting another sample of your blood, more this time so I can begin running a battery of tests. Once I isolate the factor of variance, things should progress quite swiftly."

"Do you need more money? More equipment? Is there anything I can do to hurry the process along?"

"Yes, one thing."

He restrained his own anticipation upon hearing the firm timbre in her tone. A warning.

"No more games, Louis. No more threats. You've no point to prove any more. We can afford no undue attention to focus on this project. Secrecy is our only means to success. I can't change what has already been done, but you must control yourself or our association ends here."

He tilted his head, as if bewildered by her stern statement, but he nodded somberly.

"We will work together, Doctor Kimball. And I will walk in daylight again and lead a normal life."

And if things went as planned, so would she.

***

It was possible.

After Stacy had delivered her rather odd ultimatum and gone, Louis sat back on his sofa and dared to dream.

Human again.

To breathe the warmth of sunlit air. To feel the heat of the day upon his skin. To live in a world not doomed to shadow and artificial light.

To escape the damning necessity of his curse.

To never hunt again.

Only Arabella's love had kept him going after her father's experiment had failed almost two centuries ago. He'd been so close, so close to finding redemption. Bella's faith and Cassandra's strength had bolstered him when the weariness of his existence made him think perhaps prolonging his life was a greater sin than seeking a way to revert it back to the realm of the natural. If he died in this unholy form, how could his soul be saved? How could he join the two women that he'd loved in their pure states of grace?

The thought of existing another eternity without hope of ever seeing them again was the encouragement he needed to continue on.

And now, now this bold and beautiful woman of logic and knowledge offered what he daren't believe. That he could live again. That he could finish out his normal years then go to his reward beyond.

"Dare I believe, Bella?" he asked aloud. "I have known such failure and despair before, I fear I'll not survive another disappointment."

No answer came except in the quiet corners of his heart where faith still resided.

"She is smart and determined, Little One. She reminds me of you. Perhaps that is why it is so difficult to resist—"

He broke off, sensing some things were best left unshared with the woman who'd held his heart, his hopes and his dreams of salvation. His Bella was ever the matchmaker, seeking his own happiness over her own. Hadn't she pushed him into Cassandra Alexander's arms when she knew her own days were numbered? She'd seen he had a companion to support his cause, to give him a reason to rise with the end of each day so she could seek her well-deserved rest away from the anguish of age and the merciless passage of time. She had chosen well. Cassie had filled a void he'd thought he could not survive. He'd loved her, and she'd been devoted to him.

And now the two of them were together. Conspiring, he wondered, to make Stacy Kimball his new heart's desire? Part of him wanted to surrender to their well-intentioned meddling. But part of him resisted.

He couldn't bear the pain of having and losing another mortal love. Despite the promise of pleasure a relationship with Stacy offered, its finite nature made him reluctant to give in. True, he found her attractive and intriguing, but what kind of a future could they have together?

Unless she cured him.

Unless she made him into a man who could woo and win that love.

And then, what could stop him from finding happiness again?

TEN

In the morning, Stacy filed her project report with Greg Forrester. Her area of study, acute myeloid leukemia. He approved the choice without comment once she told him of Louis's support.

Anxious to begin, she ordered the necessary equipment and arranged her lab accordingly, with Cobb a silent background observer. She was somewhat surprised to still see his shadow. Her field of research wasn't likely to interest the government. It had no political or military applications—at least, that they were aware of. But if they got wind of what she was really working on, she gave her independence about a three second life expectancy.

And what would that do to her own?

Now, to put aside the moral issues that had prevented her from finding sleep. She wouldn't think about what manner of creature Louis Redman was, or whether or not he could be trusted. She would concentrate on the work ahead and think of its ultimate value to mankind.

With Cobb a continual reminder to take care, Stacy separated her work into two areas: the expected and the experimental. The normal procedures she ran through her lab computer but those comparative diagnostics which ran an infected sample alongside Louis's she would chart on her home computer, upon her own disks. Her rationale was simple.

Anything that plugged into Harper Research's power supply was suspect—her phone, her conversations, and her computer entries. Excessive caution, perhaps, but a glance at Cobb's pseudo-casual pose near her door said perhaps not. She had no idea what was being developed on the security floor below. Rumors that it was germ warfare were expected. Whispers that it was something worse—if that was possible—made them all tread carefully.

What would they say if they knew she was tinkering with immortality?

Better they not know. Not now, not later.

As she leaned back from the computer screen to rub her neck and give her eyes a break, a cup of strong coffee appeared on the desktop at her elbow. Too tired to affect the usual irritation, she smiled up at Frank Cobb and was gratified by the look of alarm that crossed his face. A nice face, really, once she got past the all-seeing eyes and smug grin.

"You're quite welcome," he volunteered. He started to turn away.

"Are you married, Frank?"

He glanced back at her. "Are you asking, Doc?"

The lack of antagonism between them was almost as scary as the fact that he was there to spy on her. She pointed to the mellow green screen.

"Married to the job," she told him.

"Me, too."

"What's wrong with us?"

He shook his head. "I do not know."

She pushed back in her chair, the abrupt movement startling him back into wariness. What kind of jobs had he done before he came to work at Harper? Something that had him honed to a fine edge. Something more dangerous than babysitting a scientist in a security-tight lab. So, why was he assigned here, wasting his valuable talents?

She knew better than to think he'd tell her.

"I'm going home and pretend I have a life."

He relaxed at that announcement. "I've got a cold brew and ESPN waiting up for me."

She sighed. "Sounds good."

"I've got extra."

The unexpected invitation hung between them for a long, awkward minute. He seemed surprised that he'd said it out loud, and Stacy was surprised by her own response. Frank Cobb was exactly the kind of guy she usually looked for—commitment-shy, good build, great if rare smile, and no strings, with a brain thrown in as a pleasant bonus. A few hours relieving tension and stopping the clock while rolling between the sheets with him would have tempted a month ago, hell, even a week ago.

She knew exactly when the idea of exhausting sex had lost its medicinal appeal.   When she looked from Wanda Cummings' blue complexion to the sample of Louis Redman's blood. Everything in her life changed at that moment. Her focus refined, her attention centered.

Frank held up his hand. "You don't have to answer. I shouldn't have asked."

"I'm glad you did. It means we might just call a truce and be friends."

"Friends?" His brow quirked, as if the concept was unique to him. It probably was. "Yeah, okay. Friends, it is."

"Or is that against the rules?"

He grinned at her sassy tone. "Probably, but I've broken a rule or two in my life."

"No!" She pretended shock, and he looked almost embarrassed. "Well, at least I know where to find a cold beer when I need one."

"C'mon, Doc. I'll walk you to your car."

Too weary to protest, she packed up and led the way to a silent elevator ride. But instead of being steeped in adversarial tension, the mood between them was almost companionable. As he guided her through the dim parking aisles, his fingertips rested easily at the small of her back. She allowed it because there was nothing sexual involved in that touch. And because, after all the confusion and fear of the past few days, it felt good to let down her guard while knowing he wouldn't compromise his.

He unlocked her door and held it open for her, then secured the latch before he shut it. Stepping back, he raised a hand in farewell.

And Stacy knew she was no longer alone.

***

A terrible fatigue had settled in by the time Stacy entered her apartment building. Though she had mounds of work ahead of her, her only wish was to fall into bed and sleep. But sleep was hours away.

"Hi, Stacy. Haven't seen you for a while."

Stacy smiled at the perky young co-ed who shared a ground floor apartment with her rock drummer boyfriend. "Hi, Glenna. How are the classes going?"

How strange it felt to conduct a normal conversation with an average girl. No intrigue. No double entendres. Just casual words with a casual acquaintance.

When had she lost touch with reality?

"I wish I had a sliver of your brain power," Glenna was saying. "Chemistry is brutal."

"I remember." And she did. A lifetime ago, when goals were simple and death didn't dwell in a dark corner of her mind.

"Like you ever had to worry," was the young woman's warm complaint.

They'd discussed her desire to go into medicine as a nursing assistant. Stacy had made a few contacts for her to follow up on after her graduation. She was a sweet kid who could do better than the short-tempered musician with a penchant for heavy-handedness. Stacy had iced her bruises and helped dry her tears on more than one occasion.

She was the closest thing Stacy had to a friend and they hardly knew anything about each other.

They stood together at the mail boxes, sorting the wheat from the chaff.

"How's Buddy doing?" Stacy asked at last because it was expected.

"He's got a gig over in Fremont this weekend. You should let your hair down and come see him."

Stacy smiled to be polite. "Maybe I will."

"Let me know. Give me a call, and we can ride together. Gotta go or I'll be late to class."

Stacy waved, finished thumbing through her bills, then started up the stairs to her solitary haven. She knew she wouldn't call. There was no time for rock 'n roll in her immediate schedule. She had no time for a normal life until she was assured of a normal future.

Fun and future fantasies were for girls like Glenna.

As she rounded the second landing, Stacy fished in her gigantic purse for her keys. She heard them jingling just out of reach when, suddenly, the lights went out in the hall. Because it was an interior stairwell, the darkness was complete.

Muttering a curse upon the head of the power company, Stacy continued to rummage for her keys until a chill of air blew softly against her cheek.

She went still, her breath suspended. Her heart banged noisily against her ribs, creating a tight, panicked rhythm as she waited in the dark.

"Stacy."

She expelled her breath in a shuddering rush. The disembodied voice seemed to whisper in her ear. A quick revolution convinced her that she was alone on the landing.

"Who's there?" she demanded, the bravado shaking in her tone. *Where were those damned keys?* The prism ball on the end of her key chain grazed her fingertips then disappeared beneath her checkbook and TicTacs.

"Stacy," he whispered, the sound coming from everywhere and nowhere. "I've left you something right outside. Hurry. It's just for you."

Then, just like on the monorail, the cold evaporated, leaving her shivering in the overheated hall.

For a moment she couldn't move, couldn't catch her breath. Then, when a strangled gasp allowed a surge of air and adrenalin, she let her purse and briefcase fall forgotten, and raced down the steps. Shoving open the front door, she blinked into the sudden blinding brightness of the overhead security light, and with her first step forward, stumbled. Righting herself, she glanced down and choked, her scream tangling with the acidic backwash of sickness.

Glenna.

The co-ed lay sprawled half on, half off the sidewalk, her feet splayed as if in mid-stride, her outflung hands lost in the carefully trimmed yews that lined the walk. Chemistry notes spilled from an opened text just beyond the reach of still fingertips. Innocent blue eyes stared up at the sky, as blank and shiny as twin stars. And beneath the spill of her blonde hair, a seeping crimson from the gash in her throat quickly dyed the ends a terrible red.

Stacy reeled in an uncoordinated circle, her world lurching drunkenly, until strong hands gripped her by the upper arms. The scream managed to free itself, then, warbling as high and thin and foreign as an exotic night bird startled into flight. Her feeble efforts to pull away were easily subdued, but it was the brusque voice that returned her sanity.

"Doc, what the hell? I saw the lights go out inside. Are you all—"

She collapsed against him at the same time Frank Cobb saw the body on the ground. One hand cupped the back of her head, yanking her tightly into his shoulder. In the other hand, she was absurdly grateful to see a gun appear. God bless Frank Cobb for being a handy guy to have around. And for being intuitive when he needed to be.

He steered her quickly into the bushes on the other side of the walk, holding her by the shoulders as she threw up, then just holding her in the weak and quivery aftermath. She found herself sitting on the front step in the protective curl of his embrace as his calm call on the cell phone brought sirens shrieking in answer. He said nothing as she clung to his denim varsity jacket, the repetitive stroke of his hand through her hair more soothing than any words.

And when the EMTs and first squad car arrived, he exacted the information they needed from her in a firm, nonthreatening manner, keeping her close and the others at bay.

"Did you recognize the voice, Doc? This is important. Try to remember. Had you heard it before?"

Yes. Yes, she had. Familiarity teased along the frazzled edges of her memory but refused to be categorized. "I don't know. It happened so fast."

"It's all right. It's all right. Don't worry about it now."

And just as she thought she felt the soft brush of his lips against her brow, another urgent voice intruded.

"Doctor Kimball? I just heard the call. Are you all right?"

The alarm in Ken Fitzhugh's tone was the bracer Stacy needed to pull herself together and out of Cobb's cocooning arms. The young officer stood on the walk, his gaze flashing between the sheet covered body, to her, then to Frank, that last connecting jump narrowing his eyes slightly.

"I'm fine, Ken. It's my neighbor, G-Glenna."

Frank's hands massaged the caps of her shoulders in unspoken support, a gesture Fitzhugh couldn't fail to notice. Nor could Stacy miss the obvious territorial bristle as the two men regarded one another.

"Ken, this is Frank Cobb. We work together. He was . . ."

Was what? What was Cobb doing outside her apartment building?

She canted a glance up at him, and he met the question without a blink.

"He was following me home because I'd had some car trouble," she concluded in what she hoped would be a plausible lie.

"How very fortuitous."

"Yes, wasn't it?" Cobb countered.

Remembering suddenly, she squeezed Cobb's arm. "Frank, I dropped my purse and my case on the landing."

"I'll get them for you." He stood, never taking his eyes off the young officer until the last moment. The instant he went inside, Fitzhugh bent down in front of her.

"Stacy, I found something out. Listen to me."

She took a deep breath to bring her fractured attention into focus, then looked for him to go on.

"There were prints on that box that was left outside your door."

An awful certainty began to constrict within her chest, crushing her lungs, her heart, her hopes. "Whose?" she whispered.

"Redman's. This is probably his handiwork, too. You're in danger. I can't keep it unofficial any more. We need to talk about how we're going to handle this."

"Handle what?" Frank stepped between them, forcing Fitzhugh to straighten and back away. When he received no reply except the abrupt evasion of both their eyes, he moved on to another direct topic. "You didn't say how you two know each other."

Stacy put a staying hand at Cobb's waist, distracting him from further aggression. "Officer Fitzhugh and I were consulting on the same case. We'll talk soon, Ken."

Please don't do anything until then, her penetrating gaze conveyed.

"All right."

Then, Stacy's eyes teared up as the medics shifted Glenna's body to their gurney and the heavy-gage plastic bag was zippered up around her. Only a chalk mark and the bright red wetness remained beneath the flash of investigators' camera bulbs. And Glenna was gone.

Fitzhugh followed the EMTs to the now silent ambulance. Frank's hard glare remained on him until he returned to his car and drove off into the night. Then he looked down at Stacy, his expression one of cautious concern.

"What can I do?"

Taking his request at face value, she said, "I don't want to be alone tonight."

"I'll stay."

Good as his word, he helped her climb the stairs, the curl of his arm about her waist encouraging her wobbly legs to support her. He opened her door, making her stand on the threshold until he'd checked the interior. When he saw her staring at his revolver, he tucked it discretely out of sight in the holster he wore at the small of his back. She could have told her no self-respecting killer would choose to wait inside her chaotic apartment.

"Doc, you need to get yourself a cleaning lady," he advised as he led her inside.

"One look, and they run away screaming."

He responded to her pale attempt at humor with an admiring grin. With the sweep of his arm, he cleared a cushion on the couch where she dropped like a sack of Ready Mix cement. She rested her head against the back, her eyes closed as she listened to him rummaging about in her kitchen.

"Here. This will help."

He fit a glass into her hand, and she sipped obediently. And he was right. When the glass was empty, the sharp shards of panic had eased from her nerves. After a long minute of silence, she slit her eyes open to see Frank squatting down in front of her, studying her intently.

"What's going on here, Doc? What aren't you telling the police?"

In her exhausted state, she couldn't come up with a good lie. "Not now, Frank. My mind's off line until morning."

"You know something about the killer, don't you?" His hands clasped her knees in earnest. "I can't protect you if I don't know the score."

Could he protect her, even if she told him everything? Frank Cobb was a methodical man, used to black and white situations where a well placed bullet could end a threat and the rules of engagement applied to all players. A man like her father had been at the top of his game. As good as Cobb probably was in his own arena, here, he was out of his league.

"I'm going to bed."

She put her hands over his, using the connection to boost herself upright. He rose, too. When her knees buckled, she swayed into him, the contact of her forehead and his chin brief, but telling. Frowning, he placed his palm to her cheek.

"You're burning up, Doc."

She brushed off his hand and his concern. "I'm fine. Nothing a little sleep won't cure."

His unrelieved scowl said he didn't believe it for a minute, but he would take no guff from her as he slipped an arm about her waist to guide her to the bedroom. He paused in the doorway, glancing about at all the antique dolls, frilly lace and pink ruffles.

"Yikes," he muttered, winning her quiet chuckle.

"Not what you expected?"

"Maybe for an eight-year-old." Then his smile took the unintentional sting from his words. "I feel like a fish without a bicycle."

"I'm working through some unresolved childhood fantasies."

"Hmmm. My fantasies involve black leather, fur and handcuffs." He steered her toward the little-girl bed, turning her to sit on the edge of the puffy comforter.

"Glad I don't have any pets."

He was smiling as he knelt to take off her shoes and socks. His hands were warm against her skin, the contact good, real and soothing. He didn't look up as he asked, "Where do you want me for the night?"

"In here."

His gaze flashed up, carefully neutral and requesting a clarification.

"Not as a lover, as a friend." She wasn't sure that was what he wanted to hear, but she couldn't give him any other answer.

"Okay. I can do that."

"Are you sure?"

"Are you questioning my integrity and self-control? You aren't completely irresistible, you know."

"I'm not?"

Her tiny pout relaxed all the lines of his face. "Not completely. I'll just think cotton candy and hold onto one of these fuzzy bears in the tutus, and any thought of anything remotely adult will make me feel like a pervert."

"I don't like you, Frank Cobb."

He grinned. "Yes, you do." He lifted her feet, encouraging her to lie back upon the canopy bed. After covering her with a crocheted afghan, he headed for the door. A flip of the light switch plunged the room into shadow. Anxiety tightened in Stacy's belly as her protector was silhouetted against the open door.

"Frank?" She hated the pleading note that quivered in her voice.

"I'm going to check the front door again, then I'll be right back. Close your eyes."

But she couldn't. She lay stiff and anxious, listening to him moving about her living room. She heard a thump and his muttered curse. She was about to spring out of bed to check on him when he came limping into the bedroom grumbling something about an obstacle course. Smiling, she was able to close her eyes.

The mattress dipped as he settled on the opposite side, stretching out full length atop the covers. A metallic sound made her turn toward him. He'd taken off only his coat and had set his gun on the night stand within easy reach. One of her collectible bears straddled his chest, and he was glowering at it fiercely. Not exactly what he was used to when it came to sharing a woman's bed, she was sure. Feeling safe to surrender to the strength-sapping fatigue, she lay back on her side with a sigh, hoping sleep would quickly take her.

But the minute she shut her eyes, the image of Glenna's fear frozen features strobed through her thoughts. Though it was the last thing she wanted to do, she found herself replaying those fateful few minutes, paying particular attention to the man's voice.

Had they been Redman's accented tones? Even now, the memory of that sinister whisper brought gooseflesh up on her arms. She clutched at the blanket as if to offset the chill.

Why had he killed Glenna? What had he to gain by that single brutal act except her alienation?

She blinked back the burn of tears and concentrated on the sound of Frank's steady breathing. In some surprise, she realized that he was the first man to lie in this bed with her. She'd never wanted to soil the memories of her pristine past with the less than innocent habits of her adult nights.

But she was glad he was here to keep monsters, both real and imagined, away.

The mulling questions and shocks of intermittent memory made for a fitful rest. Stacy dozed on and off, jumbled dreams and hazy awareness of her surroundings blending into a surreal consciousness. She thought she smelled Louis Redman's distinctive cologne and later, heard the hum of her computer starting up. But, dragged down by the weight of her weariness, she was only an uninvolved witness, drifting through the hours until morning on a dark, drugging sea of exhaustion.

She blinked her eyes open to the brightness of daybreak. She was alone. After a moment of disorientation, she was calmed by the sound of pans banging on the stove and teased by the scent of coffee brewing. No one made coffee as satisfyingly rich as Frank Cobb.

Shrugging into her bulky pink chenille bathrobe, Stacy scuffled out of the bedroom and came to a stop. She was

Dorothy opening the door into Oz, for she definitely wasn't in Kansas any more.

Frank had been busy.

All the empty take out boxes, all the discarded envelopes and junk mail, all the plant droppings had been gathered up and twist-tied inside three large garbage bags now standing sentinel at the front door. Her sink and countertops were gleaming, and she would probably never find a glass or coffee cup again. Her sofa was a rather ugly green plaid, she noted in some surprise now that the draping of coats and clutter had been removed. Even a generous space had been unearthed on the dining room table, where a placemat she couldn't remembering owning and inviting silverware were waiting.

"Do you charge by the hour or the room?" she muttered in awe.

He glanced up from the stove where he was herding scrambled eggs onto a plate. "Must be all that pink stirred up my nesting instincts."

She plopped at the table and let him bring her breakfast and coffee. He looked temptingly rumpled, as if he'd gotten little or no sleep. Nervous energy, dedication to duty or their close proximity in the bed, she wasn't sure which.

After a forkful of eggs, she sighed, "Maybe I'll reconsider that marriage proposal."

He was pouring himself a cup of coffee. He paused in mid-motion. His expression was carefully bland as he smiled at her. "You'd better wait until you find out what my bad habits are." His gaze dropped. "Don't let your eggs get cold."

But it wasn't the eggs, it was her blood that suddenly grew chilled.

She glanced into the living room at the tidy stacks he'd made of her papers and magazines. Her briefcase was on the floor, her purse beside it. In the middle of his cleaning frenzy, had he taken the time to open it? Or was the housekeeping a cover-up for more sinister doings?

Had Frank been searching her apartment?

Had she heard the computer running while he scanned and perhaps copied the research disks from her attache?

Her stare flew up as he came to sit next to her at the table. He met it unblinkingly, his own gaze steady and unapologetic.

You son-of-a-bitch! I trusted you!

But as he nonchalantly sipped his coffee, the words to an old song taunted her.

Silly woman, you knew I was a snake.

ELEVEN

On the heels of her weariness, Stacy knew a terrible sense of defeat.

How much did Frank Cobb know and whom would he tell?

She pretended to enjoy the rest of her breakfast, swallowing down eggs that seemed powder dry and coffee that was as bitter as Cobb's betrayal until the beeper went off on his watch. He checked the digital readout then carried his empty cup to the sink.

"Would you like to ride in with me, or shall I just follow you?"

His question would have aroused no particular suspicion if he'd asked it the night before, but today, Stacy was seeing Frank Cobb through a different light, and the picture wasn't particularly flattering.

"Don't you have to go home and change?"

He brushed down his shirt sleeves and fastened them at the cuff, the gesture implying casual intimacy that made her want to scream and strike out at him. But she could play the moment just as skillfully. She kept her expression purposefully bland as she waited for his answer.

"I keep a change of clothes at work. Be prepared, my Scout master always told me."

"You snooze, you lose, right?"

He met her stare without the slightest wince of shame. "Right."

How much had she lost, besides her faith in him? How long would it take for his superiors to figure out exactly what she was working on? Could she keep him from reporting what he'd learned?

What would keep him quiet?

If money was important, he wouldn't be in his profession. Bribery wouldn't work. Neither would feminine wiles. She couldn't imagine him giving in to a seduction. Begging, arguing, reasoning—all equally futile. He wasn't a man easily swayed by circumstance or compassion. He was driven by duty. Did she have anything in the bathroom cabinet that, added to his coffee, could incapacitate him? No. Could she bash him over the head, tie him up and make him wait, to pay for his treachery? Could she keep him here with her until nightfall, until she could call in Louis to suppress their secret permanently?

If she couldn't convince him to be silent, could she allow him to be killed?

She remembered the security of his arms about her in the aftermath of Glenna's discovery.

No. She couldn't bring him harm for doing his job.

But she didn't have to lie down and let him walk over her, either.

"You go ahead, Frank. I'm still feeling a bit under the weather. I have some things to finish up here."

"I can wait."

"No. I'm sure you have more important things you have to do, too."

After a brief stalemate, he nodded. "Yeah, I do." He went to retrieve his coat where her tears had long since dried upon its shoulder. She saw the flash of his gun as he shrugged into it. Sheer folly to think she could snatch the revolver from him and hold him hostage. Where did he have the disk he'd copied? In his jacket, in his Dockers?

She was staring into the bottom of her coffee mug when he set a card down on the placemat.

"My beeper number. If you need me, for anything, just call me."

"I'll do that, Frank. You don't know how much it means to me to be able to count on you."

She said it flatly, without inflection. For a moment, he didn't move, and she almost believed he might confess the sins of a guilty conscience. But he was a professional. He wasn't allowed a conscience. And in the end, he left without another word.

How could she have been so stupid, so trusting?

She hurled her mug at the sink and was rewarded with the angry sound of shattering crockery. An appropriate echo for what she was feeling inside.

Changing seats so the computer screen faced her, she switched it on and tried to trace his treachery. He was good. He left no footprints telling where he'd been snooping or what he'd done.

How much time did that give her?

Whether it was hours or minutes, she had to make the best of them.

She worked tirelessly through the morning, entering data and charting probabilities. In the back of her mind, other possibilities provoked her. Frank Cobb's grin. The feral gleam in Louis Redman's gaze. Which would be her downfall? How was she to proceed when she couldn't turn her back on either of them? She was alone, playing a dangerous game where the rules didn't seem to apply in her favor. No rules of any kind applied to Louis.

Apparently, her knowledge of what he was didn't have the proper leverage to keep him from misbehaving. What would? How could she gain the upper hand at least long enough to finish what she'd started? She plotted out Redman's vulnerabilities while rubbing her aching temples.

Sunlight. A stake through the heart. Both too permanent. Silver, garlic, crosses. Were those fables or facts? She could only guess at his powers and, therefore, rightly feared to confront him. But there was a time when he was helpless, when he was easily subdued.

And that time was now, during the daylight hours.

***

Ken Fitzhugh would have been proud at how covertly she staked out the Easton Hotel. She had until nightfall to figure out a way inside past the security guard and Louis's ever-vigilant servant. According to the reports Fitzhugh had given her, Takeo, the servant, left the residence two hours before dusk to do errands and returned just in time to wake his master. Those stops included the investment firm, the import/export office and the market where he bought food for one. Stacy knew the direction of Redman's appetites, and that wasn't something easily purchased over the counter at a convenience store.

Louis wouldn't be careless enough to trust his security to amateurs. She wouldn't be able to charm her way past the guard by saying she had a fictitious appointment with a man who never saw anyone until after dark. Paid well to overlook his eccentricities, the guard would also be very familiar with his personal patterns. He would not let her pass unless Louis left word himself.

As she munched on cold bucket chicken, she watched the mobster, Jerome Petretti, the only other resident of the sixth floor, greet the doorman with a smile and a folded tip. The Yorkie he was walking sniffed its way around the guard's feet, earning a fleeting scowl of annoyance after the dapper gentleman had passed and he was left to step out of the cord tangling about his ankles. The dog yipped as a jerk of the leash coaxed it to follow.

And Stacy had an idea.

Hiking up her skirt and taking the sack of dinner rolls out of her pasteboard bucket, Stacy hurried across the street from where she'd parked a half block down. She held the bag out away from her as she approached the door. The guard made himself into a formidable barrier.

"May I help you, Miss?"

It was a different man than the night she'd gone up at Louis's invitation. Shifting her shoulders and twitching her hips impatiently, she said, "I'm with Jerry."

Observing the long length of her black stockings and the plunging vee of her sweater, she knew what he assumed. For once, that was in her favor.

"I'll have to call up and see if he's expecting you. If you'll wait here just a moment, please."

"Well, I don't please," she whined. "And after expecting me to trot along with him and that nasty little beast of his, picking up its business, I don't think I care to wait. Here." She shoved the bag at the guard. "You can just take his doggie's business upstairs. And you can tell him no amount of money is worth—"

The guard opened the door. "You may tell him yourself, Miss. Have a nice evening."

She minced inside on her high heels. He followed, and as the elevator opened, pushed number six for her. Making a face at the paper sack, she simpered, "The things a girl will do in the name of love."

The guard raised a brow, wisely saying nothing as the door slid shut between them.

On six, she stood in the hall, looking between Louis's locked door and the entrance to Jerome Pettretti's suite. Tossing the bag of rolls into a metal ashtray, she strode toward the mobster's residence. She wouldn't worry about the video cam. By the time Louis saw it, she hoped to have concluded her business.

Petretti answered the tap on the door himself, with one of his associates at his elbow. Both swept her with appreciative stares.

"Excuse me, boys, but I have an appointment with a Mr. Redman down the hall this evening. I was to meet his employee here about ten minutes ago, but I'm running late and must have missed him."

"Do we look like a message service, lady?" the enforcer growled.

She made a distressed face, pulling her lips into a full pout. "I can't afford to let the opportunity go, if you know what I mean," she whispered in confidence, leaning just far enough forward to entice them with a glimpse down her cleavage. "It takes me some time to . . . um, set things up, and Mr. Redman doesn't like to be kept waiting."

The two men exchanged amused looks.

"So what is it you'd like us to do?" Petretti asked.

"I was hoping Mr. Redman might have left a spare key with you, you being his neighbor and all." She batted her lashes expectantly."

Petretti chuckled. "Well, no, he didn't. We're not that friendly. Phil, why don't you go on down the hall and let the lady into Redman's apartment."

"But I thought you said—"

"He has a master key," Petretti confided to put her worries at ease. Then his gaze eased along the length of her legs. "And if you've got some time later in the week, you can leave your number with Phil."

Stacy beamed. "You are just so sweet."

She trotted down the hall at the side of Petretti's goon who expertly manipulated the lock with a thin tool taken out of a leather case in his inner coat pocket. She blew him a wet kiss and waved at Petretti before slipping inside and getting down to business.

Where did Louis Redman sleep during the day?

Time was not on her side. Kicking out of her heels, she hurried through the rooms, seeking any of the obvious hiding places in living, dining, bath and servant's bedroom. She paused before entering Louis's bed chamber, eying the big cannonball poster bed with voyeuristic curiosity. Nonsense, of course. Louis Redman didn't sleep in a bed. Focusing on that certainty, she made quick work of ransacking his room. Still, her hands had a tendency to linger over the fine material of his suits, inhaling the subtle scent of his cologne. That much fantasy she allowed herself.

Frustrated with the way the sky was darkening outside the slatted blinds, Stacy stood in the central room, thinking hard, trying to put herself in the place of a centuries old predator who had to hide himself out of necessity every day of his unnatural life.

Where would one be least likely to look?

The kitchen was immaculate, like a gleaming techno page in a decorator magazine. But what Louis dined on was not prepared upon the modern stove or pulled out of the walk-in pantry. She checked there first, but found only shelves containing just enough staples to look ordinary. She scanned the perimeter. It had to be someplace large enough to accommodate him. She couldn't picture him huddled under the double sink, then checked there, anyway.

Her gaze fixed upon the huge stainless doors of a restaurant-sized refrigerator/freezer. How many veggies did the man keep on hand to warrant such an excessive storage unit? Unless what it was storing wasn't 2% milk but rather 100% unnatural vampire.

She opened the refrigerator, surprised to find milk as well as a supply of other perishable products. And lots of what appeared to be tomato juice but was more likely type O. She stared at those containers, fighting down a shudder of dread. Determinedly, she pulled open the freezer, stepping back at the sudden rush of frigid air. It reminded her of the preternatural cold accompanying visits from the killer. Had Redman come right from the deep freeze to torment her?

Some steaks, stir-fry vegetables, and more 'tomato juice.' A better, more healthy selection that what she had in her own freezer.

Gripping one of the racks, she gave it a half-hearted tug and was stunned when the entire center section of shelves slid toward her.

Open Sesame.

Recovering herself, she eased the unit out and let it swing to the side, revealing a false back with a second door. Excitement clenching in her belly, she opened the door and stepped into what amazingly was a small service elevator. Certainly not standard in all the Easton's apartments. There were two buttons, up and down. Since the building only had six stories, she pressed down. The door closed, sealing her into a claustrophobic darkness. With a smooth purr of mechanics, the tiny car began its descent. Delivering her into the bowels of hell? she wondered.

A slight bump announced her arrival at her destination. Slowly, she opened the door, peering out into a well-lit storage room. The basement? Not quite.

Under the antiseptic glow of flourescent lights, carefully preserved in this climate-controlled room was Luigino Rodmini's history. Paintings and collectibles worth millions were all cataloged and lovingly stored. Mementos from the civilizations he'd seen rise and fall, from the wars he'd survived unscathed, from the humans he'd known and possibly loved, all there in regimented decades. And behind a double-tiered unit to store the art of VanGogh, Renoir, Picasso and others beyond price, was the most unique of all his collection. A large, simple casket where he'd lain as centuries passed by.

Seeing it made believing it settle with a yet unacknowledged punch of reality.

Louis Redman was a vampire.

When she lifted the lid, Stacy would find him resting inside.

She thought she'd accepted the impossibility of his preternatural existence. But standing in the cool, ageless air, staring at the coffin where he slept, undead, forced the fact home.

My God, it is real.

And if she continued to gawk, she would find out exactly how real.

Stacy went to the casket. Taking a deep, fortifying breath, she opened the lid, preparing herself for the horror within.

But the sight of Louis Redman peacefully reclined upon white tufted satin was anything but repellent.

He was beautiful in repose.

Exquisite bone structure seemed sculpted from pale marble. Black lashes and a stray lock of hair lay against that flawless skin in shocking comparison. He wasn't lifelike, as one always said to console the family of someone recently deceased. He appeared frozen in time, a monument crafted to exalt the man he'd once been in another time, another place. This was the face of Luigino Rodmini, who walked the streets in the era of Michaelangelo, not of Louis Redman, who made corporate deals and used American Express. Suspended in his twilight sleep, an aura of infinity enveloped him, of untouchability, of immortality.

But he would soon wake from that sleep, and finding her at his side when he was his most vulnerable, he might not be in the mood for discussion.

Acting quickly, she opened her purse and drew out the necessary equipment. Shoving up the sleeve to his black silk sweater, she tubed his upper arm and snapped a vein into attention. He never flinched as the needle pierced his skin, nor did he seem aware as she withdrew one vial, then two, then three of his unique blood.

Now, no matter what decision she made regarding Louis Redman, her own future and research were secure. She wouldn't think about Louis, not until she was far away from his influence. For even though he was deep in his unnatural rest, she was affected by him, by his dark, deadly charm and lethal looks. She thought about the sharpened salad spoon in her purse. Not exactly VanHelsing's weapon of choice but the only viable tool in her apartment. Could she, to save her life, press it to Louis's motionless chest and drive it through his heart with blows from her meat tenderizer? Thankfully, his sleep remained undisturbed, and she wouldn't be put to that test. Now, she could turn his fate over into other hands. A fate he'd made for himself by killing indiscriminately. She would not feel responsible.

But that didn't stop her from feeling a seeping sorrow when she took one long last look at his compelling features.

Had things worked out, they might have been good together.

Now, she would never know.

Having lingered as long as she dared, she restored his sleeve and readied to escape, turning toe-to-toe and eye-to-eye with the Asian, Takeo.

He may have looked ancient, but there was no weakness in his grip. His hands banded her forearms, forbidding struggle or escape. His impenetrable expression didn't alter, nor did he speak. He simply restrained her. A flat black stare said no excuses, explanations nor pleading would do any good. A man of duty, just like Frank Cobb. She'd been caught, and now she would wait for Louis's judgement.

"Ms. Kimball," came the silky drawl of his voice. "I wasn't aware we had an appointment tonight."

Takeo released her at once, knowing it was too late for her to run. Stacy turned slowly, expecting, yet still startled by, the sight of Louis sitting up inside the coffin. She couldn't discern his mood from the suave blank of his features, but saw no need to provoke him.

"Good evening."

He smiled slightly, the gesture smooth and possibly sinister. "Takeo tells me you left the freezer door open. That was rather careless, don't you think? Now he'll have to cook up everything that has thawed or throw it away. Takeo hates waste, as do I."

"I'd be happy to replace anything that's spoiled," she offered in an attempt to match his blasé manner. Failing when he lightly vaulted from his padded box to stand before her. She couldn't help shrinking away as terror's grip held her as immobile as Takeo's hands had.

"That, of course, is not the point." He glanced at the bag clutched tightly in her hands. He didn't ask her to surrender it, as if he already knew what it contained. What she had stolen. His voice lowered to a chill purr. "I thought we had reached an agreement."

"I was willing to uphold my end."

The crisp cut of her tone had him lifting one brow. "If that is true, then why are you here, stealing what I would have given?"

Anger at his nonchalant attitude nudged fear aside. "Really? Forgive me for having my doubts after your rather blatant demonstration of last evening."

Now he looked truly perplexed. "*Non capisco.* I'm afraid I don't understand."

Aggravating tears pricked behind her eyes as she cried, "Neither do I. There was no reason to kill her. No reason at all."

His expression clouded even more, making her doubt the validity of her claim for the first time even as he stated, "Of whom do you speak? I am confused. I am supposed to have slain someone? How can that be? I do not kill for fun or food, only in self-defense."

"She was no threat to you. If you were worried about me, you should have stuck to your bullying tactics instead of murdering my neighbor."

"Stacy," he vowed somberly, "I did no such thing."

She stared at him, frantically searching his handsome face for some reason to accuse or believe. "You weren't at my apartment building last night? You didn't whisper to me in the hall and send me outside to find Glenna with her throat torn out on the front sidewalk?"

"No. I did not. What reason would I have for such bad behavior?"

"About as much reason as throwing that poor girl off the pier. About as much logic as sending me the tennis shoe from the girl on the monorail after you'd murdered her, or that jogger's ponytail. But why Glenna? We'd already made our agreement. It makes no sense at all."

Her voice trailed off as darkness gathered about him. It began with the subtle sharpening of his expression, as shadow seemed to seep into the hollows of his cheeks, elongating the lines of his face. His eyes took on a metallic glitter backed by a strange phosphorescent glow. If she hadn't been frightened before, she was terrified now. She could feel the negative energy collect like lightning within massing clouds. Then it struck, Swiftly, brutally.

Across the room, a lovely Egyptian vase shattered upon its stand, shards raining to the floor. Paintings stacked along one wall fell forward in a noisy domino effect. The lights flickered above even as Louis's gaze flashed. A single fierce oath escaped him, the sound roaring from him, filling the room with deafening vibration, as the force of his rage swirled about in a ripping wind of near-cyclonic proportion.

Hands clamped over her ears while her hair flew wildly about her head and shoulders like a sheet on a Kansas clothesline in the middle of a twister, Stacy cowered, afraid the direction of his wrath would turn her way. Finally focusing on her, Louis recovered himself, making a conscious effort to regain control.

In a deathly quiet tone—the ominous calm after the storm, he said, "It makes perfect sense to me."

He took her by the elbow. She could feel the chill of his fingers right through the knit of her sweater and fought not to shy away.

"Come upstairs where it is more comfortable." It wasn't a request, no matter how courteously put. "Then, you will tell me everything."

TWELVE

It was all very civilized. Stacy drank wine and Louis the darker vintage stored for his special preference, while they watched the moon rise over the city and the heavens awake. What had awakened in Louis, from the moment she told him about the trinkets delivered from the dead girls, was a horrible sense of deja vu and danger.

As he listened to her stoic retelling of her traumatic past week, he marveled as well at her courage. Even thinking him responsible for the cruel deaths and depraved gifts, she'd come alone to risk his discovery and displeasure. How frightened she must have been—and still was. He could scent it on her, a fine, exotic fragrance he'd come to know well over the centuries. Yet, believing him to be a vicious killer, she'd still come. And she sat across from him, hiding her fear behind an admirable show of nonchalance. What a strong, determined creature she was, and he found himself impossibly drawn toward what could never be. Should never be.

Not while he remained a creature of the night.

He rose from his seat to pace as she spoke flatly about the murder of her neighbor. The recitation was chilling, not because of the actual atrocity—which was shocking enough for Stacy—but because of the suspicion gathering within his heart and mind. He paused in his restless travels as she explained how she had gained entrance to his supposedly impervious surroundings, having to turn away so she wouldn't witness the mixture of dismay and delight playing upon his features. Resourceful, as well as intelligent. A fine and worrisome combination. She wasn't going to maintain the objectivity he insisted upon if they were to work successfully together. And now, knowing what he did, he couldn't allow the distance his emotions demanded.

"So," he asked at least, "why did you take the blood from me?"

He felt her hesitation, but he knew she spoke the truth when she said, "I figured to be on the safe side, I should have enough on hand to complete my experiments."

"In case of what?"

"Just in case you were no longer available for further testing."

She met his stare straight on and without the slightest embarrassment.

Startled by her candor, he murmured, "You meant to kill me, then? Is there a stake to bring death as well as the tools to enhance life in that bag of yours?"

"I wasn't sure what to expect, and I had to be ready...in case."

"In case?"

"You woke up."

"You would have slain me?"

"If I thought it necessary. It would not have been my first choice."

The honest simplicity of her reply took him aback but also intrigued him. "But you did not. Why? You were leaving when Takeo delayed you. Had you managed to escape undetected, what would you have done?"

"I would have turned all the information I had over to the police and let them deal with you."

"You would have betrayed me into their hands." His indulgence faded.

A fire of rebellious fury snapped within her direct stare. "As I've been betrayed all too frequently. Get used to it. It's nothing personal."

"Forgive me if I consider the loss of my life as very personal."

A flicker in her gaze said she was aware of her precarious position, but she didn't back down and she didn't beg for his mercy. And because she did not, he could not be less honorable in his reaction.

"I am not behind the bothersome tricks that have been played upon you, Stacy. Do you believe me?"

"Why should I? Do you expect me to believe there is another such as yourself plaguing this city?"

His smile confirmed it. "Don't be naive, Doctor. We are all around you."

This time, her shock manifested in a very visual fashion. She sat back as if struck, her eyes round and apprehensive as her mind tried to reject what her intuition told her was true. Then a darker truth surfaced.

"You know who it is, don't you?" Her whisper was part accusation, part agitation.

How could he not answer? Ignorance would place her in unacceptable danger. Suspicion would interfere with their partnership.

"Yes, I know him."

She gave a breath of relief, as if the demon haunting her dreams finally had a face and therefore, could be dealt with. "Then why not give that information to the police? He will be arrested, the killings will stop, and then my research can continue."

"A logical, and very foolish, summation," he drawled, coming to a stop near where she was seated.

Stacy bristled at his condescending attitude. "Why? It makes perfect sense to me."

He smiled wryly at her sharp return of his earlier phrase, then explained. "If he is exposed, the fact that our kind exists surfaces as well. What guarantee have I that he won't tell them about me? And about your involvement in concealing past evidence from them? Now do you understand?"

Her frustration said that she did, all too well. "Then what do we do to stop him? His games are growing more dangerous by the day. Am I his target?"

"No," Louis assured her softly. "I am."

He felt her questions, her need to hear, to know, but he turned away from them and her, unwilling, unable to face that particular truth. When he was silent long enough for her to realize he would say nothing more on the subject, she made one reasonable request.

"If I'm to protect myself, I think I have the right to know why he's using me to get to you."

Of course, she had the right. But could he find the strength to answer? It would mean rolling out all the pain and loss of his past relationship with Cassie. It would mean admitting that he was responsible for the threat now in her life, that he was also indirectly to blame for the deaths of the faceless women being thrown in her path. It wasn't that he felt unmoved by those unnecessary losses, only that he'd managed to erect a numbness of spirit in such matters in order to go on as the night creature he was. Death was a part of that nocturnal life and had been since his youthful folly had damned him to this dark existence. It wasn't that he didn't care or feel. It was because he didn't dare open those dangerous flood gates for fear of being swept away. So he tried to make his answer succinct but honest enough to satisfy her.

"He wants to hurt me by terrorizing those I care about."

He saw her recoil and reevaluate, but she was careful in her phrasing. "And he thinks you care for me?"

"Yes." He, too, was careful not to give much away. "He must have guessed that you are important to me in some way, and therefore an obliging target." He took a deep breath before accepting his culpability. "I am sorry to have involved you in this century-old vendetta."

Her cynical smile masked her alarm. "I don't suppose you could just call him up and tell him that we're little more than strangers?"

"Even if I knew how to contact him, I doubt that he would take my word for it. If he knows where you live, he's obviously been watching you for some time. He must know that you've come here on several occasions."

"And that denotes a relationship. How silly of me to think more is required than that." She covered her face with her hands and laughed through them. Unable to gage her expression, he had no way of translating her unlikely response, so he merely waited until she looked up again. Her features were deeply etched with weariness and woeful resignation. There was little he would not have done to spare her the pain he saw on her face—except sacrifice his possible salvation.

"Who is this madman?" she asked at last. "What's his name? What does he look like? Would I know him if I saw him?"

"Did you recognize me for what I was?"

She grimaced at that quietly offered truth.

"His name is Quinton Alexander, but he would not be using that moniker. He is average, not someone you would notice in a crowd. He has fair hair and his eyes are blue, a poet's dreamy eyes. Eyes that hide his madness well. He worked for a newspaper once and fancies himself as a writer. He can appear as charming and harmless, but do not be deceived. He is evil to the soul, and he will snatch yours if he can. And if he can't, he will kill you."

Stacy swallowed hard. "Then why hasn't he?"

Louis sighed. How to explain such insanity to a woman of Stacy's pragmatic thinking. "He likes games. He likes to pretend his actions have a romantic yet tragic purpose. He is probably convinced that you need to be rescued from me, and as long as that's his belief, you will be safe."

"So I should stay away from you."

"There's the rub. It is dangerous for you to be with me, but I am the only one who can protect you from him."

"Swell."

"Exactly."

She scrubbed her palms over her face and moaned. "I need to go now. I have to be ready for work in less than six hours and be able to pretend that my idea of the natural world has not just been turned upside down. I'm going home to get some sleep. Time's running out." She stated that flatly, as if she knew it to be truth.

He didn't try to convince her otherwise. Time was their enemy, and she needed to work. As he helped her on with her coat, he recalled something she had mentioned with considerable bitterness, and asked for a clarification.

"You said something earlier about betrayal. Does this involve me?"

Her lovely face was a skillful blank, but he could sense the lie even before she spoke it.

"No. It has nothing to do with any of this."

He decided he would have to accept that at least for the time being.

"Call me if you need me."

Her smile quirked at a cynical angle. "Where have I heard that before?" She held up her hand to block his response, and vowed, "I will call. This isn't something I can do alone. I know that now."

"Be careful."

"I believe that quote is 'Trust no one.' Don't worry. I've had my eyes opened on that subject." She patted her bulky purse. "I'll go to work on these today. I am safe during the daylight, aren't I?"

"Quinton may have humans working under his influence, doing his dirty work for him when he is incapable of doing it himself. Don't assume anything."

She laughed. The sound was unpleasantly hard. "Yes, I know. Assume means 'make an ass out of you and me.' Neither of us is stupid, Louis. I won't make any mistakes."

Any *more* mistakes, she should have told him.

"While you work, I will do what I can to flush out this madman from my past. Be patient a while longer, Stacy. He will surface to brag of his misdeeds. I know him that well, at least. He is a creature of ego as well as insanity. He will want me to know his is the hand that meddles in my fate. I will be ready for him."

Swell.

Now she had the forces of darkness warring over her while she struggled to save mankind. Sounded too much like a John Carpenter plot for her comfort.

Stacy leaned against the wall of the building's main elevator, overwhelmed by the whole situation.

What would Louis say if he knew Frank Cobb had stolen her initial research? Would he still trust her and let her leave? Would he allow her to live if he thought their agreement dangerously compromised by her own carelessness? Would Cobb be another morgue statistic by night's end? Her head hurt from the strain of consequence mulling through her mind. Cobb, Charlie, Fitzhugh. Could she protect them all and still protect herself?

She had what she needed to continue her research. That's where she would concentrate. Louis Redman could wait an eternity for the results if he had to.

She didn't have the same luxury. And tomorrow she would find out exactly how long she had.

Slipping behind the wheel of her car, Stacy surrendered briefly to a swelling sense of helplessness. She dreaded returning to her apartment. She would never feel safe there again. She slumped forward, letting her forehead rest against the leather-wrapped steering wheel as exhaustion took control.

"You should be home in bed, not napping in the car."

The sudden intrusion had her snapping upright, her gaze flying to the rear view mirror.

Nothing.

But when she glanced over her shoulder, she clearly saw the silhouette of Louis Redman in her back seat.

"Don't be alarmed," he told her soothingly.

Too late.

His explanation was bland and completely logical. "I didn't want anyone to see us leaving together."

"What are you doing in my car? You nearly scared me to death." She was too tired to keep the shaky edge of hysteria from her demand.

"What kind of a gentleman would I be if I didn't see you safely home? Drive. Pretend I'm not here."

And he seemed to actually sink back into the shadows, into invisibility.

Swell. Pretend there wasn't a blood sucking vampire in her back seat.

She started the car and put it in gear. As she drove her silent and unseen passenger through town, Stacy couldn't deny that she felt better knowing he was there. She was out of her league with the forces she faced. Perhaps it was just an exhausted paranoia, but she sensed threat from everywhere. From the bum standing on the corner who rushed out to wash her windshield for a dollar while she waited for the light to change. From the grunge guitarist practicing his trade in a doorway for the change it would bring. From the street walker who stared at her for an uncomfortable moment too long as she drove by. Were they watching her, reporting her movements back to the shadowy Quinton Alexander? Or was she just too tired to think straight? For now, she was valuable to Redman, and she could count on his protection from dangers both real and imagined.

For now.

She pulled into her assigned car port, looked in the mirror, then chided herself for the habitual gesture. Yet when she turned, the back seat was empty. Her guardian was gone.

Or was he?

She chose to believe he was nearby. That made it possible for her to get out of the vehicle and walk with some degree of confidence up the front walk where Glenna had met her terrible death.

Because of her. Because of her association with a man who was not a man. A man who had an enemy who defied normal conventions of time and space, and then was crazy on top of it all.

If she had any sense left, she would run as far and fast as she could to escape the evil hovering over her and those near her.

But if she ran, she was as good as dead anyway.

She opened her door and switched on the light, momentarily surprised by the tidy condition Cobb had left her apartment in. Well, that was one benefit of their disastrous night together. She could actually see the furniture. She stepped inside and dead-bolted the door behind her, realizing there was only a pseudo-sense of security in doing so.

After placing the blood vials in her refrigerator, she turned on the playback of her answering machine while beginning to undress. The first message hit like a fist to the jaw.

"Doc, this is Frank Cobb."

She hit the delete button to spare herself the anger surging at the sound of his voice. An impersonal beep, then the next voice.

"Hey, Stace, it's Alex. I'm back in town. We need to get together about that Redman thing. I'm sitting on a goldmine here, and I don't mind telling you, the pick and shovel are in my hands. Don't make a face. I'm keeping my promise. Just don't ask me to keep it forever."

Alex Andrews. Another loose end that would drive Louis to distraction if he knew. Or to violence if it meant protecting himself. She couldn't let Louis' urbane demeanor fool her into thinking he'd lived for centuries without knowing how to protect his secret by whatever means it took. Before politically correct blood donation centers, he'd gotten his nightly meal from someplace—someplace fresh and still warm.

The centuries may have lent him a sophisticated polish, but she could not forget that he was a killer, just like Quinton Alexander. Which was worse, a murderer driven by a madness he couldn't understand or control, or a killer who did so with cold intention?

She had to rest. Her head pounded. Weakness sapped her last remaining strength, leaving her only enough energy to wash her face and slip into the oversized Mariners tee shirt she wore to bed at night. She didn't want to feel sexy when she was alone. She wanted to feel normal. Unexceptional. She padded into her bedroom in the dark, slipped beneath the covers to hope unconsciousness would arrive with merciful swiftness.

But even with the opportunity at hand, she couldn't relax her mind enough to allow slumber in. Had Frank told his true employers what she was working on? Would she go in the next morning to find her lab sealed and her data confiscated? And who was this madman, this Quinton Alexander, who stalked her with his sick sense of humor? Was it a distant stranger or someone close whom she trusted?

He wouldn't be using his real name.

Alexander. Alex Andrews. The leap was made in thoughts too tired to dismiss it as ridiculous.

But was it ridiculous?

How quickly her reporter friend had come up with information buried beneath the weight of generations. Alexander had worked on a newspaper. Coincidence or convenience? Alex's hair was brown, but hair color was easier to change than identity. If he'd done the one, why not the other?

Had her young reporter friend settled in Seattle to keep an eye on his enemy, just waiting for the chance to strike? Would she be the weapon he used to sever Louis's future and her own with it?

She would arrange a meeting between Alex and Louis. Then Louis's past wouldn't be the only thing exposed.

She rolled to her other side with a restless toss, and froze. Her eyes had yet to adjust to the darkness but her other senses tingled with alarm.

"Who's there?"

"You are not sleeping."

"First my car, now my room," she accused, trying to sound annoyed while relief shivered through her. "You make yourself right at home, don't you, Louis?"

He emerged from the drape of shadows, at first just a dark shape himself, then taking on form and dramatically highlighted features. From out of that face of hollows and haunting beauty, his eyes burned bright with unnatural fire.

"I am to blame for your agitation."

"And you thought you could ease it by popping up unexpectedly to shock me into cardiac arrest?" It sounded like more of a complaint than it was. Instead of feeling a degree of threat from his presence, she was worried about how long he'd been in her apartment. And by how much he might have heard on the answering machine.

Apparently, nothing, for he betrayed no hint of upset or concern, except over her. Toward her, his attitude was almost fatherly.

A rather incestuous notion considering how she'd been viewing him in spite of her best intentions.

"I thought I might tell you a story to help you get to sleep."

"A fairytale? One with a princess or a monster?"

He didn't respond to her teasing with a laugh. "More than one princess and definitely a monster."

She plumped her pillow, intrigued and no longer weary. "Does it have a happy ending?"

"Perhaps." His smile was sad, his voice melancholy. "But I am getting ahead of myself."

"Are you the hero of this tale?"

"Some might say hero, others, villain. You shall decide for yourself."

"Does this story begin in Italy?"

"Yes. Long, long ago, with two friends, one a scholar blessed with wealth and longing for discovery, and the other cursed by ambition and touched by jealousy." The intimate tone of his voice, and its sorrowful echo, told her that this was not some ancient tale, but a slice of his past that was still very real and close to him.

"You were the scholar."

"You interrupt."

"Go on."

"These two young friends, both so innocent of life's cruelties, had a woman come between them. The scholar called her demon, but she was more. Much more."

"She was a vampire." How easy it had become to say that name without a smirk, but rather with a sense of dread and awe.

"And she stole from these two friends their lives, their love for one another, and made them into abominations unable to withstand the light of day. The ambitious one embraced this dark life, but the scholar mourned the loss of his humanity and swore to one day find a way to reclaim it."

His tone became a hypnotic storyteller's drone, drawing Stacy into the tale of creeping horror and poignant hope as he spoke of Arabella Howland, the courageous daughter of a Regency era doctor who had restored his ability to love just as her father temporarily returned his capacity to stand in daylight.

"He used a combination of Eastern herbs and the draining powers of a radical new blood transfusion process to bleed the curse from me. I walked as a man again, feeling certain enough of the cure to wed my Arabella and conceive a child. But alas, the effects of the doctor's potions were not as long-lasting as the love between his daughter and me. Even as I reverted to what I once was, my Bella refused to leave me."

"And you lived in France, then came to America when you wife was old enough to pass as your grandmother."

"Yes. When one lives for centuries, you must be always on the move. No one must grow suspicious of our inability to age with the natural passage of time. I've lived all over the globe, always hiding my true identity behind a new name, never allowing anyone to get close enough to suspect anything. Only Takeo has been my constant companion and privy to my secret. Others have come and gone over the years, until they blur in my memory beneath the sheer magnitude of faces."

He'd become little more than a shadow again, but Stacy could picture him so clearly, the same then as he was now even as the woman he loved grew aged and infirm.

How horribly sad and strangely romantic.

"After Bella died, I was convinced I would never care for another. But that had not been her plan for me. She wanted me to continue to hope, to continue to seek a cure so that one day we could be together. Through her matchmaking, I met my second wife, Cassandra Alexander, a bold crusader who owned her own newspaper."

"And the enemy who stalks you now was related to her."

She saw him nod. "Her cousin, Quinton. He hid his madness behind creativity, and he made Cassie the object of his obsession. His father wanted Cassie out of the way so he could inherit the newspaper, but Quinton, because he loved her in his own crazed way, could not kill her. Instead, he began to seek out blonde women as substitutes, luring Cassie closer to discovering his secret by leaving her clues after each murder, hoping to either win her love or disgust her so that he might then kill her without remorse."

Her voice hushed, Stacy asked, "And which did he do?"

"I was able to rescue Cassie from his intentions, but he fell victim to his own darkness, becoming a companion to the same demon who spawned me centuries before. We have sparred several times since then, and his hatred has grown more explosive after his paramour turned away from him when she found him to be a coward who could not be trusted."

"And Cassie?"

"My beloved Cassie loved life as she loved me. She, like Arabella before her, chose not to join me in this dark existence. She fell victim to her own mortality some seventy years ago, and since that time, I have been alone."

Seventy years.

Stacy's heart broke for his solitary sorrow.

"I have loved two extraordinary women in my life, both of whom sacrificed much for me. I could never—would never ask that of another."

Wondering what such a sacrifice might entail, Stacy distracted both of them from that course of conversation. "And your ambitious friend? What of him?"

"Gerardo." He spoke the other's name with a deep and eternal fondness. "We have come to terms with our past mistakes. He now shares his life with a woman who accepted his dark gift and has adopted her son, Gino, as his own." He smiled as he mentioned his namesake, but the sadness still steeped in his tone, striking a kindred note within the geneticist.

"So if your wife Cassandra has died, why does her cousin continue his warped idea of vengeance?"

"He blames me for many things—for his failure to win Cassie's love and his father's respect, for the loss of his wicked companion, for forcing him into hiding throughout this past century. I thought I could ignore his threat, but he will not allow that to happen. And I cannot allow him to threaten what is most important to me."

For one ridiculous second, Stacy mistakenly thought he referred to her. Sillier still was her sudden, unfounded wish for it to be true. Except the fervor with which Louis spoke had nothing to do with love but rather with longing.

"I will not allow him to cheat me out of attaining my humanity. You must find the cure, and if I must destroy him to see that it is done, so be it."

Her weariness returned in an engulfing wave, and with it, a sense of loneliness deep enough to drown in. She was a tool, nothing more. A means to attaining his end just as he was hers. It was the strangeness of her mood that coaxed her to think there might be more.

Tomorrow, her objectivity would return and Louis Redman would cease to be a romantic fantasy. But for this achingly empty night, she had pretended he was both rescuer and hero. His bittersweet tale of love won and lost appealed to her own poignant view of happiness. One could not hope to have what one could not forever hold. In that, she and Louis were very much alike.

Take away the pain of emotional involvement and only work remained. That's where she would focus. That's where she would succeed for the both of them.

"You are tired," Louis surmised gently. "Sleep well and know that I watch over you."

As if that would give her comfort?

Obligingly, she closed her eyes. She went from wide awake to barely able to hold her thoughts together in the space of a heartbeat.

Louis, he was doing something to her, using some vampiric magic to soothe her cares away. Her last remembered threads of consciousness concerned the two women Louis had loved enough to wed and weep over. Women who were strong and supportive, and by his own unvoiced accord, reminded him of her. She fell asleep wondering how she would compare to them.

Dreaming of finding a cure that would allow her and Louis to live happily ever after, not as princess and monster, but as husband and wife.

THIRTEEN

Frank Cobb wasn't at his post.

For the first time since he'd been assigned as her 'assistant,' he wasn't lurking at her doorway, watching her every move.

Probably because there no longer was a need.

Had he told them everything?

The certainty that time was short goaded Stacy into a marathon work session. A meticulous process under the best of circumstances, her efforts were slowed as she carefully took longhand notes on a legal pad instead of using her computer to graph results. If her findings weren't compromised already, she couldn't risk some cyber-snoop getting hold of her data before her testing was conclusive.

Was this work she did crossing the boundaries of moral decency? Could it be considered transgenic—bringing specific genes across the gap between one species and another? But Louis was human, wasn't he? Or at least, he had been. She wasn't engineering alien biochemicals to threaten human existence...or was she? Was she dabbling where science should never go? Or was she simply using the knowledge at hand to defeat the ravages of nature?

When conscience wavered, she did what she always did to suppress it. She brought up the image of her mother whose vital life had been eaten away by chemotherapy and the ugly side effect, Kaposi's sarcoma, the rare skin cancer it could not control. When the issue of human rights and dignity raised its flag, she rallied behind that picture. Where was the decency in what her mother had endured? What right had anyone to tell her she should not do anything in her power to thwart man's most deadly diseases? She wasn't a theologian; she was a scientist. These were her tools, her talents. And she would not apologize for her methods when the haunting visions of cancer wards filled with pediatric patients denied her rest.

She was doing the right thing.

Stopping only when her eyes felt crossed from hours of squinting through the microscope eyepiece, she took a short break to refill her coffee mug and roll the kinks from her shoulders. She tried for the half-dozenth time to contact Alex Andrews, but he hadn't checked in at work and wasn't picking up at home or on his cell. She settled for leaving yet another message.

And when she returned to her lab, Frank Cobb was there glancing over the notes she'd taken in her own undecipherable shorthand.

"Looking for something in particular, Mr. Cobb?"

He regarded her without batting an eyelash. "You didn't come in yesterday. I was worried about you."

"Your concern was what sustained me."

Not knowing how to respond to her cynical drawl, he remained cautiously aloof.

"And where have you been this morning?" she asked. "I thought you might have been reassigned now that you're no more use to them here."

His eyebrow arched. "What, you no longer need me to make coffee?"

She wasn't buying into his charm. Her guise of good naturedness fell away. "I mean now that you've accomplished what you were sent here to do."

"Which was what, Doc? Take care of you?"

She skewered him with a sour look. "Why do I doubt that that was your main agenda?"

"I don't know. Why do you?"

She muscled him away from her desktop, flipping her notebook shut just in case he could understand her hieroglyphics. "Stay away from my work, Cobb, and stay away from me."

"I was with the police this morning," he mentioned casually as he moved away from the table to assume his station at the door. He slit a gaze toward Stacy to weigh her reaction. She counterbalanced him for cool.

"Really? Did they have more questions about the other night?"

"No. This was about another matter. There was a hit-and-run fatality early this morning, and I was acting as the center's liaison."

"Someone here at Harper was in an accident?"

"No. He was freelancing. Harper's name was mentioned, and I went to help them figure out the connection. The poor slob was knocked right out of his shoes. His papers were scattered down the whole block. What a mess. Killed him instantly."

Cobb watched her expression with his snake-in-a-coil intensity. Uneasiness rippled up her spine and got her heart beating faster. What wasn't he purposefully telling her? Why had he brought it up at all? Unless...

"Freelancing as what? A researcher?"

Cobb's laugh was short. "If you can call that kind of work legitimate research."

The other shoe was about to drop, hard.

"He was a stringer for *Gab Magazine*. Alexander Andrews. You must have known him. You had him out there digging up dirt for you."

The room lost its focus and began to shift in great, dizzying swoops. She grabbed for the edge of the table, missing. Her knees buckled, twisting at an awkward angle, the left one banging into a drawer handle to bring an exquisite shock of pain to cut through the sudden fog of her awareness.

"Whoa, there."

Cobb's hands cupped her elbows, keeping her from finding the floor in a graceless heap. She let him swing her into a chair and didn't resist as he forced her head between her knees. Sickness and sorrow beat against her temples.

"Easy. Breathe deep."

"Alex is dead?" she managed at last, her voice as wobbly as the tears distorting her vision.

"I'm sorry. If I'd known the two of you were close, I wouldn't have broken it to you like that."

She shrugged off his belated compassion and his massaging touch. Sitting up was a mistake. The room swarmed with pindots of color like darting fireflies. She shut her eyes and swallowed down the rising nausea.

"What happened?" she asked weakly. "Someone hit him? Did he step into traffic?" She could picture a distracted Alex working on some scheme, walking off the curb into the side of a bus. Poor Alex. His dedication had finally taken its toll. And to think she was ready to accuse him of being immortal.

Now, she wished it had been true.

"No. From what the police said, he was on the sidewalk. The car swerved up, banged into him and drove off without even slowing down. No skid marks, nothing. And unfortunately, no witnesses."

"An accident?"

Her doubt must have shaded her question. Cobb gave her a direct look. "You know some reason why it wouldn't be? What was he working on, Doc?"

She forced herself to gain composure. Tears could come later, but now was a time for caution and control. She couldn't let Cobb guess at any correlation between Alex's death and the information he'd been gathering for her. And she hoped to God that there wasn't any.

"How should I know what story he was after? We weren't really friends. I got to know him when I was doing police work. He said he was going out of town for something. Maybe that's the story that got him killed."

"An interesting choice of wording. Killed. You think it was some mysterious story and not the background checks he was doing for you on Redman?"

It took all her self-discipline not to be thrown by his abrupt demand. Her reply was admirably measured. "I asked him to find out some things about a man who was donating a huge sum of money for my research project. There's nothing strange about that."

"But, admit it, there's plenty strange about Redman, isn't there?"

"If you mean he's a recluse with some serious privacy issues—"

"Did Andrews find out anything about Redman that would make our bashful friend consider him a...liability?"

She recoiled from that hypothesis, refusing to consider it. She'd been giving Louis the short end of the stick too often lately only to be proven wrong for her suspicions. "No. He was doing the check for me as a favor. Louis—Mr. Redman—didn't know I'd hired him."

Unless Louis had overheard the message on her answering machine.

She resisted her own awful doubts by going on the defensive. "Besides, if anything was wrong, why haven't the police been here to talk to me?"

"I took care of that."

"Took care of it?" A chill crept along her skin. "How?"

"That's my job, Doc. I keep you in the shadows. The police believe Andrews was acting on his own, trying to get a story on Redman's donation."

"But I left messages for him—"

"Erased."

A tremor swept her from head to toe. *Erased. Just like that. Just like Alex.*

What else did Cobb take care of in the line of duty? Had he tapped her phone? Is that how he knew that Alex was trying to contact her? Is that how he'd managed to suppress evidence before the police got to it?

Had he suppressed Alex, too?

"Who do you work for, Cobb? Harper or the Feds?"

He took the sudden shift in topics without any betraying discomfort. "Harper signs my checks."

"To do what? Babysit me? Spy on me? What?"

His gaze never flickered. "To protect their interests. And yours, when you'll let me."

"And what exactly does that mean?"

"It means I make sure the work goes smoothly and without interruption."

Despite herself and her wish for self-control, anger brightened in her gaze, threatening to spill over into betraying trails of dampness. She blinked hard and pushed on fiercely. "Were Alex and his tawdry magazine an interruption?"

"No." He shrugged, as if one reporter held the significance of a pesky gnat, to be swatted without thought of consequence. "Maybe an inconvenience."

"And you took care of it. Did you take care of him, too, Cobb? Is that part of your job?"

There. She'd slapped it down in front of him as clearly as if she'd demanded to know if Harper had paid him to run down Alex Andrews before he became an embarrassment. And she waited for him to respond. To say yeah or nay.

His silence and complete lack of expression terrified her more than either answer could have.

"Doctor Kimball?"

Her gaze flew wildly to where Phyllis Starke stood in the doorway. The room's tension deflated in a gush. Never had she been so glad to see the sour-faced woman. She'd asked, but she was afraid to hear Cobb's reply. Afraid because knowledge would force her to act.

It took her a moment to realize how formally she'd been addressed. Starke never treated her with any degree of professional courtesy or distinction so the title, coming from her was more alarming than expected.

"What is it, Phyl?"

"Mr. Forrester would like to see you."

"I'll be right there."

"I'm supposed to wait and bring you with me."

Perplexed and beginning to experience a squirm of wariness, Stacy nodded. She snatched up her note pad.

"You won't need that," Starke told her curtly.

But there was no way Stacy was going to leave it behind so Cobb could pour over its contents.

"I might want to jot down some things."

She tucked the pad into the pocket of her lab coat and preceded Starke down the hall. She could feel Cobb's penetrating stare, like a gun sight, aimed at the back of her head. When she got into the elevator and turned, she could see him standing where she'd left him, but as the doors closed, he leaned toward her computer.

Damn him!

She marched into Forrester's office with Phyllis trailing behind her.

"Mr. Forrester, if I'm to continue my work here at Harper, I must insist that Frank Cobb be removed immediately."

Forrester's bland smile gave her a prickle of warning. "Is something wrong with Mr. Cobb?"

"He disrupts my research, and I don't trust him." How utterly petulant and prima donnaish that sounded. Did it also convey her fear and suspicion?

She would have to be careful. She wasn't sure who her enemy was.

Forrester frowned in a gesture of appropriate concern. "Well, I suppose if he upsets you that much, I could assign someone else."

"That's really not necessary, Greg. I don't need an assistant or a babysitter."

"But I'm afraid it is necessary, Doctor Kimball." The chill in his tone ended her protest. It was a fight she couldn't win. Her wishes didn't matter. He, or his government investors, wanted someone watchdogging her every move. And at least Cobb was an evil she recognized.

"I withdraw the complaint," she murmured. "Cobb is adequate. I guess I'm just not used to working with someone looking over my shoulder."

"It's for your own protection, Stacy," he told her with a benign, grandfatherly air that was as genuine as Starke's new found respect.

"But this is a security facility. What is he protecting me from?"

"Perhaps from your own impulsiveness, Stacy. We wouldn't want anything to distract you from your dedication, that's all. You are one of our finest researchers, and we value your input here at Harper. Let's just say we want to do our best to guarantee the relationship continues."

Was he threatening her? Panic and outrage sparked together as flint and steel.

"That's what I want, too, Greg. I'm very grateful to Harper for supporting my projects in the past."

He smiled, a crocodile showing teeth. "And we value your loyalty. It's our prime goal to see that your work is successful. I think we're only beginning to guess at its long-term ramifications. That's why we've moved you up to a priority concern."

The ramification of that statement unnerved her. She needed an immediate clarification before knowing how to react. "What do you mean?"

"To provide you with an optimum environment, you'll be working out of one of the lower level labs. You'll have the most up-to-date equipment, more room, and unlimited resources. And no one will disturb you."

"But I like my lab where it is."

"I'm afraid arrangements have already been made." He pushed a new badge across the desk toward her. "Here's your new ID giving you clearance. Mr. Cobb can answer any questions you might have on using it. Let me forewarn you, though; we have some very sensitive projects being developed on that level, so security is at a maximum. Because of the scanning processes, you may not remove any data on disk. It will be erased."

There was that word again.

"But I do a lot of my after hours work at home."

"I'm afraid that will no longer be an option. If you need to stay late to complete a study, we have facilities available for you to spend the night. Mr. Cobb can make those arrangements for you."

A very handy fellow, her Mr. Cobb.

She could feel the velvet-lined trap about to snap as her neck stretched forward. Then Forrester triggered the pressure plate for her.

"One more thing. Just a routine precaution, you understand. Before you leave each evening, you will meet with Ms. Starke and fill her in on the progress you've made. You will present her with copies of all your findings and notes."

"Why?" She couldn't help blurting that out.

"Just in case something unforseen happens to you. It would be awful to lose you to some random accident and even worse to lose what you've managed to accomplish. This way, the research can continue without delay."

She got the message. If she made trouble, she was expendable. Her smile was a frozen grimace. "That's a very responsible action to take. I've been reminded lately of how fragile life can be."

Forrester nodded agreeably, missing the reference. Or perhaps he wasn't.

Was Harper working purposefully to cut her off from the outside world? To greedily grab onto her research for the betterment, not of mankind, but of Harper itself? She thought of Frank Cobb conveniently on the scene where Glenna was killed, ingratiating himself into her confidence, into her room so he could steal her data, tapping her phone so, coincidentally, the threat of Alex Andrews would go away. Granting her no escape from the government's hand in Harper's pocket and nowhere to turn for help.

Except Louis Redman.

With his money and power, he could pull the project from Harper. He could set her up in another lab, outside of the country, away from their control. She could work without encumbrances, without fear of discovery and could walk away, thumbing her nose at their autocratic rule.

If they would let her walk away.

She was thinking terrible thoughts about a company—about a government agency—that could hold her prison against her will or worse. Worse was the very real possibility that it was true. Who would know? Who would protest if Stacy Kimball disappeared off the face of the earth? They could make up any story they wanted and have it believed. And if anyone doubted what they were told, they could become statistics, too. If they knew she was about to bolt, taking her study with her, they would take measures to prevent it. Measures that would have her knocked out of her shoes on the sidewalk.

Only Louis had as much at stake as she, herself. But would he risk exposure to reach their mutual goal? If he made waves, could he be caught in a tidal backwash? If Harper knew the potential of what she was developing, would they let one millionaire benefactor get in their way? Unlikely. He would come under their scrutiny. What kind of pressure could a company like Harper exert if they discovered his secret? How would they use that knowledge in tandem with her project?

It would mean disaster.

She would have to do everything possible to keep Louis far removed from Harper's clutches. She couldn't compromise him, not even for the sake of her study.

Because of the danger if the research fell into the wrong hands.

Because of the attraction she could deny but couldn't resist.

She thought back. Had she mentioned Louis directly in any of her notes? She didn't think so. Even if they did know the content of her study, they wouldn't know the source. And if she could keep it that way, she could continue her work with minimal distraction and minimal danger to Louis.

And then there was the time element. Setting up a new lab, creating new protocols, new specimen controls would take time—providing she could get what she already had safely out of Harper's clutches.

Time was something she did not have.

Better she play along, using Harper as they were using her in hopes that she and Louis could outsmart them in the end. Discussing options with Louis now would mean revealing facts about herself that she preferred to keep to private. For now, she could maintain a balance of control. For now, she wouldn't have to involve Louis in the equation.

A time might come when she'd have to tell all, but that time was not today.

She picked up the new ID badge and pinned it to the front of her coat. "If there's nothing more, I'd like to get back to work."

"I wouldn't dream of keeping you from it a minute longer than necessary." Greg Forrester grinned and she wondered how she had ever thought of him as harmless.

She followed Phyllis to the elevator and was startled when the other woman stayed her hand before she could push the button for the research floor.

"You don't need to go there."

"But I have to gather up my notes, my belongings."

Starke waved off her protest. "Everything's already been moved."

They didn't waste any time.

When the doors opened to the lowest level, it was like stepping out into a military compound instead of a science lab. Cement floors, bare lights and uniforms. Nothing that welcomed, nothing that inspired, nothing but intimidation and the threat of an unseen power. The Gestapo came instantly and disquietingly to mind.

Stacy, who had never considered herself easily frightened, fought down a tremor of real fear in order to force herself from the elevator.

The first challenge to their right to be there came within ten feet. A guard stepped forward to check their badges and punch their names into his computer. He waved them along. At the first bend in the corridor, they confronted a sealed security door. Badges were run through the identi-plate and their thumbprints scanned. The door clicked open, inviting them onward. As they went down the hall, she heard a low frequency hum and caught a glimpse of a vacillating light. They were being x-rayed.

Forrester was right in his warning. So much for smuggling any data out on disk.

"This will be your lab," Phyllis told her, gesturing to a solid door with a small, prison-sized window in it. To enter, the ID key had to be used.

Stacy tried to keep her expression impassive. Yes, the lab set-up was superior, all sterile white and polished steel with all the highest tech equipment, ample space...and her own private guard. Frank Cobb stood in the center of the room, his features as impersonal as the setting.

"Is all to your satisfaction?" Starke asked with just the right bite of jealous irritation.

Oh boy, could she have gone off on an angry bender. Satisfaction? Being herded like a criminal to the bowels of the Center, x-rayed, fingerprinted—she was lucky they didn't insist on a cavity search. Her freedom, her creative choice, her options...gone. This was not her place of work. It was her own personal microscope slide where she would be watched, monitored, and stripped of independence. If only she had the privilege of telling grim-faced ghoul Phyllis Starke to take her job and shove it.

But, a confirmed and desperate realist, Stacy said nothing. Her nod was the best she could do in response.

"I'll leave you to your work then. I'll be down at 4:30 sharp to go over your progress."

"I'll be looking forward to it."

One thing about Starke, sarcasm was never wasted on her. With a glower of contempt, she stepped out of the room. When Stacy heard the vacuum seal on the door, her spirit was sucked out as well.

She glared at Cobb. "From assistant to jailer. I hope it was a nice promotion for you."

He absorbed her venom without a blink. "I've tried to set up all your work areas the way you had them upstairs, so you wouldn't be disrupted."

"Disrupted." Her laugh slashed bitterly. "No, I am a hearty species. I can take root again and flourish no matter how rudely I've been jerked from my native soil. Even in this artificial dirt."

Cobb was too much of a professional to express regret or opinion. He wisely got out of her way.

Once she'd arranged everything to suit her meticulous work habits, Stacy put her upset behind her and immersed herself in the task at hand. Since Harper and their government Big Brothers obviously knew the potential of her work, she didn't waste time concealing her purpose from them. But if they wanted more, they were in for a struggle. She had no choice but to use their facilities to a quick and hopefully successful end. But she didn't have to reveal her sources. And she didn't have to pretend to like it.

And at 4:30 sharp, as her harsh-faced supervisor went over her daily accomplishments, Stacy sat stoically while Starke assessed her findings.

"Where did you get the samples you're using?" Starke glanced up over the data sheets to pin Stacy with her glare.

"What difference does it make?"

Starke laughed. "I'm not stupid, so don't assume I don't understand the connotations here. Your project is all hush hush, but I'm capable of reading between the lines and am not without my own sources of information. Where did you get these blood samples?"

"Originally, from the morgue, under the fingernails of a murder victim." She saw no reason to lie.

"But who was the sample taken from?"

"If the police don't know, how should I?"

Starke looked over the figures again, anticipation and agitation animating her sallow features. "How did you come by them?"

"A friend of mine is a pathologist. We used to work together. I do freelance consulting for him sometimes. He thought I'd be interested in the unusual properties he discovered."

"He knows about this, then?"

Alarm froze through Stacy's gut. She thought of Alex Andrews knocked out of his shoes on a public sidewalk. *Hit and run, my ass.* There was nothing random about his death and she'd be damned if she'd allow anything similar to befall Charlie. He didn't deserve it. No one did.

"He doesn't know anything. This is way out of his league. I told him it was a genetic anomaly."

"And he believed you?"

"He's too busy not to. The living aren't exactly his field of interest."

Stacy waited, tension making her muscles ache and her head pound. Finally, Starke set the papers aside. "I guess he's of no importance then."

Stacy released her suspended breath in a carefully regimented stream.

"Mr. Cobb will see you home."

At that final insult to her freedom, Stacy rebelled. "That is not necessary. I have my own car here."

"He'll follow you then. And in the future, he'll pick you up and see you home."

"I am perfectly capable of driving myself—"

Starke cut off her protest with the efficiency of a scalpel in the hand of a surgeon—Doctor Frankenstein, most likely. "We've been informed of the unfortunate trouble at your apartment complex."

Stacy slid an accusing glare toward Cobb who received it impassively.

"In light of that," Starke continued, "we feel it's in your best interest to cooperate on this point. You will cooperate, won't you, Doctor?"

"I'm not one to make waves, Doctor," she drawled icily in return.

"Good." Stake nodded to Cobb then gathered up all of Stacy's notes.

"I need those," she was quick to claim.

Phyllis's smile was pure artificial sweetener. "I'll have them copied and returned before morning. We can't be too careful with information like this. It's better we have it safeguarded in more than one location."

And for whose best interest was that?

Certainly not Stacy's.

Stacy stood aside while Cobb opened the door to her apartment for her. She waited in the hall as he made a cursory sweep of her rooms, her mood growing more volatile with impotent fury the longer it steeped. When Cobb paused before the flashing light on her answering machine, she was ready to tangle.

"I don't think that's for you, Frank."

He stared at the beckoning strobe of green then up into the fire of her gaze, clearly at odds. If he chose to push the recall button, there was little she could do. It wasn't as if she could overpower him. And he had a gun.

"Thank you for the escort, Cobb," she dismissed softly. "I'll see you at 6:30."

Then she waited, wondering a bit frantically what she would do if he decided not to be obliging.

Finally, he started toward the door, leaving her with at least one scrap of privacy. Unless, of course, her phone really was bugged, and her superiors already knew who'd left the message on her machine.

Her jaw tightened as he passed her in the doorway.

"Lock this," he told her. "And don't lose my number. I've got a faster response time than 911."

"Why? Are you sleeping in your car at the curb?"

His opaque stare gave no answer and got her wondering if maybe he *was* camping out nearby.

She latched and deadbolted the door behind him, and, for the first time since that morning allowed the rivulets of her distress to shiver freely through her.

What the hell was she going to do?

What could she do in the prison camp Harper had become?

Tossing her purse at the over-stuffed sofa, she stalked to the side table to retrieve her message. Her heart took a painful lunge when Alex Andrews' breathless voice wavered from the machine.

"Stacy, just a quick warning. Someone else knows that we know. I think I'm being followed. You be careful. I think tonight we need to talk about going to the police."

Tonight they wouldn't talk about anything, not ever again.

She dropped heavily onto the couch, burying her face in her hands. Tears of frustration and loss wet her fingertips, but instead of bursting forth in cleansing sobs, her anguish bunched up tight in the back of her throat, burning there like Cobb's betrayal.

A light touch to her shoulder sent her scrambling back in terror.

"I'm sorry about your friend."

She stared helplessly up at Louis Redman through the glaze of her grief. It didn't matter how he knew for the moment, only that he was there.

"Now," he continued, "how are we going to keep you safe from the threat we can see and the threat we can't?"

FOURTEEN

As Stacy sipped the tea Louis had made for her, she contemplated the ridiculousness of a vampire brewing camomile in her kitchen. And as she did so, an almost hysterical laughter swelled inside her until she ached from holding it back. How far her life had detoured from the norm.

Louis appeared at ease in her cluttered rooms. He'd forgone the tailored Armani suits and Italian loafers to blend casually with her surroundings. He was sleek yet still elegant in snug black jeans and pullover sweater. The running shoes gave her pause. With his preternatural powers, did he ever need to rely upon fleetness of foot? More a fashion statement than a necessity, she decided, finishing the last of the herbal drink. By then, its soothing warmth had spread through to heat chilled extremities and calm an anxious mind. She regarded her visitor with a directness that gave him pause.

"We need to find this Quinton Alexander."

He blinked at her bluntness. "For what purpose?"

"To keep you safe and uninvolved and to assure that my work will continue."

"We have discussed this."

"Well, we need to discuss it again. The last time we brought the topic up, I wasn't a prisoner in my own lab, and the government wasn't breathing down my neck."

Louis didn't answer right away, and when he did, it was with a question. "How long will it take you to finish your work?"

"With trials and the paperwork necessary to authorize human test subjects—" She did laugh then, the sound harsh and brittle. "I forgot. With the government in charge, the red tape won't be a problem. A day. A week. A month. Maybe more. It depends on how long it takes me to break down the various components and isolate the affected gene. It's hit or miss for the moment. Things will go quickly once I know what I'm looking for."

"How long before they know exactly what it is you are doing?"

Again, the strained laugh. "If they had a clue, I'd be shackled to my work station twenty-four hours a day. For now, they think everything's theoretical, and they're giving me the rope to either hang myself or square knot a new rung on their ladder to immortality. The closer I get to the findings we need, the harder it's going to be to hide things from them. Then things could get unpleasant. There's the danger that they pull me off the project or—"

He gave her a sharp look, alerted by the fraying words at the end of her sentence. "Or?"

She regarded him with a wry candor. "I'll simply disappear some day. They hate loose ends, you know, and no one is irreplaceable. Eventually, I'll become a liability, just the way Alex did."

"Alex?"

"My reporter friend. The one who dug up all the background information."

There. Now he knew. Stacy leaned against the yielding back of the sofa, letting it absorb some of the tension that began massing in the room. She couldn't read his distress upon the impassive angles of his face. It was more a feeling of seismic energy gathering, increasing pressure until eventually a weak link would give and release the uncontained magnitude of his emotions. She prepared for the dark surge.

"Did Harper get that information from him?" His question was silky, deceivingly smooth, like several fingers of Jack Daniels straight up. The kick would follow when least expected.

"I don't know. Alex was an old pro. He wouldn't have left his notes or his sources exposed. But we have to assume that they'll discover the truth eventually. Unless we distract them in another direction."

"With Alexander."

"It's the only way."

"A dangerous way. He will not be voluntarily...cooperative."

"Then we'll have to convince him. For now, we have to concentrate on keeping as many of our secrets as possible. My phone is tapped. My computer has been breached, too. We'll have to be very careful not to give them a reason to clamp down on security measures. Our enemies need to be isolated and identified, so we can deal with them as efficiently as possible. Just like a dangerously mutated gene. Why are you smiling? Do you think I'm over-reacting."

Louis fought to restrain the mobile curve of his mouth, but it was difficult. She reminded him so much of both the women he had loved. And lost. That cold dash of reality wiped the fond amusement from his face and heart. His reply was terse.

"No. You are being cautious, and caution is warranted." He moved toward the windows in the dining area, careful to remain in the shadows lest prying eyes were watching even now. And they probably were. "So you believe your employer will take no steps to protect you?"

"They've already sold me out. As long as they keep a current record of my research findings, I'm expendable."

"Then we must make sure that at least one piece of the puzzle remains out of their grasp, so they have no excuse to terminate you."

He saw her wince at the word 'terminate.' Smart woman. She understood the danger she was in and would be careful.

"We must also assume," he continued, "that Quinton will escalate his attacks on you. He is a clever fiend who is difficult to predict. Insanity always resists the path of logic."

She paled, considering her plight. She was alone, unable to call in her bodyguard or the police to rescue her. But instead of turning to him to beg for his assistance, she squared her shoulders and braced to support her own defense.

"How can I keep him from making a midnight snack of me should he get bored playing his game?"

"Be wary of both friend and foe until you know how to recognize him. Knowing him as I do, it is unlikely that he will make a move against you this soon. He will toy with me through you. He's only guessing at our relationship now, but if he suspects you can be a tool to hurt me, he will use you mercilessly. So, for the time being, it is best you stick to your regular routine. If you feel threatened, you will move in with me."

She bristled up at that. Whether from his presumptive claim or from a confusion of the heart, she didn't like his suggestion in the least.

"I have to relent to being a prisoner during the day because Harper has the facilities I need, but I will not become your prisoner by night."

He smiled slightly, wondering what she was so afraid of. Him or herself? "I am really an excellent host. It wouldn't be a terrible captivity."

But she wasn't mollified. "Whatever time I have left will be my own."

"Will it? You are very brave or very foolish to think yourself safe here. If Quinton comes, do your really think your human friend can overpower him? Do you think you could find the strength to fight his will should he choose to exert it over you?"

Pridefully, independently, her chin shot up, and her lush lips opened to proclaim what he knew to be a dangerous untruth. What he must now show her to be a deadly misconception.

He moved. Using the supernatural speed of his kind, he crossed the room like a puff of wind, standing one moment at the window, and the next toe to toe with the arrogant doctor. She never saw his progress. He simply was there in front of her, a startling apparition she could neither anticipate nor escape. Fear widened her intelligent gaze until all was submerged save alarm and a desperate panic. Her attempt to scramble backward was thwarted by the sudden bracketing of his arms on either side of her shoulders as he leaned close to intimidate and purposefully terrify. His lips curled back so that she would see the terrible fangs.

"And if I were Quinton Alexander, you would be mine," he hissed.

Her hand moved to her throat, a gesture to suppress her scream perhaps. Or so he thought until a small silver cross appeared between her slender fingers to drive him back with the force of a compelling shove. Averting his head as pain and sickness held him helpless, he marveled at the tenacity threaded through her quavering voice.

"Perhaps not strength of body, but certainly strength of mind."

"If you'll lower that crucifix, I will applaud you properly."

Slowly, he turned back toward her. The fright eased from her expression, replaced by something he found much more unsettling. Her eyes gleamed with a smug confidence, a sense of well being that he hated to deny her, but in order to keep her safe, he had no choice but to destroy it. She still didn't understand the nature of evil she was dealing with. This was no clinical strain of contagion to be looked at through the safe distance of a microscope. It was an infection running wild, to which no one, least of all her, was immune. She had to realize her vulnerability, or she would fall victim to her own false pride.

She needed to be afraid, for in that fear came strength and wariness to guard against threats from all directions.

Even his.

He met her superior stare, letting his admiration shine through at first. Then gradually when she was relaxed and certain of her triumph, he dazzled her with the seductive power of what he was. So easy. She suspected nothing.

And that's how Quinton would defeat her.

Seditious charm overcame her barriers, a fog seeping up to envelop and quietly disorient in a haze of thick vampiric mastery. She had lost herself, without knowing how or where, to his will-devouring power.

The mocking curve of her mouth slackened to a malleable parting, inviting without knowledge or consequence anything he might offer. Her gaze grew limpid as he reduced her self-control to an eager reflection of his own. He touched her cheek, and she leaned into his palm, the gesture a blatant request for domination.

He wanted her. Had wanted her from the very first.

Unable to resist, he bent down, until her soft breath teased him beyond the capacity for reason or restraint.

It had been too long since he'd allowed himself to know love.

And he was dangerously close to falling into it again with the bold and beautiful Stacy Kimball.

Knowing the danger, still he plunged ahead.

She tasted of twilight fantasies and sweetened tea. He dipped inside to sample more deeply and was as lost as she. She made a quiet sound in the back of her throat, not of surrender but of sultry pleasure. Her hands came up to rest upon his shoulders, rubbing briefly, gliding together to lace through his dark hair. Pulling his head toward her.

Somewhere in that sensual tangle of tongues and wills and wishes, the unnatural magic became a very human desire. And the lesson he'd thought to press upon her was dealt back at him with a bittersweet cruelty.

He had no defense, either.

Once he'd stopped manipulating her with his irresistible control, he was sure she would draw back in outraged dismay and disgust.

She didn't.

Her arms enfolded him, close then closer still, until he was kneeling between the spread of her knees, bracing himself for balance against the cushioned back of the couch. She kissed like a woman who enjoyed her own sexuality and didn't mind if her partner knew it. A somewhat disconcerting revelation to a man raised with courtly manners and wives from repressed centuries past. There was nothing he needed to show her. She was skilled far beyond the techniques gleaned from his own passionate encounters.

But if there was nothing more he could teach her about pleasure, perhaps, he realized as she finally eased away, there was much he could show her about love.

Confusion darkened her naked gaze, cloaking it like a maiden who belatedly discovered her immodesty. Though obviously knowledgeable in carnal matters, she seemed oddly shy when faced with her own emotions. Those feelings shone ripe and vulnerable in her gaze, edged with fear, not of what he was, but who he was—a man capable of breaching her flirtatious barriers. Louis recognized and understood that caution, having practiced it for most of his five hundred years. During his two momentary lapses, where tender sentiment had overcame safety, he had found paradise and pain. Looking upon the woman before him, he wasn't sure if he was ready to endure that paradoxical combination again. At least, not until his humanity was restored.

How unkind of him to woo her as a monster when he had nothing he could give except unrealized promises.

"Forgive me," he murmured softly, rocking back on his heels. "That was unfair of me."

Stacy scrambled for a saving clarity of mind over heart. She adopted a manner both gruff and defensive to rebuild the walls her brief lapse of judgement had allowed to crumble. Even as she tasted him upon her kiss-swollen lips, he watched the anxiety and denial darkening her stare.

What upset her so? There was no fear of him there in that anguished gaze. Rather a tempered refusal to recognize her own longings, her own weakness where emotion was concerned. She was afraid of herself.

"You proved your point." Her voice was raspy with self-castigation. "I'm not invulnerable. But I'll do better now that you've brought those failings to my attention."

Failings.

Stacy saw him smile wryly at her choice of words. Had it been his plan to embarrass as well as instruct her as to her weaknesses? Forewarned was forearmed. She would keep the barriers high and unbreachable about her.

Especially now that she knew there was more at stake than her profession or her life.

Louis Redman had become a serious threat to her vow of uninvolvement. Love 'Em and Leave 'Em Kimball. That was her credo, her mantra, her only protection. Until her work was successful and her reward was a normal life.

In that, she and Louis were much alike.

"I'm tired. You should go now."

He stood without argument and stepped back to break the magnetic pull between them. "I will return tomorrow, and we shall decide upon a plan. You are not safe. That must be our first priority."

Her answering smile quirked with a hard-bitten cynicism. "We can't have anything happening to me before my work is complete, now can we?"

The stoic blank returned to his glorious features, resisting any display of inner sentiments. "No, we cannot. Good night, Stacy Kimball. Sleep well."

"You can't leave by the front door. I think my apartment building is being watched. Perhaps it would be best if you—"

But her concern was for nothing. She'd glanced toward the door then back...at empty space.

Louis was already gone.

She uttered a jagged little laugh and sagged back against the cushions. Her fingertips moved along her parted lips, finding her mouth soft and damp with residual passion. And it had been passion sparking between them. Any other term would pale as a description. And she'd enjoyed the taking, the giving of that desperate yearning. When she realized what she was doing, she jerked her hand away.

What was she contemplating?

The man was a monster who lived off the vitality of others. A parasite, a disease. Certainly not a suitor whose attention she should covet and secretly encourage.

Her only commitment should be to her work. Any other distraction could be only that, a fleeting and impersonal sidebar. And because she feared Louis Redman was already much more than that, she needed to be extra vigilant against the temptation to let emotion rule.

Think about work. Think about goals.

When considering them, she remembered a particularly unpleasant piece of business she'd meant to do before news of Alex's death had shaken her off course.

She needed confirmation for something she already intuited. Knowing wouldn't change anything, but it would push up her time table—time being the only variable she couldn't control.

Rolling up her sleeve, she took a blood sample from her inner elbow.

What she did wasn't an exact determination. The conditions were far from perfect, and her home equipment was far too inferior. But it would give a rough verification of what she already believed to be true.

Placing cells from her sample onto a glass slide, she then exposed it to a chemical stain. After the dye had a chance to work under the cover slip, she secured the glass under the clips of her not inexpensive home microscope.

She stared at the telltale black spots until they began to swim before her eyes.

Then she wept.

It wasn't a long, violently cathartic cry. It wasn't like the first time, when she'd been so surprised, so shocked, so denying. She'd expected what she ultimately saw. The news, though bad, hadn't caught her unprepared. It simply battered her already bruised spirit with a looming shadow of defeat.

A single droplet fell upon the curve of her bosom, a small, bright red dot quickly joined by another, until the pattern spread at an alarming rate.

Stacy grabbed up a wad of tissues, holding them to her nose, discarding them when they were saturated and replacing them with another compress. Finally, the flow slowed then stopped. Mechanically, she washed her face and rinsed at the stain on her sweater that would probably never come clean. Such stains never went completely away.

Even as emotionally prepared as she was for the news, she needed a way to fill the gaping void certainty had bored within her soul. She needed to reach out and touch a friend.

She picked up her cell phone and dialed. The brusque annoyance in Charlie Sisson's voice was just the bracer she needed.

"Hey, lover." She smiled so he wouldn't hear the sorrow she was hiding. "Did I catch you in the middle of something?"

"A perforated stomach, if you must know."

"Sounds fun."

"Wish you were here. Is there something you wanted, or is this just a social call? I've got about a million miles of intestines to get through this evening."

"How appetizing." Then she grew serious, conquering her self-pity by shifting her concern to another. "Charlie, has anyone been by asking questions about that supposed jumper...or about me?"

His answer was more than a little disturbing.

"Some Fed-types were sniffing around earlier, but I blew them off. Said I'd meet them for breakfast after my shift's over. Why? Trouble?"

"Nothing I want you to involve yourself in, okay? Don't do anything heroic or stupid like that."

"Me?"

He sounded incredulous, but she knew better. There was a streak of superhero a mile wide in Charlie Sisson.

And that's what she was afraid of.

"Charlie, I'm not kidding around. I know how you like to meddle in things."

"You've got the wrong guy. I'm Mister Conscientious Objector. I just cut 'em and gut 'em. I don't comment on 'em."

Closing her eyes, she leaned against the phone in relief. "See that you stick to that motto. Stay out of this one, Charlie. I'd hate to think of you stretched out on one of your own slabs."

"Gotcha."

She ended the connection and felt suddenly so alone. She hadn't told him even though he was one of the few who knew her history. She'd learned from experience that such pain was better kept private. There was no comfort anyone could give her, only awkward condolences.

She'd done what she could to protect Charlie and Louis.

Now, how was she going to protect herself?

***

Frank Cobb frowned as he played back the tape. He'd thought it might just be a glitch in his headphones that prevented him from hearing any other voice but Stacy's. But the recording was equally bewildering.

He could have sworn she was speaking, not into the phone, but to someone in the room with her.

So why was her voice the only one audible?

Who had been in the apartment with her?

Redman was his first and best guess. But she'd never used his name aloud nor made any reference that could be traced to the elusive zillionaire. And without proof, he had nothing. Instinct wouldn't sway Forrester or his employers, not with so much at stake.

At least he had a name. Quinton Alexander. Find Alexander and hopefully more pieces would fall into place in the puzzling whole. The sooner he figured it out, the sooner he could move on to something more in tune with his expertise. Being a Peeping Tom didn't fit into his training regimen. Usually, he'd be complaining up a storm about the inactivity and the waste of his talents. But he'd said nothing because he intuited that there was more behind Stacy Kimball's little games of deception than scientific espionage. He couldn't buy Forrester's claim that she was selling Harper's secrets. It was a cover up, but covering what, exactly?

C'mon, Doc. Throw me a bone here.

He would replace the bug. Faulty equipment. That's what it was.

What else could explain it?

He settled back into the negligible comfort of the Company's panel van, fitting the earphones over his head to listen while the recording tapes whirred in their tireless vigil. In another hour, he'd be replaced and could return briefly to his tiny boarding house room where he would shower and collapse for a couple of hours of intense sleep. He didn't have to take a turn at eavesdropping. He'd volunteered. A usually boring and slightly unsavory job, but on this case, he'd wanted to stick close to the subject. His superiors called it an obsession with duty.

He feared it was becoming another kind of obsession altogether.

Then he heard her crying.

He'd been through private wars and private hells, but this one woman's tears almost undid him. His first instinct was to rush inside, to offer his help, to offer his shoulder, to offer his life if it would stem the tide of those noble tears.

Crazy impulses.

He was getting soft. Maybe it was time to step back and remove himself from her case before his objectivity was compromised.

Then there was silence on the other end of the headphones, and he was able to restore his much-needed detachment.

He repressed a smile as he listened to the doc talking with the coroner on her cell. Smart girl, staying away from her compromised phone lines. But not quite clever enough to divert suspicion away from herself.

She was involved up to her pretty, steel-blue eyes.

Stacy Kimball was building a damning case against herself, and he was collecting the evidence to convict her. That was his job.

And tonight, it stunk.

FIFTEEN

"I brought bagels."

Stacy peered through unfocused eyes at Cobb and the sack he extended. She would have slammed the door in his wide awake face, but the wafting aroma of coffee curbed the urge.

"What are you doing here, Cobb?"

"I'm your taxi, remember?"

"But that's not for another thirty minutes."

"So I brought breakfast and brilliant over-the-table conversation to perk you up. Do I get to come in?"

She considered snatching the coffee and leaving him in the hall, but manners learned once upon a time prevailed upon her better behavior. One did not shun Greeks bearing gifts.

Or was that the proper lesson one learned belatedly from sly Trojans?

"Make yourself at home, Frank. I'll be out of the shower in five."

Cobb stepped in with a Cheshire smile. What trouble could he get into that he'd not already caused?

Besides, he'd brought coffee.

Reaching into the bag to pull out a piping hot paper cup, she carried it with her into the bathroom. When she emerged five minutes and twenty seconds later, Cobb was seated at her table putting the finishing touches of blueberry cream cheese on a cinnamon raisin bagel half. He looked innocent.

She didn't believe it for a second.

She took the bagel from his hand and, after a bite, drawled, "Did you have time to finish searching my drawers?"

His smile was pure wickedness. "I thought I'd wait until you were in them. The job's much more rewarding then, don't you think?"

"You just keep thinking and wishing, Cobb."

He sighed heavily. "The story of my life."

"Pure fiction."

"Better than science fiction," he replied, "which is the direction yours seems to be taking lately."

"Your heartfelt concern for my well being brings out all the best in me." She made a gagging gesture with her forefinger. She'd started to turn away when he gripped her other wrist. It wasn't a particularly gentle hold.

"I am concerned, Doc. You're involved in stuff that can turn nasty overnight. I don't want to be the one—"

"To what?" She jerked free of him. "Run me down on the sidewalk like you probably did Alex Andrews? That kind of concern I can live a lot longer without!" She tossed her half eaten bagel into the bag without giving him a chance to respond. It's not like he would confess to anything anyway. "Let's go. I don't want to be late and get the warden worrying."

***

There was no such thing as an exact science. The one thing Stacy enjoyed about it was its constant state of flux. It was the ultimate mystery, the final frontier for exploration. It could be frustratingly coy with its answers, or open its arms wide to offer the opportunities of a lifetime.

Her lifetime, at least, in this case.

In the matter of a single day, after years of roadblocks and dead ends, her research showed her the possibility of decades to come.

No longer having the luxury of following infinite avenues, Stacy was forced to narrow her study into a single path, a single case, a single trial. Once she'd mastered the secrets of one, she could start expanding them to suit all.

She could hardly contain her excitement as she peered through the eyepiece, watching as the gene sample from Louis Redman overcame and altered the diseased specimen to match its properties. Healthy properties. She'd done the test three times and each arrived at the same results.

Close. So close she could taste it.

So close she could almost feel the regeneration going on inside herself.

But was it just a temporary fix or reparation done on a genetic level? That was her next step. It was so hard to walk slowly, in baby increments, when she felt the need to run, to rush forward.

Slow and steady. Slow and steady wins the race.

"Is that what you're working on?"

The sound of Phyllis Starke's voice triggered a hostile takeover of her mood. Purposefully, Stacy turned the knob a notch too tight and was rewarded by the snap of the slide she'd been viewing.

"Oh, damn. Phyl, you shouldn't sneak up on me like that. Now I've got to waste all of tomorrow duplicating these results all over again."

She unclipped the damaged slide and, before her supervisor could prevent it, destroyed the smears upon it. Starke's thunderous expression told of her angry suspicion that the act had been intentional. But she couldn't prove anything. And as long as she couldn't, Stacy was relatively safe.

"At least your notes are still intact."

Stacy smiled up at the glowering woman. "Nothing new to add until I finish with this experiment. You know how slowly things can move at this stage."

Starke's glare narrowed. "Yes, I do. I know exactly how these things work."

A threat. Starke wouldn't be easy to fool or stall.

"We spoke to your pathologist friend and the investigators on that murder case."

Stacy fought not to betray a reaction. "And? Anything new?"

"Nothing," she spat out in obvious irritation.

Hiding her smile as she shut her computer down, Stacy murmured, "Something will turn up. It always does."

"And when it does," Starke purred viciously, "I will be there to take the appropriate action."

"Is she always such a bitch?"

Stacy slanted Cobb a look as they walked to his car. "Why Frank, what a disrespectful way to speak of your employers."

"She doesn't sign my checks. What's the story? Perennial PMS, or is it just you?"

"I wish I could claim all the credit but she was a bitch long before I came on the scene."

Cobb grinned. "But you push her buttons, right?"

He shook out a cigarette, and when she reached for it, he held it out of her grasp, making her jump for it figuratively. Teased by the curative taste of nicotine, Stacy spilled it all.

"She was bopping Forrester to get her promotion. From what I hear, that was the only way she could compensate for bad team evaluations. And now she's annoyed with me because she thinks I've taken her place in the sheets."

"Doctor Kimball telling tales out of school? Shame on you."

She snatched the cigarette and let him light it for her before he did his own. "It's not gossip when she was the one who so delighted in letting everyone know about it."

"And have you?"

She glanced at him to clarify the purpose of his nonchalantly asked question. "Have I what?"

"Given her a reason to be annoyed?"

"That's none of your business."

No apologies. "Well, you can understand my jumping to conclusions, can't you?"

She whirled, placing herself directly in his face, hers heating with outrage. "Oh, yeah, I understand. Starke is a professional prude and, therefore, decent. I have big boobs and like short shirts and—what a jump of logic—that makes me a slut." She shoved him, causing him to stumble back. "You've just sunk to a new low in my opinion, Cobb."

"Can't blame a guy for wishing it was true."

She made a snorting sound and stalked away. "You are such a guy."

"That's an insult, right?"

They'd reached his car, a low-slung '68 Vette in black. Very discrete, she thought wryly as she dropped down into the passenger seat, feeling as though her fanny was dragging the ground. As the engine purred to life, Cobb gave her a solemn look.

"Don't underestimate her, Doc. She's already making noise with Forrester about being willing and able to take over your project."

Alarm knifed through her belly. "And just how do you know that?"

He smiled. "That's none of your business. Just be glad I'd much rather be chauffeuring you around than her." He shifted into reverse and ended the conversation.

But Stacy couldn't afford to forget it.

***

The shrilling of her cell phone woke Stacy from a fitful nap in her recliner. Fumbling for the phone, she mumbled a fairly coherent greeting, then was wide awake.

"Stacy, it's Ken Fitzhugh. Can you meet me down at the Pike Place Market at about 11:30? I've got some information on your reporter friend who was killed yesterday."

"What—"

"Meet me, okay? I don't want to go into it over the phone. Can you come alone?"

Rubbing the sleep and the sting of Alex's loss from her eyes, she muttered, "Sure." Then the click on the other end kept her from asking for more particulars.

With all that had happened, she hadn't had the chance to get back to the young officer to address his claim that Louis's fingerprints were on the first 'gift' she'd received. Had the eager policeman jumped the gun with the results, or was he purposefully misleading her?

Or was Louis somehow involved?

The vehement denial she felt over that last option left her unsettled. Louis Redman was a vampire. Didn't that already make him a killer? Why did she want so much to believe he was a benevolent one?

He could be lying to her. He wanted the research she was doing. Why should he be any more honest about obtaining the desired findings than Harper had been? Would he be above saying anything to get what he needed from her? Didn't the threat of the unseen and unknown spectre of Quinton Alexander light a fire under her, hurrying her to get to the hoped-for conclusion?

Did Alexander exist, or was he a tool Louis wielded to scare her into compliance?

Suddenly, she wanted very much to hear what Fitzhugh had to say.

Now, to escape the apartment without Louis or Cobb knowing about it.

She dressed quickly, shunning her usual flashy attire in favor of shabby chic. Baggy jeans, a loose flannel shirt, her hair tucked up under a SeaHawks ball cap felt like an invisible disguise. Leaving a note for Louis on the dining table asking him to wait, she slipped out of her apartment and went downstairs to the one Glenna had occupied.

Buddy Jacobs looked like hell. If Stacy had any doubts about his feelings for her neighbor, his bloodshot eyes and stubbled cheeks told her everything. She embraced him briefly and muttered the appropriate sympathies while he seemed lost with what to say or do with himself. Taking advantage of his misery seemed like a loathsome endeavor. Until she remembered Glenna's frequent bruises. He should have treated her better when she was alive.

"You look like you need to get out for a while," she prescribed. "Come on, Buddy. It'll do you good. How about coffee down at the Market? My treat."

She suspected it was that last part that got his attention. Glenna had been the breadwinner, and her boyfriend was probably experiencing the pinch to his pocket. Unworthy thoughts, she knew, but brutally true.

"Get your coat," she insisted, giving him a nudge. "We'll take your bike."

With the lanky musician as escort and his helmet and darkening face shield on her head, Stacy made a clean get away. Her sense of victory was short-lived. The danger she faced was real, and she was alone.

But the lure of discovering even a piece of the puzzle was enough to warrant the risk.

***

The stalls at Pike Place were empty, the catch of the day on ice and the boardwalk washed clean. The scent of fish and salt lingered sharply on the air, along with milder aromas of produce and pungent herbs. Novelty shops were long past closing time, and the only passersby were the Seattle night people—the panhandlers looking for a spot to sleep; the Goth youths with their ghostly white faces, black garb and multiple piercings; and night owls like herself.

It had been disgustingly easy to ditch Buddy.

Their coffee hadn't even cooled in the cup when he was approached by a leggy woman he described as a blues singer. After she had hugged him tight and pressed a consoling kiss on his lips, complete with tongue, they were obviously singing the same tune.

Stacy vowed she could find a way home, and Buddy was indecently quick about taking her at her word. He and the singer were gone in an instant.

Glenna deserved better.

It was approaching 11:30.

She walked the length of the Market, but there was no sign of Fitzhugh. Figuring he might have been delayed by a call, she refused to worry. The night was pleasantly warm, and the physical activity felt wonderful. Her stroll led her to the end of the empty fruit carts and fish lockers to several restaurants still serving drinks to diehard revelers. Music filtered out onto the breeze. Mellow oldies, hip hopping rap mingling with baleful teenage angst. The potpourri relaxed her mood as she circled a broad wooden deck to overlook the Sound.

Chill water temperature combining with warmer air stirred up a slow rising blanket of fog, but even that felt restful. A gray, enveloping buffer to reality blowing soft upon her exposed skin. She leaned her forearms on the rail and lifted her face to the mists crouching low over dark waters.

"Stacy."

The soft call jolted her with remembered terror, but when she turned, it melted in relief as Officer Fitzhugh jogged toward her.

"Sorry you had to wait. I don't like the idea of you being out here alone, but I couldn't risk what we had to say being overheard."

"Who's listening, Ken?"

He leaned against the rail beside her, looking so young and very distressed. "We are. I came across a request for taps on your phone."

Alarm jumped inside her. "A request from who?"

"I can't find out. It must go all the way to the top. Redman's involved and so is the government. The files on those attack victims, they've been purged from the computer system. The print match on Redman is gone, too. It's as if someone's extremely anxious to clear a path, but I don't know where it's leading."

"But who and why?"

"What kind of research are you doing, Stacy? That's got to be the link. Redman must have some tremendous importance to the government, or they wouldn't be covering his trail so well. They even had that gossip reporter killed."

Anguish burned behind her fierce stare. "But is Louis a victim or an accomplice?"

"Louis?" A slight edge of hurt that she would speak of him with such intimate familiarity colored Fitzhugh's tone. "Stacy, are you sure you want to hear all this? Are you and Redman involved somehow?"

"No, of course not," she protested quickly, perhaps too quickly. "We live in totally different universes. He funded my work, but if he's a killer, I'll be the first one to blow the whistle on him."

"It might be dangerous for you to get close, Stacy."

"There are other things that scare me a lot more, Ken. Like the thought that maybe someone is setting Louis up to take the fall."

"Why would anyone go to all that trouble? Facts don't lie. I smell conspiracy all over this one. Either Redman's manipulating Harper, or the government's playing one against the other. I don't know, but maybe it's time you got out of there. I don't want to see you getting hurt."

She smiled at his puppy dog look. "I'm where I need to be for right now. I can't explain, Ken. You'll just have to trust me."

"I want to, but—"

The rest was cut off by a beep from his police radio. He held up a finger to put her on hold while he walked a few feet away to answer his call. He tucked the radio back in his belt and turned to her apologetically. "I've got to go. There's some trouble over at Hing Hay Park."

His carefully veiled expression alerted her. She gripped his arm.

"What kind of trouble, Ken? Another attack?"

He covered her hand with his own gloved one, pressing lightly. "I don't know that for sure. I asked to be notified of any call of that nature coming in. I've got to go. Can I drop you someplace?"

But she could see his eagerness to hurry off and, because of the situation, didn't want to delay him.

"You go on. I can catch a cab."

"I'll call if it's anything...you know."

Yes, she knew. She forced a tight smile and waved him on his way.

Another murder.

She sagged against the rail, sickness roiling inside her.

Please don't let it be anyone I know.

"*Stacy.*"

Just a whisper.

She turned, thinking Fitzhugh might have forgotten something but, seeing no one, assumed her mind played a trick upon her. It was just the music or the distant partiers. She looked back out over the water, but her pose was no longer leisurely. The peaceful ambiance was broken.

"Stacy, I have a gift for you."

She whirled, flattening her back against the rail while her gaze raked the mist-cloaked deck. Only empty tables, their umbrellas folded in tight. Only pindots of light leading back toward civilization.

How isolated she was. What an easy mark.

Quickly, she headed toward the lights and faint laughter. She'd broken into a brisk jog when something brushed against her face like the thick tangle of a cobweb. She reached up frantically to pull it away, clutching the gossamer fabric in one hand as she ran now, strides long and powerful, carrying her away from the waterfront and toward safety.

From the market, Seattle's streets soared upward for more than five blocks before tapering off. Stacy ran, effortlessly at first, driven by panic, but then as her breathing labored, it was a struggle to go onward and upward. The storefronts were dark and uninviting. No traffic passed by. No cabs to carry her away from the nightmare.

She heard faint strains of laughter mocking right behind her.

With a cry, she lengthened her stride. She'd been on the women's track team in college, a way to outrun her problems, in some Freudian sense, she supposed. But now it was the means to out distance a demon, and she pushed as hard as she could, chest burning, thighs screaming as they pistoned up the dramatic slope toward the glow of an OPEN sign.

She ducked into the espresso bar, collapsing into the nearest seat under the startled looks of late night yuppie customers. Gasping, side cramping from the abrupt sprint, she didn't care what they thought. Gratefully she gulped at the water a perplexed waitress set down before her. She ordered a cappuccino and sank back into the leather booth while tension quivered through her.

He'd been there, with her in the darkness.

He could have snatched her life away with sinister ease and no one would have been the wiser. For no one knew where she was except Fitzhugh, and he wouldn't be checking on her any time soon.

Had he been lured away by a false report so she would be vulnerable?

Stupid, stupid, stupid.

Remembering at last, she lifted her hand to see what it held so desperately. A scarf. She stared at it blankly, as if she'd never seen the pastel Monet colors before. As if she didn't know it had come out of a colorful box in her top dresser drawer. It had been a birthday present from her father, the last he'd ever sent her.

He'd been in her bedroom. He'd gone through her things.

He'd left the scarf as a warning...warning that she was going to be next.

The game was about to end.

SIXTEEN

The cab dropped her off at her front door. She could imagine Cobb's look of surprise if he was, indeed, camped out in the tight bucket seats of his sporty car. It was after one, and exhaustion of body and spirit numbed her to all but the thought of sleep. Confrontation was the last thing on her mind, but the minute she turned on her lights it was there, unavoidable and in her face.

"Where have you been?"

She skirted Louis Redman on her way to the kitchen and a stiff glass of Scotch. "I took a friend out for coffee. That's still allowed, isn't it, or do I have to apply for permission from one or all of my jailers?"

Louis watched her kick back the large swallow of alcohol. It did little to still the trembling in her hands or the strain shadowing her eyes. She walked a thin, tensely strung tightrope, and he needed to know the cause.

As she moved past him to take a seat in her ratty recliner, something fluttered to the floor. He bent to pick up the brightly patterned scarf.

"What's this?" Hers, he could tell by the faint scent lingering upon it, but there was a greater significance. The fragile fabric was damp from her sweaty palms.

She stared at the twist of silk as if it were some colorful viper coiled about his hand. And the walls began to crumble.

"He spoke to me."

Her hoarse whisper said more than her words, but he insisted she clarify. "Who?"

"Alexander. He was right beside me down at the waterfront. He gave me this. It's mine. He must have gotten it from out of my linen drawer. From out of my bedroom. He was here, in my rooms."

The tremors spread in rivulets along her limbs until she had to grip the arms of the chair to control them. Her lips quivered then firmed with a fierce determination to deny the fear.

"He's coming for me next, Louis."

Her gaze rose, all liquid emotion. He couldn't give the false encouragement she sought. Not when she was right about the danger. He could say nothing.

"I've been looking it in the face for so long, you'd think I'd be used to it," she continued, "but I don't want to die, Louis. Not now. Not when I'm so close to the answers."

He came down to her, offering comfort because he couldn't offer assurances. Her arms slipped instinctively about his neck as her cheek sought the sheltering lee of his shoulder. She didn't weep. He wished she would to release the pressure terror exerted on heart and mind. But her strength came from a stubborn pride, refusing her the luxury of tears. So he simply remained on his knees, holding her in silent support, damning himself for bringing this horror into her life. Damning himself for wanting what she offered so badly, he hadn't the character to remove himself from the equation to assure her safety.

He told himself as he breathed deeply of the fragrance in her hair, that his departure would solve nothing at this late date. Her research was under scrutiny. Quinton Alexander was stalking her and already tiring of the game. His own presence became both problem and protection. The danger wouldn't lessen in his absence, but perhaps he could keep her from further harm by remaining close.

But he hadn't protected her tonight. Alexander had managed to slip past guards both human and preternatural to strike fear into her heart. That would not happen again.

"You will never have to face your fears alone," he murmured against the soft pulse at her temple. "I will be there."

Her head turned slightly. He felt the warmth of her breath stroke along the line of his throat in a whispery caress as she considered his vow.

"Stay with me, at least for tonight," came her hushed request which revealed more of her vulnerability than she would normally allow. That trust in him was humbling, and he would not betray it.

"Nothing will harm you on this night or any other."

She leaned back, the intensity of her gaze probing his, weighing his sincerity. And when he didn't buckle beneath that unswerving stare, her hands relented in their desperate clutching, easing to cup the back of his head, her thumbs notching beneath the curve of his jaw as she came forward to kiss him. The gesture of needy thanks gradually gave way to an evolving demand for comfort, one that surpassed simply being held to plead for more intimate assurances. And if she were to believe him, to believe in him, he couldn't pull away.

Nor did he want to.

They stood together, Stacy's palms clasping the sides of his face, their gazes lost in one another's as the moment steeped in anticipation. In those dark, jade green depths, she found an answer to what she sought so desperately.

A connection. A link to another's heart.

Hers was a life of such isolated loneliness, at first from necessity then by design. Relationships were fleeting, a momentary release, like a sugar high that felt great during its indulgence but quickly dissipated because it lacked real sustaining substance.

Nothing about Louis Redman was sugar-coated.

He was mysterious, dangerous, not even a man by precise definition.

But tonight he was the answer to the fear and emptiness inside her. And perhaps tomorrow, he would become the answer to her dreams.

And she pursued him without further hesitation, sensing he would not make that first overture until he knew she was ready. She was ready. She'd been ready since the first time she'd experienced the polar pull of his magnetism at the fund raiser and knew she couldn't stay away.

Her hands skimmed down his arms, fingers entwining on the right, removing the scarf from the other to let it filter to the floor forgotten. Wordlessly, he followed her to her room.

He glanced about, but there was none of Cobb's alarm at the surrounding fluff and femininity. Perhaps because Louis had been wed and had raised a daughter, such things were shrugged off as insignificant. After that cursory gaze, he had eyes only for her.

He smiled faintly as he took in her attire.

Blushing as she took off her ball cap to release a waterfall of blonde hair, Stacy murmured, "Not very fashionable, I know."

His fingers were already undoing the buttons of her bulky flannel shirt. "The well-wrapped gift is more fun to open. If you know the content ahead of time, it tends to lessen the surprise."

Was he chiding her for her daring wardrobe? He quickly kissed her frown and that concern away as he pushed the shirt from her shoulders. She shivered at the deliciously cool feel of his palms upon bared skin.

"It's been a long time for me," he told her as his mouth tasted the curve of her cheek and the whorl of her ear with teasing nibbles.

"It's like a bicycle." When he paused, she explained, "You never forget how."

"I rather like the idea of learning all over again."

Seduced by that sentiment, she melted against him as he fumbled with the fastenings to her bra. Smiling to herself, she reached back to give assistance then sighed as he charted her bare back from waist to shoulders with slow, massaging circles that kneaded the tension from her. The urgency building inside her then had nothing to do with anxiety.

She would forget what he was and think only of what she needed from him. What they needed from one another. Comfort, reassurance, security, and yes, for this night love. There was no great risk in loving Louis Redman, no reason to fear commitment might be demanded. They were alike in their solitude, giving to each other for only this moment, knowing there could be no permanence, no obligation.

At least not yet.

She could lower her guard and respond as herself for the first time.

And in that aspect, it *was* like learning all over again.

Eager to explore and enjoy, Stacy tugged his sweater over his head then gloried in the rugged terrain of the densely muscled arms and mid-section that could have easily belonged to a body builder. Or a god. Her fingertips revered rock-hard abs and swelling pectorals. The human body had always been her favorite subject, but delighting in Louis Redman was far preferable to any of the anatomy lessons she'd done in the past. Though one could argue that he was technically no more alive than her previous cases, there was nothing inanimate about his response to her.

His hands skimmed around her torso, sliding up beneath the fullness of her breasts. And Stacy's passion knew a moment's pause.

She'd developed at an early age and had been mortified by her generous proportions. When other girls were still in undershirts, she was sporting an ample C-cup and the fantasies of every boy in seventh grade—along with a goodly share of its teachers. She'd compensated for her embarrassment by boldly displaying her charms in tight sweaters and daring halter tops, dismaying her parents with the number of times she'd gotten sent home from school for the sake of decency. She had never learned to appreciate her shape, but had honed it like armor to hide the shyness of an awkward intellectual. The tongue-tied chemistry major never garnered the same attention as her eye-popping curves. And as it became obvious that men were more interested in her dramatic exterior than in the more slowly developing woman inside, her body became a threatening rival and finally a shield behind which she could safely hide.

But Louis's gaze never left hers to fixate upon her twin competitors. His hands caressed them as part, not paramount, of the entire woman. And for the first time, Stacy felt comfortable, complete and adored.

"What was it that attracted you to me, Louis?" Her fragile ego needed to know.

As his touch continued to chart her swells and valleys, he murmured, "You had the sexiest mind and most beautiful soul."

"You didn't like the way I looked?" Her vulnerable surprise made him smile.

"Your looks distract from the true value of the woman you are. You purposefully create a confusion of signals to keep admirers away. Did you really believe that none would see beyond the obvious?"

Her gaze grew lambent with sultry cynicism. "Until you, none had."

"Good."

He followed that pronouncement with a kiss that curled her toes and startled butterflies of excitement in her belly. Until this point, she'd had sex, but never had she made love.

Their hands hurried the remaining clothes off bodies that desired nothing more than the feel of flesh upon flesh. Louis took her down upon the bed, layering himself above her like a cool evening breeze that teased her skin into a shiver of sensory anticipation. Though she was anxious to take the strength of him inside her, he refused to rush the sensations to a premature end. His kisses were slow and thorough. His fingertips learned her form with a cartographer's skill, until each area knew a newly discovered expectation.

He paid homage to each masterpiece as well as every flaw, suckling at her breasts, laving the hollow of her collarbone, nibbling at the backs of her knees and massaging the soles of her feet until her body was in a sensitive state of bliss, becoming a single excited erogenous zone. His fingers glided between her thighs, not as a destination but as another region for masterful exploration. He soothed over the pearl of her femininity then dove deep for other treasures, leaving her gasping for breath and a saving sanity as he moved on to pay equal attention to the languid line of her outstretched arm.

The only area left as a virgin frontier was the arch of her throat.

Even as he worshiped her as a man to a desirable woman, Louis was all too aware of the erotic pulse throbbing below her aggressive jawline. He felt its enticement with her every swallow until it became a lure he could not escape or ignore. He nuzzled the side of her neck, scenting her vitality, tasting her potent humanity with the drag of his tongue along that elegant curve. And abruptly, passion took a darker turn. One she did not ask for or deserve.

Though hunger pounded through his veins, swelling them with ravenous need until they burned from neglect, he couldn't violate her tender trust. He would not force the vileness of what he was upon her.

Not unless she understood and was willing to go beyond the perimeters of mortal ecstacy.

The suddenness of Louis's thrust inside her startled a cry of unexpected wonder from Stacy as she arched to accept him more fully. The sheer intensity of their joining brought her agonizingly close to completion.

Too soon. Too soon.

She breathed into the fiery sensations until a vague feeling of control ebbed back into her quaking limbs. She touched him, smoothing her palms over shoulders shaped as if in cool marble. Her nails dug in as their hips found and perfected an ancient mating rhythm, and thoughts of control spiraled out of reach. Then, there was only volcanic tension, building, building, reaching higher and higher until she grabbed on fiercely as the coalescing pleasure blew like Mount St. Helens. The breath left her lungs in an explosive huff, as seismic tremors threatened to shake the ruffles out of her coverlet. And a second later, Louis reached his own soul-shattering release, groaning her name from behind gritted teeth.

The silence afterward befit the stunning aftermath of a cataclysmic event.

Until Stacy's cell phone rang.

She would have cheerfully ignored it except Louis withdrew, and the sudden sense of emptiness had her grasping for balance. Her hand fumbled about her for her jeans, withdrawing the slim fliptop from a side pocket.

"Yes?"

"Stacy? It's Ken."

"Ken? Yes. Hello." Did she sound as disconnected from planet Earth as she felt. She struggled for a grounding tether. "Yes, Ken, what is it?"

Beside her, Louis rolled onto his back to stare impassively at the ceiling.

"I wanted to let you know it was a false alarm. Some kids playing a prank or something equally stupid. I had to be sure you got home okay."

"I'm fine," she murmured huskily.

"I hated to run out on you like that—"

"Really, Ken, I understand. I'm just glad it was a prank and that no one came to any harm."

"Me, too. Are you all right? You sound—strange."

"Just worn out. I'll talk to you later."

And she hung up on his inhalation as he was about to say more. She wanted nothing more of that outside world intruding upon this magical night. She set the phone on her night stand, putting away the distraction it represented as she turned back toward Louis.

Oh, but he was gorgeous. And for the moment, he was hers, body and needy soul.

"Sorry for the interruption."

As he brushed the tousled hair back from her brow, Stacy picked up on the sudden somberness of his mood.

"I was not there when you needed me this evening," he murmured regretfully, claiming her soft skin and tender heart with the stroke of his gentle caress.

"I didn't ask you to be. It's not your fault. You couldn't have known."

A pause. "Yes, I could have. And should have."

The mood already broken, Stacy gave up on trying to recapture it. Her sated lethargy disappeared as she came up on her elbow, all attention. "How?"

He dodged her direct demand. She didn't know why, but his evasion was obvious.

"You are in danger, Stacy. I think you are right about Quinton getting ready to strike."

This was not the direction she wanted their evening together to take. "Must we talk about this now?"

His stern glance was her answer. "When he does," he continued, "if you are to survive it, I must be there. You must be able to reach me instantly should the need arise."

A faint smile crooked at that. "You have a cell phone in your casket, do you?" Then, more seriously, "You can't be with me every minute. What if he has someone snatch me during the day? What then? How will I let you know? You can't have your manservant guard me. That would leave you vulnerable, and you're in as much if not more danger than I am. It's a noble sentiment, Louis but I don't see how it could be effective. You can't be on watch twenty-four hours."

"There is a way."

His hesitation alerted her to the gravity of what he was about to suggest. "What way?" She gathered her sheet up around her, feeling suddenly exposed and vulnerable.

He sat up, putting his back to her as if he couldn't bear the thought of seeing her reaction. Though his words came low and matter-of-factly, his tension telegraphed itself through the taut line of his shoulders.

"When a vampire initiates a human with his bite, a certain telepathy develops between them. They are aware of each other's thoughts. They can feel when the other is near...or in danger."

If he expected her to respond with fainting horror, he misjudged the scientist in her. "How fascinating. Yes, I can see the benefit in that. That way the vampire can call to his victim when the need arises."

"I prefer 'initiate' to 'victim.'"

She ignored his wry correction. Her mind raced ahead with the possibilities. "If you initiated me, I could reach you mentally at any time."

"And if I am able, I would be there with you in a matter of seconds."

"And how is this done?"

"I would need to take your blood."

She sat up straighter, eager to begin. "I have a tourniquet and syringe in the other room."

He checked her enthusiasm with a staying hand and a dash of dry humor. "I'm afraid it will have to be accomplished the old-fashioned way."

"Oh."

She stared at him but was seeing Wanda, Lisa, Brianna and Glenna with their sightless eyes and punctured necks. He must have read her reluctant horror, for his mood grew gentle with empathy.

"It will not hurt, Stacy. You needn't fear that I will lose control and not stop in time. I've no reason to harm you and every reason to help. You must trust me. Do you, Stacy?"

Determinedly, she brushed her hair away from her throat. "Go ahead."

He smiled at her self-sacrificing tone. "No need to fall on your sword, Little One. It's not as unpleasant as all that."

Chagrined, she exhaled, trying to expel her anxiety along with her suspended breath. When she was able to respond with a shaky smile, he stroked her cheek with the back of his hand.

"Your bravery is by far your most attractive feature," he told her.

"That's not what most men say. But, I know, you are not most men."

"And they are fools."

He leaned toward her and, unconsciously, she braced herself. Instead of getting right to business, he detoured to her lips, letting his kiss linger to seduce her from her fears. She relaxed into it, parting for him, opening to him, luxuriating in the taste of passion as it rose between them, a delicious distraction. Her head tilted to one side as his tongue traced the delicate shell of her ear, waking helpless shivers of urgency. He licked down the long arch of her neck, sucking on the ridge of her collarbone, dipping into the sensuous well behind it, feathering upward until she felt his...bite.

Swift and sudden pain jolted through her, followed by a honeyed rush of submissive pleasure. She sighed into it, into a feeling unlike any experienced or imagined. Freedom. Exquisite, relieving freedom. She floated upon a sea of soft sensation, where the tidal flow and ebb became the joining of their heartbeats. Though Louis was taking from her, Stacy wanted to give more. More of herself, more of her will, more of her soul, for that was what he drank when he drew purposefully from her veins. He swallowed up her sense of separateness, of isolation. And they became one.

Stacy swooned upon his shoulder as the insistent tempo of his heart became the primal rhythm of her pulse beats, matching, echoing in perfect harmony. And through that entwining cadence came the whisper of his voice, not aloud, but intimately within her mind.

Stacy, can you hear me?

She tried to nod but her head was so heavy, the effort too great.

If you can hear me, reach out to me with your thoughts. Reach out to me.

Louis?

Yes. It's Louis, and you are no longer alone.

Such a lovely idea. No longer alone. She drifted, holding that sentiment close, letting it wrap about her, warm and comfortingly just the way Louis's arms were as he laid her back upon her bed. When he straightened away, protest struggled up through her complacency.

"Don't go."

"I was going to get you some water."

"I don't want anything but you. Please stay." The need for him to be close, to remain at her side neared desperation. She stretched her hand out to him, relieved only when his enfolded it.

"You must take care of yourself, Stacy. Your work is important, but your life is more vital still. You have not been completely truthful with me."

She said nothing, afraid to guess at his meaning. Then he explained himself with an inescapable demand.

"How long have you been ill?"

SEVENTEEN

"How did you know?" Again, she gathered the sheets about her as if she could hide within them, covering her imperfection from the intensity of his gaze. But she could conceal nothing from him, not now.

"I sensed it before, but taking your blood confirmed it. Is that why you chose the direction of your research, to find a cure for yourself?"

There was no use pretending.

"I'm a fighter, Louis. Known treatments couldn't help, so I decided it was time I found a new way to go about it."

"I am that way?"

"I hope so. If my research works, and if my time doesn't run out first."

She wasn't talking about Quinton Alexander. This was a more insidious, a more destructive enemy, one without a face, without mercy. All the protection in the world wouldn't keep this killer from claiming her but, perhaps, her own skill could. And he would do everything in his power to aid her.

"Fate has a strange sense of humor," she told him, wrapping her arms inclusively about her upraised knees. "What are the odds that catastrophic disease would strike two members of the same family? I guess we were just lucky."

"Not luck, Little One."

"I was working at the coroner's office, so you'd think I'd be immune to death. But having to stand by and watch someone you love just fade away, watching your father turn to alcohol for comfort. At first, she had mild, flu-like symptoms, then she went right into full-blown AIDS. She was prone to infections, so her room had to be completely sterile. We had to wear a plastic apron to visit her. I couldn't wash the smell of antiseptic solution off me. Finally, she developed pneumocystis and hope ran out.

"My dad, this big, burly cop, was reduced to being her nurse when the insurance ran out. He tried to keep working, to ignore the fear and suspicion, the rumors of how she had contracted the disease. It made him so angry. He kept getting into fights. The drinking got worse. He lost his job. Too many days off. Too many disciplinary warnings." She paused to wipe at her eyes, but the tone of her voice never wavered from its quiet, clinical rendering.

"When she finally died, there was this huge feeling of relief that our lives could go on again. And then the guilt over being glad she was gone. My dad never got over it. He took a security job out of state just to escape. I haven't seen him in two years. There were phone calls at first, then a few letters. Now, nothing. I couldn't call him out of the blue. I couldn't tell him about me."

"And so you've gone through everything alone."

"What's the point in starting a new relationship you won't be around to finish?" She shrugged philosophically. "It wasn't so bad. Relationships rarely live up to their PR anyway."

That bold-face lie made his heart ache with admiration. How brave she was, and how personally he felt her loneliness.

"I didn't believe it at first," she continued in a distancing monotone. "I had a full blood count, blood film reports, bone marrow examination, chromosome analysis, the whole nine yards. Leukemia. There was some suggestion that it might have come from exposure to the radiotherapy I saw my mom through, but why did it matter. Knowing why wouldn't make it go away. I jumped into the first available clinical trial, using a combination of drugs to kill the abnormal cells. The intensive chemotherapy made it impossible to work, so I took a leave of absence from the police force and finally had to quit all together. By the time I hit remission, I had another goal in mind. I wasn't going to let it take me like AIDS did my mother. My field of study changed from the dead to the living. With good risk AML, there's about a 60% chance of being alive and well for up to five years, but with poor risk, that chance of survival without a bone marrow transplant or a stem cell transplant is extremely low. I'm a poor risk. I'm going into relapse, Louis, and there's no way to effectively stop it. I could start up the treatments again, but then I'd be no good to anyone—not to you not to me. It would mean being transfused three times a week because the drugs affect the production of normal blood cells. I'd have a catheter in my chest to take samples more easily and fill me with antibiotics. Later, they'll have to use the tube to feed me when the chemo makes me too sick to eat.

"I won't be useless. I won't just lie down and die while those in my field pursue gene mapping that might take up to ten years to perfect. I don't have ten years. There aren't any viable candidates for transplant, so that leaves finding a cure."

"So you came to Harper."

"Yes. After I rounded out my medical degrees, they were thrilled to have me. I don't kid myself about who's behind their funding and why, but sometimes you just have to overlook the bad in hopes of grabbing onto a little good. It's like making a deal with that devil we discussed earlier. The sacrifice is worth the benefits of success."

"Is it?"

Her expression toughened. "Harper can give me what I need. If they demand a price, I'll pay it. Hey, if I'm alive when the bill comes due, I'm not going to complain about the interest rate."

"What will they do with your research, Stacy? Have you thought of that?"

"Bad things. Things that will make them a lot of dirty money. But I can't let that matter. Not now. Not when I have a chance to wash that antiseptic smell off my hands for good."

"There are worse things to have on your hands, Stacy."

She gave him a perplexed look. "You've had blood on yours for centuries. Why should you care if mine get a little stained?"

"That stain never comes clean. And the price is hard to live with."

"But you do. You live with it. So will I. I will live, Louis. I will have my life back. I will have the things I deserve, like family, children, things only a future can give you."

The same things he'd once hoped to have and hold forever. How could he begrudge her? Then he thought of the price Arabella had paid—her father's life, her ability to walk after an attempt to kill him went awry, the pain of growing old beside an eternally youthful husband. The price of loving her still hung heavily upon his heart.

"And you will turn your back on the consequence of the price you've paid?"

"Won't you, Louis? Won't you happily accept the cure and walk away just grateful to be returned to the state of humanity you so desire? You know you will. Don't pretend otherwise. We want that future, damn the cost. That doesn't make us monsters. It makes us human. If I can keep the research from being bastardized by the government, I will, but it's not my priority. I can't afford that luxury of conscience. I'm a scientist and I'm dying. If I can use the one to prevent the other, you can be damned certain I will."

The fierceness in her gaze extinguished with the gentle brush of his hand over her hair. "I do not judge you, Stacy. Who am I to do so? I want what you want. I don't deny it. I am hungry for that taste of humanity. I have starved for its lack these centuries past. I understand your urgency, your desperation, your fears. You are not alone any more."

She filled his embrace without a sound. There was no quiver in the strong shoulders that bore the burden of her mortality. As he held her, as he shared her determination, Louis truly understood at last the quixotic woman in his arms.

Her lifestyle was a rebellion against things over which she had no control. Her slovenly apartment defied the sterility of her mother's deathbed. Her promiscuous manner and shocking clothes held the threat of a commitment at bay when she feared she could not keep it. She smoked and ignored the eating habits that would extend her time. She spat into the wind with a gesture so bold, one couldn't help applauding its challenging bravado.

How well he understood her. They lived parallel lives.

Didn't he shun contact with mortals, afraid his attachment would lead to the inevitable agony of loss? Didn't guilt over the sacrifices made by the two women he'd loved haunt him every time he lay down alone as dawn claimed a world he was forbidden to roam? Yet here he was, tempting fate, alongside this brazen woman who refused to surrender to odds beyond her wildest hope of conquering. Because he still was enough of a romantic to dare to dream. Because the eternity he longed to share with those he loved was in a realm beyond this dark dismal Earth he walked alone.

"We will have those normal lives we deserve," he promised with the forcefulness of one who had the power to make it so.

"Then keep me alive, Louis. Protect me long enough so I can see both our dreams realized."

"I will, Little One. I will. Now rest and know that I will not leave you."

And secure in knowing that he was there, she was able to do just that.

***

It was an agony to get out of bed. The fever was back, burning through her like a furnace to consume her strength as fuel. Popping antibiotics, Stacy dragged herself to the shower and stood, letting the water wash the sluggishness from her mind. She hurt deep in her bones. That ache lent a prodding urgency to ambitions. Time was running out.

Louis knew the truth about her. Strangely, it left her feeling stronger, not vulnerable. She'd been struggling against the fear, against fate for so long, she'd forgotten what a luxury it was to share the burden. And now he was with her, not just in word but in mysterious deed. They were as one. She could feel him within her, as if a part of his essence resided in her soul. And again, strangely, she didn't see it as an invasion but rather a completion of who she was. As if another facet of her life had just been discovered, a door opening upon possibilities and potentials she'd fiercely denied.

She was no longer alone.

She met Cobb on the steps coming up to get her. She brushed past him without a word and headed straight for his car. She had no patience for clever banter. Her thoughts were racing through the protocols she would run in the lab that morning.

Perhaps this would be the day knowledge would grant her a full lifetime.

As they drove through town, Cobb's casual comment neatly severed her train of thought.

"Who's Quinton Alexander?"

She shot a look at him. but he watched the road behind his mirrored sunglasses. "Where did you hear that name? Listening at keyholes?"

"It doesn't matter if I can't find out who he is and what danger he presents to you."

Her apartment was bugged.

That knowledge stabbed through her, a violating shock of surprise and alarm. What else had he heard? The sense of invasion shortened her already frayed temper.

"Maybe you should have kept your car off the sidewalk long enough to let my friend Alex find out for you."

"I didn't kill your reporter. I had no reason to. He could have been...useful."

"Ha! He never would have told you anything."

"Grow up, Stacy. We were already negotiating a price. He was about to give us everything."

Stacy stared straight ahead. Tears of denial and a deeper certainty that Cobb was telling the truth blurred her vision just as his words distorted her faith. She should have known Alex would try to find a way to make a fast buck off his investigative prowess. He'd only promised her that he wouldn't go to the press. Selling out to her employers, who'd already guessed most of it anyway, must not have seemed like a betrayal when they were waving a bunch of zeroes in his face. What was thirty pieces of silver compared to a condo in Key West? Bitterness burned in the back of her throat and laced her reply with acid.

"I guess you'll just have to do your own legwork now, won't you?"

"Unless you'd care to enlighten me."

"I don't think so, Cobb. I'm assuming you have all the legal approvals for the wire taps and other goodies you've placed in my private dwelling, right? So that if I sic a lawyer on you, you won't be looking at, say, five to ten years in an exclusive bad boys club. You know Harper would never admit to authorizing such a thing. They'll leave you swinging in the breeze."

"Goes with the job, Doc."

"It's a crappy job."

"Don't I know it. So who's Alexander?"

She sighed heavily. What difference did it make now if he knew? "He's the manic who's been leaving bodies all over town. And I'm next on his dance card. So what are you going to do about that, Cobb?"

He slanted a sidelong glance at her to see if she was making some poor joke. "There's always protective custody."

"Guess again."

"How comfortable is your couch?"

"You'll never know."

"I've got to be close if I'm going to take care of you."

"You should have thought of that before you became such a jerk."

She sat back with a pathetic slice of satisfaction in knowing she'd rocked his confident boat. A faint smile etched her lips as she considered the scrambling to come.

Let them try to find Alexander. That would keep them off her case. Let them try to deal with the reality of what he was. She didn't have the energy for it today. She needed all of her focus concentrated through the lens of her microscope. She had dreams to rescue.

Let Cobb worry about the demons.

EIGHTEEN

She had the day to herself to work and explore the ramifications of her findings. Cobb disappeared as soon as he saw her through security. Probably to intensify his search for the illusive—and inhuman—Quinton Alexander. No one looking over her shoulder. No one's gaze burning a hole in her back, or sneaking peeks at her computer screen and scribbled notes. The perfect time to produce. If only she could.

Nothing went right.

She destroyed her first three samples through careless error. Her hands were unsteady, her mind unclear. Fatigue was a three hundred pound gorilla on her back making it such an effort to simply move from work station to keyboard that she had to rest up to enter the results. And then, looking at the figures in retrospect, they made absolutely no sense at all.

She wanted to weep. She wanted to curse. She wished Cobb was there to bear the brunt of her frustrations. She wished Louis was awake so she could feel his presence more personally and take strength from it.

She had to finish while her mind was clear, while she had control of her system.

She knew the leukemia drill. A two-fold drug cocktail that would cause nausea, vomiting and inflamed muccous membranes. Fevers, infections, agonizing pain in her joints.

A low platelet count that led to bleeding. Intensive chemotherapy would sap her remaining strength, along with constant transfusions and the frantic yet futile search for a bone marrow transplant match. She'd have to be isolated because of the threat of infection. Her food, even her water, had to be cleansed and bland. She wouldn't be able to work. She would lose her independence. She would lose hope. And because her risk was poor, she would die.

Unless she could gut it out until the answers came. She would not go peacefully to some sterile hospital bed knowing she would never leave it again.

Then, that afternoon, after the sandwich she hadn't been able to keep down, she struck gold.

Uttering a shaky breath, she went through the steps a second time, just to make sure her overanxious mind wasn't toying with her. But there it was, a stabilized alteration of her blood cells with no sign of AML abnormalities.

She slumped over the keyboard, her forehead resting against the computer screen as she suppressed the wild need to either laugh or cry. But she could do neither.

If they bugged her house, why wouldn't they treat her lab with the same caution?

She couldn't let them suspect she was on to anything. And she had to find a way to smuggle her disks out without erasing the data they contained. She would work through the night, studying to see if the integrity held. And if it did, tomorrow she would be running unauthorized human trials. On herself.

Phyllis Starke arrived at 4:30 on the dot to snoop through her day's accomplishments. For once, Stacy saw her as a possible confederate instead of as an enemy. She drew the immediately suspicious woman aside for a tete-a-tete.

"Phyl, I need to talk to you, privately."

She glanced around. "We're all alone here."

Right. Stacy betrayed none of her wry disbelief. She leaned in closer, assuming an intimate pose. "I haven't been feeling well lately."

Starke eyed her candidly. "You look terrible."

Trust Phyllis to sugarcoat it. But that was all right. Things were going in the right direction.

"Well, I think I know why, and I have to ask you a very important favor."

"What?"

"I think I've been ill so much because I'm...I'm pregnant."

Phyllis jerked back as if the condition was a dangerous contagion. "How?" she demanded.

"The usual way, I assume. Anyway, if I am, I can't go through these x-rays twice a day without endangering the fetus. Is there something you can do, quietly, woman-to-woman?"

"Why don't you just tell Forrester?"

Stacy lowered her head, taking full advantage of every nasty thing Starke had ever thought of her. "I can't tell him, Phyl. Not until I'm sure."

"The baby's his?" Her shock was so great, Stacy almost felt sorry for her.

Saying nothing to alter her assumption, Stacy pleaded woefully, "You won't say anything, will you? I mean it may be nothing but indigestion."

But Phyllis's narrowed gaze fixed upon her flat abdomen with an angry intensity. "I can see your difficulty."

"But will you help me?" She played out the desperation ploy, wondering if she was wasting her time fishing for sympathy in a dried up pond. But she had to keep casting out, hoping to snag something, some charitable or maternal instinct. "I know you and I haven't been friends or even particularly friendly. But if this got out, especially to Greg—"

She didn't need to elaborate. Phyllis saw the writing on the wall. If Stacy was knocked up by the boss, there was no chance that she, herself, would ever get a second shot at him. The longer the news was kept under wraps, the longer she had to seduce the fickle Forrester back into her embrace.

"And if you're pregnant, what would you do?"

"I'm Catholic. I don't have many choices. I guess I'd have to leave Harper before the secret got out. I wouldn't feel right about breaking up a marriage because of my carelessness."

Those words were a sweet symphony to Phyllis.

"I won't say anything."

Stacy expelled a gusty sigh of relief that wasn't feigned. "And the x-rays?"

"I'll take care of that. When will you know for sure?" The hardness was back in her tone, that rift of hatred and an older woman's envy chafing just below the carefully professional surface.

"I have an appointment at the end of the week. If you could shut things down for that long at least, I'd be so grateful to you."

The word grateful conjured up all sorts of future potential in the other's mind. For once, Stacy was glad for the greedy ambition blinding Starke to her duty or decency.

"If you'll give me a minute to make a backup of my disk for you, we can both go home."

"Fine. I'll go see the x-rays are turned off."

Quickly, Stacy ran a full copy for herself, secreting the disk in the side of her bra. Then she deleted several pathways on the computer and copied a second, incomplete disk to placate Harper a little while longer.

Hopefully, by the week's end she wouldn't need to play these games.

By then, she shouldn't need Harper at all.

***

Cobb was oddly preoccupied on the drive to Stacy's apartment. With excitement and anticipation bubbling like a wellspring inside her, she missed his irreverent banter as an excuse to relax and unwind. Her nerves were jumping, her muscles twitching, her fingers drumming a restless tattoo upon the top of her briefcase. Inside, was the answer to her every wish—a normal life expectancy and maybe, just maybe, a chance at happiness with a certain reclusive beast made man again.

It felt strange to consider a lasting relationship with a man, even stranger because the man in question now lived out the daylight hours sealed out of sight in a casket. She'd guarded herself from having private ambitions for so long, letting down the barriers was like opening a rusted door. Would the struggle be worth the reward? She hoped so.

But once freed of his curse and his need of her, would Louis Redman still be in her future? No guarantees there. Unfortunately, all her experience was in getting men not to fall in love with her when fleeting lust would do. She wasn't sure she knew how to invest in the long haul banalities of the day to day. The night to night. A shiver of longing rippled through her when she thought of lying down with Louis Redman—and waking up with him in the morning. He'd been gone before her alarm went off this morning, and his absence filled her with a sorrowful despair. Because of his bite or because she'd felt so secure with him beside her?

Were her feelings for Louis genuine or a product of his vampiric claim?

Another risk she would just have to take.

Cobb pulled up outside her building and cut the ignition.

"You don't have to come up," she said somewhat peevishly, annoyed that his lack of communication had left her in an emotionless lurch.

"Yes, I do."

His flat summation should have warned her, but she was too tired to read more into it. She trooped obediently up the stairs behind him, passing over her key so that he could give the rooms his all clear pronouncement. But then, instead of bidding her good night, he confronted her with the reason for his taciturn mood.

"Put what you'll need to get by for the next few days in a bag."

"Excuse me. Are we eloping?"

But it was nothing that intriguing.

"You're a target here. I'm taking you someplace safe."

"Someplace like where?"

He grimaced slightly at her strident demand, having known it wasn't going to be easy. "There are some guest facilities at the Center—"

"I am not going to be a prisoner at Harper."

"You'll be out of danger there and near your work," he continued as if he hadn't heard her protest, or didn't want to recognize it.

"I'm willing to renegotiate your sleeping on my couch."

"Too late for that. Get your things."

"You can't force me to go with you."

His stare was direct and uncompromising. "Don't make me."

"Harper is not going to take away my life, Frank. I won't allow it."

"They're trying the best they know how to save it. And so am I," he added more softly. His voice gentled, growing persuasively reasonable. "C'mon, Doc. Pack light. I can come back and get anything you might miss."

"I don't want to go with you."

"I'm afraid you don't have a choice."

That was it. The bottom line. No choice. She couldn't take Frank Cobb in hand-to-hand even if she was crazy enough to attempt it. Harper had won this round.

Uttering an explicit oath, Stacy went into her bedroom and yanked an overnight case out of her closet. Indiscriminately wadded handfuls of undergarments were followed by carelessly flung work clothes. Still muttering, she stalked into the bathroom to cram her necessities into her vanity case. Cobb stayed pointedly out of the way, content to let her wreck havoc upon inanimate belongings instead of him.

A knock on her door made Stacy pause in her irate tirade. Louis wouldn't knock. So far, even though night had fallen, there'd been no sign of him. Could he sense Cobb's presence in her apartment? Perhaps she should try to contact him along the fragile new lines of telepathic communication she'd just learned. And tell him what? Help, I'm being held prisoner...

The knocking grew louder, taking precedent over other concerns.

She walked into the living room to find Cobb standing by the door, gun in hand. After first recoiling at the sight, she responded to his gesturing with the barrel for her to answer the door.

"Who is it?"

"Fitzhugh."

"The police officer," she whispered to Cobb in an aside. He nodded and tucked his revolver out of sight as Stacy opened the door to emit the youthful lawman, hoping he'd come to do more than ogle her with his moonstruck gaze.

"Ken, has something happened?"

That something glittered within his pale-eyed stare as he said pleasantly, "Not yet."

And he struck.

Stacy could only stare in horrified surprise as Fitzhugh's back-handed blow smashed the side of Frank Cobb's face, sending him flying into the far wall with enough force to leave the outline of his body in cracked plaster.

Then the stranger before her smiled serenely and said, "It's time I introduced myself. To coin a phrase from the Rolling Stones, 'Pleased to meet you. Won't you guess my name?'"

***

Mortality.

Louis arose from his daytime confines with that thought on his mind, as he had most of his five hundred years of captivity. Only this evening, it was different.

It was obtainable.

All his doubts about Stacy Kimball's ability had fallen away, leaving a confidence that fueled more than the transient hope he'd clung to for past centuries. She could restore him to his humanity. She could give him back the kiss of daylight upon his upturned face, the pleasure of enjoying a meal not drawn from living veins, an escape from fear...and the freedom to love again.

His gratitude for Stacy went beyond her scientific skill. She'd awakened him to long dormant emotions, making him feel alive before he was actually living again. Smart, brave, determined—all the qualities shared by two others who had briefly companioned him within the all too finite boundaries of marriage. She trusted him enough to expose her vulnerabilities and to risk her career and very life. She'd lowered her strict rule of noninvolvement, coming to him willingly, accepting his gift of passion even before his dark immortal embrace. A special woman of rare courage and an infinite supply of untapped desires. Could she devote herself to him with the same zeal she applied to her position at Harper?

"Bella, Cassandra, tell me what to do. What I feel for this woman is love, I'm sure of it. The same love I felt for the both of you. It is unfair for me to ask or expect you to understand my desire to grow old with her when our own time together was cut short by your mortality. I need your blessings. As you loved me, wish me happiness."

He hadn't expected an answer, not in the physical form. But it came, a deep abiding sense of peace, of acceptance. Their unselfish support of his choice, their approval of his actions, gave an infinite relief.

He would feel no betrayal in going on with his life, at last.

The thought of Stacy committed to their shared future inspired him to a restless anticipation. He would go to her. Though it was too soon to initiate another linking kiss, he was eager to reestablish their more intimate bond. He found himself as greedy as a child who'd been given a wonderful gift. He couldn't bear to set it aside even for a minute.

So, he rose from his crypt with the expectations of a courting youth, only to be shocked from his randy fantasies by a harsh slap of reality.

Stacy's cry pierced through his brain in a shaft of white-hot urgency.

"Louis, I need you!"

***

Had he heard her?

Stacy's gaze flew frantically to where Cobb sagged, dazed and bleeding, against the shattered wallboard, no help to her for the moment.

It was up to her to stall the inevitable.

"Quinton Alexander, I presume."

"At your service, Doctor Kimball. A pity we don't have the time to truly get acquainted, but your annoyingly diligent friend there has made it uncomfortable for me with his questions. I fear it's time I moved on, lest loose lips announce my whereabouts to those I prefer to remain hidden from. That, unfortunately, would prove quite fatal."

"What do you want with me?" Stacy demanded.

"Why, dear Stacy, I want you to die."

He smiled then, a broad grin that revealed his hideous fangs and the true evil inside him. How had she ever been fooled by his mild manner?

Stall. Stall.

"Surely you have time to boast about how you maintained this charade. Your Officer Fitzhugh was quite convincing."

His arrogance wouldn't allow him not to take a minute to preen. "Yes, I was good, wasn't I? Become that which you hold in contempt, I always say. Wearing the symbol of the authority I disdain was endlessly amusing, as was investigating the same murders I committed. Using my late and very tyrannical father's name, Fitzhugh, was also most enjoyable, though I doubt that he would have appreciated the irony. Well, enough chitchat. Time to tie up loose ends and move on."

Knowing herself to be that loose end, Stacy was anxious to delay his plans.

"If you think my death will in some way hurt Louis, you're wrong. He could care less about me. I'm not the prize he's after. It's my research he's interested in, and that will continue with or without me."

That took the killer aback. His eyes narrowed as he considered her claims and pronounced them unworthy. "I don't believe you. I know my enemy well, and know you are the kind of woman he can't resist."

"But he has. He's immune to your games. The victims were nothing to him, just as I'm nothing to him. You've been wasting your time, *Ken.*"

Her amusement at his expense was too much for him. With a roar, he gripped her by the forearms and thrust her away. Her airborne flight was interrupted by the yielding cushions of the couch. He was straddling her there before she had the opportunity to flee. She scented death in his fiercely panted breaths and saw her demise in his manic glare.

Louis, where are you?

"I would have preferred that he held you in some affection, but it really doesn't matter. After I tear out your throat and use your blood to point my colleagues in his direction, I'll let them do the rest while I quietly slip away. That was my original plan, anyway, before you proved such an entertaining distraction. And an annoying one. You've managed to cover up much of what I wanted revealed. You were supposed to have run screaming to the police, sending them to my enemy's door. But you didn't, did you? Instead, you chose to ally yourself with him. Well, if you won't tell the authorities where to look, I'll have to be more obvious. They've proven highly ineffectual to this point, but I suppose I have you to blame for that, don't I? I hadn't counted on your willingness to conceal the evidence to protect a creature who deserves to die. But Louis will soon follow you to the grave he's denied for so long, leaving me to enjoy the last laugh."

"Don't laugh too soon," she sneered.

Alexander snarled as his arms were gripped from behind. Though no match for him, Cobb distracted the fiend long enough for Stacy to pull out her crucifix and press it into the ghoul's forehead. The sizzle and snap of flesh burning was overwhelmed by the vampire's screech of pained surprise. He slapped her arm aside, breaking the connection.

Howling madly, he rose straight up in the air, bashing his assailant into the ceiling with a near spine-snapping violence. Still in mid-air, he gripped Cobb by the collar and flung him off as if discarding a heavy cloak. Her bodyguard went tumbling into her dining table, his elbow fragmenting her computer screen as the whole thing collapsed beneath his weight.

Then the enraged Quinton Alexander turned to her in full blown fury. The imprint of her cross glowed where it had cut into his brow, oozing noxious fluids.

"You should not have done that, Stacy. After all we've been to one another, I would have been kind."

With a desperate cry, she lunged off the sofa, darting toward the door as if it held some hope of salvation. Alexander's hand closed about the back of her neck, jerking her up short even as she screamed. She squeezed her eyes shut, expecting to feel the sting of his teeth in her throat at any second. When the savage attack didn't come, she dared to open her eyes.

There, in her open doorway, stood Louis Redman.

"Come, you coward," he taunted the seething Alexander. "Isn't it time you stopped hiding behind women and faced me man to man?"

"I'm fine right here," Quinton hissed, tightening his hold on Stacy until she was close to swooning. But she wouldn't gratify him with an outcry. "Like old times, eh, Louis?" Quinton panted in a rapturous rage. "We meet again over the fragile form of a mortal woman. How easy to destroy her. One twist of my wrist. One strike of my fangs. Should I end it quickly, or should I let you suffer, not knowing when it will come? Like I've suffered these past decades, hiding, waiting for the past to catch me? You turned Bianca against me, just as you turned Cassie away from the fondness we shared."

"You create your own misery. It stems from the ugliness in your soul. Don't try to blame me for the symptoms of your madness. I accept none of your guilt. Stacy has no part in this. Let her go."

"So the two of you can be together? I don't think so. The idea of your happiness sickens me. I will end it, here, now, leaving you with nothing, just as I've had nothing since you interfered in my life."

Louis drew slowly closer. "You drove those who loved you away. Cassie cared for you, Quinton. You are the one who turned her against you with the same cruel and brutal games you've been playing with Stacy."

"It's because I love them."

"You don't love Stacy. You don't even know her. You only want to use her to hurt me. Well, come on then. Hurt me. Step out from behind her and face me, *uomo d'uomo*."

The stalemate continued. Stacy could feel the fury pulsing through Alexander's panted breaths, through the crush of his fingers as Louis goaded him beyond reason, pushing him toward an irrational act.

"Your childish games bore me, Alexander," Louis drawled at last. "Bianca will not come to your rescue this time. Even she who made you is tired of your inept attempts to gain attention. You are worth no recognition. When I've destroyed you, you'll be quickly forgotten."

"You are wrong there," Quinton raged.

"Am I?" Louis questioned with a supreme *ennui*. "I think not. I'm going to swat you like the bothersome gnat you've become."

"But not before I've snapped her neck."

"Then do it," Louis snarled impatiently, "and move on to me."

Using Stacy as a shield, Alexander began to move backwards, going further into the apartment to increase the distance between him and his tormenter. Louis followed, maintaining the threatening distance.

"What's wrong, *codardo?* No stomach for confrontation when it's a fair match? Your father was right to despise you for your craven weakness. How could you have ever thought that my Cassandra would love you?"

A frightening shout of impotent rage burst from the crazed monster as he threw Stacy into Louis with a strength that left her winded and dependent upon his arms to sustain her. Louis had no choice but to hold her, giving Alexander the necessary time to escape.

But as the vampire whirled, planning to leap through the window to freedom, he was met with the impaling thrust of one of the broken table legs, driven through his chest with all Frank Cobb's remaining energy. Cobb collapsed upon the flailing then eerily still Alexander. And for a moment, no one moved.

Then, slowly, gingerly, Cobb sat back, observing through disbelieving eyes what he'd captured. His gaze lifted to Stacy and Louis.

Clutching at Louis, seeking to protect him, Stacy made a soft plea. "Frank, it's not what you think."

Bleeding from the terrible gash that split his face from cheekbone to jaw, Cobb's smile was gruesome. "Really? And what do you want me to think has happened here, Doc? Nothing out of the ordinary?"

He laughed a bit crazily then sighed, his shoulders slumping.

"Frank—"

"You don't need to worry that I'll expose any of your secrets. The media will never hear a word of this from me."

"What are you saying, Frank?"

Dare she hope...

But he didn't respond to her directly. He was studying Louis through hard, emotionless eyes.

"You're off the hook, Redman. I've got what I need to satisfy the honchos at Harper. I'm bringing them their test subject on a silver platter, along with the brilliant scientist who's going to make all their greedy dreams come true."

NINETEEN

Harper came to clean up with a frightening efficiency. An unmarked ambulance arrived to quickly carry out the restrained and discretely covered body of Quinton Alexander. The official-looking attendants remarked to all who asked that the victim was a guest who had suffered from a seizure after a party on the third floor got out of hand, turning into a domestic squabble. He was loaded into the back with none of the onlookers any the wiser, and gone with lights flashing.

While the remaining team of four sanitized her apartment, Stacy stitched and dressed the gash on her bodyguard's cheek. He sat unflinching through the ordeal, his wary and speculative gaze fixed on a silent Louis Redman.

"It's going to leave a nasty scar," Stacy advised as she gently taped down the length of gauze.

"It'll make me look dangerous," Cobb replied with a lopsided smile.

"You're already dangerous. I can give you the name of a good plastic surgeon, if you like."

He shrugged stoically then touched cautious fingertips to gauge her handiwork. "Nice field dressing, Doc."

"It's been a while, but it's like riding a bicycle." She glanced up at Louis, who'd been purposefully withdrawn from the situation. His returning gaze glimmered as he caught the reference.

"Any allergies?" she asked, popping the top of her antibiotics. When Cobb shook his head, she passed him two pills. "Take those."

He dry swallowed them without comment. From the look in his eye, she could tell there were plenty of other things he wanted to express an opinion on.

"All clean," one of the crew told him.

"Do they work by the job or the hour?" Stacy asked in a low aside to earn a faint smile from Cobb.

"You couldn't afford them."

Cobb stood, wavering slightly but able to push off Stacy's stabilizing grip as the last of Harper's crew left the place looking like nothing out of the ordinary had ever happened. "I should go and make sure our new guest is comfortable. Is he...what I think he is?"

"Not of the Transylvanian branch of the family, but no less dangerous," Louis stated with enough dry humor to coax another reluctant smile from Cobb. Stacy could see he really wanted to dislike the suave enigma but was having a hard time doing so.

"Any special precautions I need to know about how to keep him from turning to dust or us into appetizers?"

"Keep him out of the sun, chained in a coffin if you have one. He'll be weak and manageable for a while, but I wouldn't recommend underestimating him."

"I won't make that mistake again."

The two men regarded one another with reassessing candor. Finally, Cobb said, "I assume you can keep her out of trouble for a while." When Louis nodded, he turned to Stacy. "Thanks for the nip and tuck, Doc."

"Thanks for the nick of time, Cobb."

He saluted her with his forefinger and hobbled toward the door.

"You should get x-rays," Stacy called after him. "You might have broken ribs."

"Wouldn't be the first time. Good night, Doc. Be here bright and early to pick you up."

When the door closed behind him, there was a moment of awkward silence. Then Louis made a welcoming gesture with his arms. Stacy was burrowed against his chest in an instant.

"I was so scared," she blurted out as delayed shock finally chipped away the last of her calm veneer. There was no need to pretend any more. Not with Louis.

"He can't harm you. He won't harm anyone, ever again. Nothing stands in our way now."

Something in that phrase triggered a memory she'd repressed in all the confusion. That of Louis callously goading Quinton to kill her. Slowly, she backed out of his embrace, careful to let none of her upset betray itself in her expression. Her tone was deceivingly quiet.

"And you will be human again. That's the important thing, isn't it?"

Perhaps their supernatural bond made him extra intuitive, or maybe he was just sensitive to her moods. He frowned. "An important thing, yes, but not the only thing. What's wrong, Stacy?"

"You told me once that you would do anything to escape your curse. I guess I really didn't believe you until now."

His concerned scowl deepened. "What do you mean?"

Holding back her heartbreak, she said with a brutal frankness, "I have only myself to blame. After all, you told me that you expected those who loved you to make sacrifices for your sake. I imagine it's a hard habit to break, especially when it's so conveniently in your favor."

Incredulity was soon replaced by shock and injury as his features, for once, plainly revealed his dismay. Sensing the depth of the pain her accusation caused him, Stacy would have wished the words back, except she had to know the truth.

He was quick to conquer his emotions. His face returned to that handsome mask, but his tone was rife with anguish. "I would not have sacrificed your life to save mine. I cannot force you to believe that."

How she wished she could accept that somberly delivered sentiment. But before her was a creature who had lived for centuries off cunning and deceit, doing awful and unimaginable things in order to survive to the next setting sun.

Louis saw the distrust darkening her heart against him. He tried to explain, and in doing so, hoped to erase that look.

"I could see Cobb readying to strike even as I spoke the words. Between us, we would not have let Alexander hurt you in any way. You were in no real danger."

Her expression tightened in disbelief. No danger? He was asking her to deny the terror that even now etched shadows beneath her eyes and sent tremors through her limbs.

But she didn't have to believe, not of her own volition. He could make her. He could have used his vampiric charm to beguile her from her distrust and misery. He could have, but he respected her too much to employ such trickery. She would have to make up her own mind about what kind of man he was, for without that faith, there was no point in continuing. And he wanted things to continue with Stacy Kimball, very badly.

She was being genuine in expressing her fears. He could be no less when calming them.

"Do you know the difference between me and Quinton Alexander and others like him?"

She shook her head, willing to listen while reserving judgement.

"They revel in what they are, in the power they have over humankind. They feed with a conscienceless abandon because they feel themselves superior and answerable to no one, not to man nor God. They are evil, soulless beings who wallow in darkness and despair."

"And how are you different?" A clinically asked question that contrarily held limitless possibilities.

"For centuries, I have struggled against the nature of the beast inside me. I have not always won, but I have never given up the fight. I have never forgotten that I was once a man who had hopes and dreams and desires, all stolen from me in a moment's folly. Though they were out of my reach, I never stopped yearning for them, for the humanity I'd lost but never forsaken. I have a soul. I have a God. I have had one wish; to be reunited with those I've loved when I leave this world. If I remain in this unchaste state, that will not happen. That is why your work is so important to me."

"So that you can be with your wives on the other side. I see." She was trying so hard to be neutral but was failing wretchedly.

"No, Little One, you don't see." He tenderly stroked back her hair, his gaze warming as he beheld her confusion. "That is why your work is important to me. Not why you are important to me."

He watched her silken throat move in a jerky swallow and pressed on, determined to break through her self-imposed barriers. Only then would they be free to love one another.

"You claimed that I took advantage of those who loved me. Are you among that number, sweet Stacy?"

Her response was pure defensive bluster. "Of course not. I think of myself as your doctor."

"Then we are about to break several of your physician's codes."

Her ripe lips mouthed a protest that went unspoken as his kiss claimed her. After a token denial, more for her own sake than his, she gave in gracefully, taking fully from the well of his regard.

"I think of you as my doctor only as a distant second to a very, very desirable woman."

Those murmured words created a meltdown within her.

"You are important to me, Stacy Kimball, not only because you can give back to me that which I have lost, but because you have restored in me that which I have forgotten. I'd forgotten how wonderful it felt to taste a woman's kiss, how delightful it was to banter intellects then surrender souls. Though I longed for humanity, I'd forgotten what it was to be human until you woke my heart to joy. That is why I cherish you, my love."

This time, she came into his arms without reservation or regret. Her kiss matched his for its hunger and impatience. Her hands were just as eager in their removal of his clothing as his were with hers.

Naked and entwined, they fell atop her frilly bedcovers, enjoined at the lips, at their hearts and then, with a glorious thrust, their bodies. Hot sensations possessed him, he who had been cold and barren of feeling for so long. He needed her on so many levels he could no longer separate them. Sustenance was no longer drawn just from her tender throat but from the heated way her femininity embraced him. She was salvation, not only of the body but of the spirit. The soft, urgent little sounds she made when they were enjoined to the fullest called to a part of him so shadowed with neglect he'd nearly forgotten its name.

Its name was love.

He loved her. And he loved her with all his heart, with all his strength.

After the tension and the fear and the horror of the past few hours, finding release in Louis's passionate embrace was beyond paradise. Here, Stacy found safety at last. Here, she could respond naturally, emotionally, even irrationally. And she loved it. And she loved him. Wildly, feverishly, without reluctance or remorse, in the room where she'd invited no other for the purpose of passion, in the heart where she'd allowed no one but him to linger, with the body she'd given but never surrendered. Until now.

Her cries echoed the rocketing emotions bursting free at last.

As Stacy drifted in the sacred circle of his care, one idea formed then would not be dismissed until she spoke it aloud.

She gazed up into the magnetic green eyes glowing verdant and deep with sated pleasure.

"Louis, if for some reason I am not successful—"

"Hush, now. You mustn't talk of that."

She kissed the fingertips he pressed to her lips then brushed them determinedly aside. "If the experiments don't show promise or if I—if I don't have time to start over again, I want you to promise me something."

"And what is that, my love?"

My love.

The endearment would have derailed her thought process had the subject been less vital.

"Louis, if it becomes clear that I will not live long enough to finish what we've started, I want you to promise to make me as you are."

His recoil was emotional as well as physical.

"Please," she cried, cupping a hand behind his head to still his retreat. "Hear me out. I have given this a lot of thought, and it makes sense."

"Nothing about your death makes sense."

His argument made her smile tenderly. "But it does. It will give me the time I need to perfect a serum to restore both of us to a normal existence."

He frowned darkly. "And if you cannot?"

"Then I won't suffer the way my mother suffered." She touched his cheek. "And neither of us will be alone."

"Stacy—"

"Please don't tell me I'm acting illogically or emotionally. I am neither of those things. This is a very rational decision, and if you'll listen—"

He couldn't listen. He silenced her explanation with another kiss. A kiss speaking of all that went unsaid between them. She could taste his reluctance, his admiration, his fear. And his love for her. Yes, his love. She turned her head away at last, breathing quickly, faintly into the wild rip and ebb of desire.

"Promise me, Louis. Promise that you will do it."

He cupped her face between his palms so their gazes met and mingled with a tender intensity. "I promise you, I will not let you go, in life or in death. Does that satisfy you?"

"Yes, Louis. That satisfies me."

And he went on to satisfy them both until the lateness of the hour and the approach of dawn forced them to part.

Stacy managed a few hours of fitful sleep, dreaming alternately of Louis's vow and Quinton Alexander's threats, both weighing on her future with drastically diametric results. Behind that restless slumber was the strain of knowing she had to perfect serums that would serve both of them, allowing them to enjoy that future together, be it finite or eternal. And when she woke alone, aching and exhausted in every bone, she dragged herself from the bed determined to follow the course of action their desperate situation prescribed.

She had no time left.

A monster, Quinton Alexander, was in Harper's hands. Her remission was at an end. Damning factors conspiring against her chances for success. But she wasn't a quitter. And she had every motivating reason to push herself beyond the sake of health and personal safety.

That reward was happiness with Louis Redman.

Staring at the shattered shell of her computer took a degree of starch from her resolve. She couldn't run her numbers and projections here. So, she would have to do the necessary analyses at the lab, quickly, as covertly as possible.

And then she would have to deal with Quinton Alexander.

Louis was right. They couldn't give Harper the potential to develop such a weapon against the natural order of humankind. Their purpose wouldn't be for the good of man or the future of their world. They would squander the knowledge and twist it into something so deadly and unstoppable she couldn't allow her imagination to explore the ramifications of such destructive magnitude.

Quinton Alexander would have to be destroyed.

Then she and Louis would disappear.

There was no other answer, no other scenario.

Harper would not let her go voluntarily. And if they discovered the truth about Louis, if they hadn't already learned of it from their vindictive guest, he would never be safe. He would be hunted down, captured like a test animal and kept in a coffin cage. He would be studied and bled, and eventually he would die horribly at their hands, his redemption unmet, his soul unsaved.

That couldn't happen.

Focused on that determination, she met Frank Cobb on the stairs. The side of his face looked like Doctor Frankenstein had put him together from spare parts.

"You look like hell," he told her first.

"And you, hell warmed over."

That was the extent of their small talk on the way to the Center. Frank had things on his mind and so did she. Their silence was oddly companionable, as if they were old, battle-scarred veterans heading back toward the front.

The truce held until the steel elevator doors closed behind them.

"Have you got Alexander secured?"

"I can't discuss that with you."

Stacy gaped at him. "What do you mean?"

"Just that. It's a need to know situation, and you don't need to know."

"I don't—That psychopath nearly killed both of us, and you're telling me I'm no longer involved?"

"That's exactly what I'm telling you."

"Look, Cobb—"

"No, you look, Doc. The threat to you is over. Your involvement is over. If you've got any questions, I'm sure your sour-faced supervisor will be all too thrilled to handle them for you. Until then—"

He broke off to catch Stacy in mid-swoon.

"Doc? Stacy, are you all right?"

She lacked the strength to lift her head from his broad shoulder. "Just pushing too hard, is all." Her voice was as thready as her energy. That weakness obviously scared Cobb to death.

"Maybe you should pack up your troubles and take a long vacation."

She struggled to step back, supporting herself on the waist-high rail at the back of the elevator. She must have looked truly terrible to shake him from his stoic manner. For that, she had no remedy or excuse. Her smile wobbled. "Soon. Soon I'll be able to. Until then, I've got work to do."

He said nothing, his concern relayed in the tightness about his mouth and the frequent glances slanted her way. Then the doors opened, and the time for chitchat was gone.

At the first security checkpoint, she was met with a firm rebuff.

"I'm sorry, Doctor Kimball," the guard told her flatly. "Your clearance has been revoked."

"But my work is down there, my lab, all my equipment."

He wouldn't budge. "You'll have to speak to Dr. Starke, ma'am. I can't let you pass."

Dawn breaking upon her naivete, Stacy whirled on a stoic Frank Cobb. "You knew about this."

He didn't blink at her accusation. "I wasn't sure."

"What's going on here, Frank?" she demanded, fighting down the first prickles of panic that shortened her breath and gave her voice a slight but betraying vibrato. "Why am I being kept from my work?"

"I can answer that," came a sweetly acidic drawl.

Stacy confronted Phyllis Starke in an unrestrained fury. She'd had enough of the woman's petulant ego to last a lifetime, and a lifetime that wouldn't last beyond the foreseeable future if she couldn't get past her. "What's going on here? What game are you playing?"

"I thought you were the one who liked games. This is no game, Stacy. I assure you." Starke's smile was pure malice. "I've taken over your project."

TWENTY

Panic brought a sweat to Stacy's brow as she rode the elevator up with Cobb. He was her escort back to her old lab where she was to begin at once on a new project of less strategic importance.

Don't faint. Don't faint.

Sickness swirled in black and red polkadots. She fought to keep her breathing even and her balance stable. And Cobb kept a covert eye on her while pretending not to. It was his alarmed attention that woke her to her situation. He was expecting another episode of weakness, for her to come unglued, with him there to pick up the pieces.

Well, he was wrong.

Sucking a deep, vengeful breath, she hissed, "She won't get away with this. I'll go to Forrester."

"The order must have come down from him. He's the only one who could invalidate your clearance from the private sector." He softened his tone as if that would soften the reality of the blow he delivered between her eyes. She swayed but refused to buckle completely. Not in body. Not in spirit.

"They won't get away with stealing my research."

"It's their research, Doc. They own it all."

She denied his fatalistic claim with a fierce rebuttal. "They don't own me. That was my project. Louis gave Harper the funding with the stipulation that I do the work."

"I think your little project has gone far beyond Harper's interest in Redman or his money."

"What do you mean?" When he didn't answer, she gripped his arm. "Frank, what do you know?" Then more fearfully, "What do they know?"

His discomfort became a deadly calm. "I guess it's no great secret. Some brass from D.C. is flying in tomorrow to meet with Forrester. It's going to be a whole new ball game after that, with all new players. Sorry if they pulled the rug out from under your career, Doc."

"It's not my career I'm concerned with, Frank, it's my life."

Her gritty statement caught his attention, but she became equally close-lipped as the doors opened on the regular lab level. As she stalked down the hall between the row of fishbowls, Herb Watson stuck out his head, unable to resist the opportunity to vent his glee.

"Hear you got kicked back upstairs, Stacy. Gee, that's a tough break."

Even before she could wince away from his nastiness or begin to think of a suitable return barb, Cobb went toe to toe with him, growling, "Wipe that smirk off your pasty face before I take great pleasure in doing it for you."

Blanching, Herb slithered back into the safety of his own sterile corner.

"That wasn't necessary, Frank," Stacy chided half-heartedly, secretly warmed by the unexpected chivalry. "You probably scared him out of the next five productive years of his life."

"No great loss, I'm sure." And he took her arm with gentle deference to guide her on their way.

"Dang you, Cobb," she grumbled. "Just when I'm ready to wish you off the face of the Earth, you go and do something noble and ruin everything."

"Sorry not to live down to your expectations."

Stacy stood in the doorway to her lab, looking about in dismay. Everything was in meticulous order, except everything was new. Nothing in the lab was hers. Not the CPU, not the virgin notebooks, not even the coffee cup.

And this time there were no flowers of welcome. She was officially off the team.

A soft sound of helplessness escaped her.

"Sit."

Cobb shoved a chair behind her knees, dropping her efficiently onto the seat. While she sagged there like one of her collectible rag dolls, he came around to sit on the edge of the desk, leaning down so their faces were close. He kept his voice low. Did that mean the lab was bugged, too? She lacked the energy to feel indignant.

"What do you mean it's your life? That's figurative, right?"

She supplied a wan smile. "I wish."

For a second, she saw right to the soul Frank Cobb would claim not to have. She watched his conscience writhe like a moth on a mounting pin and took ruthless advantage.

"Frank, help me."

He didn't move.

Placing her hands on his knees, she petitioned with quiet earnest, "Help me."

"How?"

It wasn't much, but it was a toehold.

"I need my notes. I need my samples."

He reared back, a mask of impassivity slamming down over his expression. "I can't."

"Then I'm going to die, Frank. My future is in that research. Why do you think I was willing to risk so much? It wasn't for the promotion or the prestige. You have to be around long enough to enjoy them. It was for the chance to give myself a normal life expectancy."

He took in her pale features, the sunken eyes, the bruises on her hands and jaw that hadn't been there last night. He did the math and didn't like the common denominator that kept coming up.

"You have leukemia." He said it flatly, bleakly.

"Yes, and it's a death sentence unless I get my notes back. You told me I could trust you. You told me I could call you anytime I needed you. I need you, Frank."

He vaulted away from the desk and stalked the room in short, angry strides. "You don't know what you're asking." His voice was a rough, angry growl.

"Yes, I do. I'm asking you to do what's right instead of what you're told. And I have to trust you to make the right choice."

Could she? Knowing he was a snake, could she take him in again?

He glared at her, his eyes wild and dark-centered, a creature caught in a trap of its own creation. "Well, you've made a mistake, Doc."

And he was gone. As nearly all hope was gone.

Damn you, Cobb. Just collect your salary from Uncle Sam and keep your eyes closed.

But cursing Frank Cobb wouldn't accomplish anything.

Slowly, almost blindly, Stacy turned on the computer and inserted her bootlegged disk. All the data was there, but without the samples as a control, the information was incomplete. She would have to start all over. All over again. She didn't think she'd have the strength to see the process through. Or the time.

She'd failed Louis and herself. And all the others who might have known the same hope of survival with the results of her study.

Blinking away the burn of defeat, she began reconstructing her findings. By mid-morning, she had barely scratched the surface. As she leaned back in her chair, closing her eyes for a brief respite, she was startled as something slapped down on the desk in front of her. She stared at her dog-earred notebook and a tray of labeled slides. She looked up, eyes welling with emotion.

"Don't ask and don't thank me," was all Cobb would say before taking his place at her doorway.

After blowing him a kiss, she wasted no time. Flipping open her confiscated notebook, she began entering data into her program.

And by lunch time, the evasive first puzzle-piece fell into place.

There was no time for celebration or safety protocols. She worked quickly, with a detached determination. As rapidly as she could, she prepared an injection then tied a length of tubing about her arm.

"Doc, what are you doing?"

Before Cobb could take a step toward her, she found a vein and sent the untested serum coursing through her bloodstream. She saw his features register shock and distress. And as her body began to convulse, he caught her before she hit the floor, easing her the last few feet down. The tile was cool beneath her as the serum began its burning change. From a distance, she heard Herb's anxious voice.

"What happened? Shall I call someone?"

"She's just fainted. Give her a minute to come around," Cobb assured him.

And through the violent flicker of her eyelids, she watched him carefully gather up the evidence of what she'd done—tossing the syringe, releasing the tubing and turning off her computer screen.

Frank Cobb was a handy guy to have around.

She smiled as consciousness left her.

***

The scent of Calla lilies washed over her.

They covered the still figure at the front of the viewing parlor, long cut stems curving up to graceful ivory cups, laid upon the body like rushes on an ancient floor. Stacy approached, steps muffled on the aisle runner, movements slowed by dread and grief. The smell thickened, twining about her other senses, choking them until all that remained was the sweet, clogging odor and the pain of loss.

The viewing room was empty. Row upon row of vacant chairs respectfully faced front. Such a long walk, she remembered thinking. A walk toward a destination she feared to reach.

She could see the woman's profile now, silhouetted above the flowers. An intelligent brow, straight nose, the bleached white angle of one cheek and artificially reddened lips. Despite all the whispered assurances heard at previous funerals, there was nothing lifelike about the body. Death was death, the absence of living, and the two could never be mistaken.

Her gaze was distracted by the arrival of two mourners. One she almost didn't recognize in his somber suit and high gloss shoes. What was Frank Cobb doing at her mother's visitation? He slipped into a seat on the far side of the room to stare straight ahead, features composed in impervious lines, cheeks suspiciously shiny. The shock of seeing that dampness was displaced by her perplexity. Why would he be weeping for a woman he never knew?

The other man was Louis Redman, sleek, dark, elegant as always. He carried a single calla lily, bringing it to lay with a quiet dignity atop the others. But when he set it down, something spilled from the fluted bowl of the flower, something dark, something red.

Blood.

It continued to flow, discoloring the other pale blossoms, pooling along the edge of the casket to finally drip, like raindrops from plugged gutters, to the white runner below.

And as she hurried forward, she met that spreading stain, stepping gingerly across the crimson pattern as she reached for the offending flower, needing to end the alarming tide.

She never completed the gesture. For in that space of fractured seconds, she got a closer look at the face so meticulously made up in an effort to mimic what was no longer there within her. Life. A life cut brutally short.

Her life.

It was her face, not her mother's. A face ravaged by the effects of her disease. Cheeks sunken, skin drawn, hair all but gone from the chemo. A face of suffering and defeat.

With a cry of denial, Stacy began raking the lillies off the coffin lid. Armload after armload, they stacked up about her feet, suffocating her with their cloying smell. The room began to spin and her breathing to labor.

She sat up with a gasp.

"Are you all right, Doc?"

She glanced at Cobb in confusion. "I don't know. What happened?"

"You injected something and had a seizure. You've been drifting in and out for about fifteen minutes. What did you put in your arm?"

"Hopefully, my future. Help me up, Frank."

With his support, she was able to regain her chair. Her balance was unsteady, her insides in a turmoil.

"Wave to your neighbor," Cobb advised, glancing up through the glass wall where Herb Watson kept an anxious watch. "He's been worried."

She lifted a hand to Herb, signaling that she was herself again. Reluctant to surrender his curiosity, he went back to his own work.

"What are you doing?" Cobb demanded when she picked up an empty syringe.

"I need to test my blood. Pray for a miracle, Frank."

Moments later, she peered through her microscope until tears blurred the image on the slide. What she saw was unmistakable. What she saw was a complete destruction of abnormal cells, as the properties she'd separated out of Louis's blood aggressively took over.

"Stacy?"

"It's gone, Frank. My cancer's gone."

"In remission, you mean?"

"No. Gone. *Adios.* Bye-bye. Outta here, gone." She dropped back in her chair, slumping as the enormity of what she'd accomplished swamped her like a small craft on a high sea.

"You've found a cure for leukemia." His voice hushed with awe and amazement.

"At least. At the very least. I'm not sure yet what else it means."

She sat up, grasping a clean slide and drawing a deliberate line along her forearm. As she watched, the sting of pain disappeared as quickly and completely as the cut. Cobb seized her wrist, examining the unmarred flesh in incredulity.

"My God."

"Now you know what has Harper panting in anticipation," Stacy told him soberly. "They're not going to develop a cancer vaccine. They're going to pump this into the military. It'll never save a single civilian life. Imagine, soldiers on the front line, their bullet wounds healing, practically invincible as they march on their enemies."

"My God," he whispered again as consequence sank in deep and dire.

"Frank, I can't let them develop this research. They'll use it for all the wrong reasons."

His expression became a purposeful blank. "How are you going to stop them?"

"Steal it. Destroy all evidence that it ever existed. Without my notes to guide them, it'll take them years to duplicate what I've found, and by then the cure will be on the market and under the proper controls."

"I don't think I want to hear this. And I don't think you ought to be planning it."

She gave him a long, belatedly cautious look. Yes, perhaps he was right. The less he knew, the better for secrecy's sake and for his own career longevity. But he could help her without being involved, if he would go that far.

"Where are they keeping Alexander?"

"We've already discussed that." He stood, an inanimate professional once more. "I'm happy for your success, Doc. Just don't expect me to compromise my position."

"I expect you to think and do what's right. You know I'm right, don't you?"

"I know you're talking about destroying government property, and that it's treason for me to listen without reporting it." He sounded angry with her, for her intentions and for placing him in such an awkward situation. "You're not dealing with a batch of philosophical eggheads here. It's the military. They follow orders and don't ask hard questions of themselves. If you get in their way, they will hurt you. And I don't want any part of that."

She gripped his forearm, feeling the muscles tense beneath the wrap of her fingers. "But you won't report it, will you, Frank?"

He said nothing, jaw tight, gaze hard.

Frustrated by his blind obedience to what he believed to be his duty, she cried, "If you won't help, then stay out of the way. I'll ask that much of you, at least."

He pulled free of her grasp but not of her demanding gaze. "I'll give you until the brass shows up tomorrow. After that, what you and I think or want won't matter."

"Thank you."

He made a noncommital sound and stalked from the room.

That left Stacy with only one goal to accomplish before setting off an Armageddon within the bowels of Harper Research. She brought out the samples of Louis's blood and began the separation process again.

She had her life back. Now, she would give Louis his.

And if they were to have a future together, she would have to start planning now, while she waited for the anticipated results of her testing. There were other details she couldn't afford to ignore for long. With a call, she would set the gears in motion, thinking as she did so that this was a difficult day to be one of her friends.

"Charlie, I need a favor. A big one."

***

Phyllis Starke looked upon the object in the center of the room with a gleam of dispassionate greed.

Now, Greg Forrester couldn't afford to ignore her. She would deliver what Stacy Kimball had failed to. She would complete the study and wallow in his approval. He would realize, at last, her true worth, her true loyalty.

But why stop at Forrester? What degree of loyalty had he shown her? Her features pursed bitterly as she considered the humiliation of being passed by in both promotion and his attention. He didn't deserve the faithfulness she'd shown him. With what she could learn and develop from Stacy's notes and this convenient donor, she could have whatever and whomever she wanted. Perhaps one of the generals who would arrive in the morning. Yes, that notion pleased her immensely. Uniforms, especially ones covered in medals of valor, held an undeniable appeal for the power and command they represented.

And she wanted power. Blind, ambitious, and unscrupulous power.

But first she had to discover how to unlock the key to Kimball's research.

The bitch would tell her nothing, but Phyllis had all the tools at hand to complete the study despite Stacy's stubbornness. Who would have thought the little sex kitten was working on the secrets to eternity. She smiled to herself.

After tomorrow, Stacy wouldn't matter. She would be gone. Not fired, just gone, the way loose ends who knew too much tended to disappear. And she would not be missed, not by Phyllis, anyway.

And after Stacy, maybe even Forrester, himself. She thought covetously of that big horseshoe-shaped desk bathed by the day's sunlight and the company's respect.

To begin her study, she'd need blood from the creature Cobb had delivered the night before.

"Open it," she ordered one of the sentries, gesturing to the metal casket sitting chained in the center of the lab. When neither moved, she raised her voice a decibel. "You heard me. Unlock those chains. This is my project now, and I am in charge. Do what I tell you, or you'll walk sentry duty on some foreign fenceline for your remaining years of service."

They might dislike her, but they were carefully trained. They understood the chain of command and the threat of consequence. One of them came forward. The soldier's reluctance was obvious as he approached with the key, but he did as told, freeing Phyllis to open the heavy lid.

She peered inside, not quite prepared for what a member of the undead might look like. She was surprised.

A handsome young man. No one would guess him to be a killer. Nor would anyone suspect he held the secret to immortality within his veins. Curiously, she put fingertips to his throat.

"No pulse," she murmured to herself.

She heard the involuntary gasp from the guard beside her and impatiently waved him away.

"Go stand by the door, you ninny. He can't hurt anyone. I am in perfect control of the situation here."

"But it's almost dark, Doctor. I must warn you to be careful."

"Of what?" she snapped, tolerance waning as she readied a syringe. "He's got enough sedatives pumped into him to arrest an elephant."

"No, he doesn't."

She glanced at the guard, sure he was mistaken. "What do you mean, he doesn't?"

"Mr. Forrester didn't want him full of drugs that could affect the results of the tests."

A tremor of fear quickened. "You mean he's—"

"Awake, Doctor," came a low croon of amusement.

She glanced down to see the monster's eyes were not only open but bright with smug malice. As she watched, unable to move, he broke the bindings on first one arm then the other. With a determined heave, he sat up, snapping the chains about his chest as if they had been made of construction paper by a first grader.

"Don't just stand there, idiots," she screamed at the guards. "Shoot him!"

Puffs of powder and blood exploded across Quinton's chest, ruining his blue uniform shirt but not his good humor.

"Oh, my dear doctor, you haven't done your research. Bullets can't harm me. But I, contrarily, can do considerable harm to you."

As she stumbled back, shrieking wildly, his hand speared out, closing about her throat, shutting off both sound and air. And as the two guards stood gaping, their emptied revolvers dangling impotently, Quinton jerked the doctor up and sank his teeth into her neck.

Finally, as her thrashing grew feeble and the gurgling sounds she made dwindled to a soft groan, one of the soldiers had the presence of mind to pull the alarm switch.

Too late to save Phyllis Starke from her own ambition.

TWENTY-ONE

She'd been working for seven hours straight but a healthy vitality flushed through her, making it seem like minutes. The weakness was gone from her body, from her mind. Never had things been clearer, her goals so near, so tangible. Not only had the serum cleaned away the abnormalities, it had also imbued her with a potent sense of power and energy. Some of Louis's preternatural strength? She would enjoy exploring that possibility at a later date.

For the moment, she had no time for tangents. Her concentration narrowed until the outside world, with all its woes, ceased to influence her. She forgot about Greg Forrester, about Quinton Alexander, about Frank Cobb. Her thoughts had room for only one man. The man who would become her future.

On the edge of her lab table stood a row of vials. Half contained a pure concentrate of the serum she'd used on herself. The others held the miracle she'd just completed. One of those, she would give to Louis.

"Is it ready?"

She gasped as she turned, unused to his ability to appear at will whenever and wherever once the sun had set. A quick look around told her that the lab floor was abandoned by its nine-to-five laborers so there was no one to question Louis's presence.

Surprise gave way to excitement. And to a deep inner warming that centered around her fast-beating heart. Vampire magic? Or just plain magic? She took a breath to suppress emotions, to become the consummate professional once more. Never had that task been so difficult as when Louis Redman was near.

"I think so. If all my research is right, your cure is here in these vials. It should be tested first."

Louis glanced at the vials then back into her eyes. "You didn't take these precautions with your own cure." Then his voice lowered to an emotional rumble. "I felt the change in you. Is it true? Are you free of the disease?"

"Yes." That single word trembled with the force of her relief.

His green eyes glowed with happiness and impatience. "Then what do we wait for? I wish to be whole again, too."

Stacy hedged. It was one thing being cavalier about her own life but quite another when it came to risking his. "The process was much more complicated in your case, Louis. I can't be sure of the results. I want to test it first."

"How?"

She could hear the richness of urgency in his tone and knew it wouldn't be easy to hold him back from something he'd desired for centuries. But she'd already thought of that and had the solution ready.

"We have a test subject below. Not a voluntary one, but a handy one. And after what he did to my neighbor and those other girls, I'm afraid my ethics aren't bothering me at all. And besides, if the properties are altered in his blood, he'll be useless to Harper, and that will be one less problem we have to deal with."

His hand brushed through her hair as his expression grew serious. "You know we can't stay here, don't you?"

She smiled up at him. "I know. I have nothing that I'll regret leaving behind and everything to look forward to."

"Then let's find Quinton."

"We have no security badges. The lower level is guarded round-the-clock."

Smiling mildly, Louis stripped off two sheets from her self-stick note pad and pressed one to the pocket of his navy blue silk shirt and the other to the lapel of her lab coat. When her brows crinkled in puzzlement, he explained, "To anyone we encounter, it will look like a very official badge giving me free run of the facility."

"Okay," she murmured, choosing to believe he had that power to cloud minds because it would make things so much easier for them. "He's being kept on the security level below us. Cobb wouldn't tell me exactly where, but I'm sure the number of guards present will give us all the clue we need. Louis..."

"What is it?"

"We have to take care of Quinton, one way or the other, tonight. Government officials are coming in tomorrow, and after that, we may never get close to him again."

He nodded, understanding the importance of her plan. The knowledge of Quinton's dark existence as well as the potential of Stacy's vaccine could never fall into their hands.

Picking up several of the vials and a capped syringe, Stacy took a breath and smiled grimly at her elegant companion. "Let's go."

As the doors shut them into their own private space in the elevator, Louis turned to take Stacy in his arms. His words rumbled with tender emotion. "I have asked dangerous things of you, Little One. Are you sure you want to continue? I can take care of Quinton."

"You haven't asked anything that I wasn't willing to give. I'm not backing out now. We're both in this together. What affects you affects me. I'm not afraid."

"Sometimes I think you should be. I know I am for you."

His words were a curative science could never replicate. She touched his taut cheek, tracing his high cheekbone with her thumb, the gesture tender and telling. Then she stepped back to gain the more dispassionate distance the situation demanded.

"Tomorrow we'll be away from here, on our way to a new life. I'll gladly take any hurdle they throw in my way. They're trying to steal my work, to distort it to fit their plans. And they're interfering with my future happiness. They're the ones who should be afraid."

He kissed her then, a necessarily short but exquisitely revealing kiss that weakened her knees and strengthened her resolve.

They would have to move fast. First Quinton, then the remaining research. There must be no clues left for Harper to follow.

The rest of the elevator ride was spent in an anticipatory silence, but just as the doors opened to the security floor below, the shriek of the building's alarm made a harsh greeting. Louis gripped Stacy's arm.

"What is it?"

She shook her head in uncertainty, but instinctively she knew.

It was Quinton.

Smoke billowed down the hall in a dark, noxious cloud. From out of it, several uniformed guards appeared. Behind them was Frank Cobb. The guards rushed on as if they didn't see the couple emerging from the elevator. Cobb stopped before them.

"Frank, what's happened?"

Cobb's expression was all grim business. "He got loose. Starke couldn't wait until daylight to begin her experiments. She's dead."

That blunt summation made Stacy wince. She had no fondness for the woman who'd done everything possible to discredit her and her career, but she wouldn't have wished Quinton Alexander upon her. Upon anyone, for that matter.

"Where is he?" Louis demanded.

"I don't know. He started a chemical fire in the lab to cover his escape. One of the guards pulled the alarm. If the security system isn't shut down within two minutes, there's a self-destruct in place."

"A what?" Stacy looked between the two men in dismay.

"It's assumed if no one is left to disarm the system, national security has been compromised. The building will lock down, and the underground levels will be gone in seconds. The ultimate clean sweep. No culpability for the government. No questions for Harper to answer." He pushed her back into the elevator. "Get out of here."

"But my work. I can't let them have my research. If they reset the system, they'll still have everything, and we'll never be safe."

"Then I guess I'll just have to do the right thing, won't I?"

Calmly, Cobb withdrew his sidearm and with a firm deliberation fired four shots into the security panel. Sparks fountained, and the scent of crisped circuitry burnt the nose with its acrid stench. All the lights gave a last flicker of life then the panel went dark. There would be no reviving it in time. In a matter of a minute, there would be nothing left to find. All evidence of her work would be gone, along with Harper Research's marriage to the government.

"I'll get everyone out," Cobb told her. "Go. Don't stop for anything. I'll meet you at my car." He looked to Louis. "Make sure she gets there."

"I will," Louis promised, pushing the button to close the doors.

"Frank!"

But the doors closed just as he turned toward her with a small, lopsided smile.

Once he was sure Stacy was out of danger, Cobb turned to the task at hand, shouting to the remaining guards to leave the building. Then he, too, took the elevator up.

Greg Forrester met him where the doors opened on the executive floor.

"What the hell happened, Cobb?"

"Your experiment got out of hand. I suggest you exit the building while you still can."

"What about Starke and Kimball?"

"They're dead."

Forrester flinched, but he didn't question Cobb's gruff claim. "And the...the vampire?"

"Gone."

Uttering a fierce oath, Forrester gripping Cobb's arm. "Find him, Cobb. I want him back. This opportunity is not going to escape me. I don't care if you have to go to the ends of the Earth, you find him."

"Yes, sir."

***

The ride up in the elevator seemed interminable. Each second brought destruction closer. Gripping onto Louis's arm, Stacy prayed they wouldn't be trapped in the steel prison. Finally, they came to a smooth stop and, with an atonal ding, the doors opened. They bolted from the elevator and ran toward the nearest exit doors. They had to get out of the building and off the property before the complete lockdown, which would happen in stages throughout the facility. Once they were through the door stenciled with the Harper logo and outside the main building, Stacy whispered words of thanksgiving.

On the parking level, she and Louis raced down the dim, nearly empty aisles toward Cobb's vehicle. Halfway through the garage, a tremendous shock wave rumbled through the structure. Stacy pitched against Louis, grabbing on tight as concrete dust filtered down atop them. The sprinkling system came on automatically, its fine spray drenching them and quickly puddling the cement floor. Pushing her wet hair out of her face, Stacy pointed ahead.

"There. The black one."

They started to run toward the car. Stacy's gaze flew about the dim and now hazy cavern.

"Where's Frank?"

"He can take care of himself, Little One."

A soft voice interrupted.

"But who will take care of you?"

Louis turned toward the speaker. Suddenly, he was no longer at Stacy's side. He flew backward, across the aisle and into the back of Forrester's new Mercedes. The shriek of the car alarm echoed off the low ceiling and had Stacy clutching her hands to her ears as she looked from where Louis sprawled across the dented trunk lid to his smug attacker.

"Hello, Stacy. Didn't think I'd let you leave without saying good-bye, did you?"

Quinton Alexander's fangs gleamed white and terrible as he grinned.

"Run, Stacy," Louis shouted. "Hide yourself."

She ran. Out of the corner of her eye, she caught a blur of movement as Louis launched himself across the open space to knock Quinton to the wet floor. They rolled together like a pair of wolves, growling, snapping, looking for weakness, and Stacy didn't look back until she'd found a safe place to crouch behind the bulk of a Suburban.

Huddled behind one of the massive tires, she peered out from under the vehicle. Her breath plumed in the cold, misty air. She shivered from the continued spray above and from the terror coursing through her. But thoughts of her own safety were a distance second.

What could she do to help Louis?

From her low vantage point, all she could see was the scuffle of feet as the two age-old enemies grappled with one another. She saw Louis's Italian loafers leave the ground, followed by the sound of shattering glass. Then there was silence.

She waited a long moment, trying to quiet her breathing, trying to decide what to do. Would her interference be help or hindrance in Louis's fight against the crazed Alexander?

Perhaps she could step out and distract the beast long enough for Louis to get the upper hand.

If only she knew where they both were.

Their psychic link. Yes. She could contact Louis and—

But what if Quinton could pick up on those same telepathic vibrations? She didn't know enough about the shared phenomenon to risk both giving herself away and perhaps dangerously compromising Louis at a critical moment. Better she trust him and wait.

But waiting had never been easy for Stacy.

She started to edge forward, to rise up for just a quick look...

The sound of crunching of metal forced her to drop back out of sight. Someone was running across the rooftops of the few cars scattered about in the lot, leaping the sometimes fifteen to twenty foot span between them. Louis or Quinton? Dare she stand and cry out? Or would that make her a ready target for Quinton's sick revenge?

What good would curing herself do if she were to die in this steamy garage at the hands of a madman, if she couldn't grant Louis his wish for mortality?

She felt a rush of air behind her.

Hairs rose on the back of her neck in a horrifying prickle. Slowly, she turned her head to face the hideously grinning Quinton Alexander.

"Peek-a-boo," he taunted, his hand shooting out to fist in her hair.

She cried out as he dragged her to her feet and shoved her forward, out into the open aisle. There, she saw Cobb squared off like an old-fashioned gunfighter readying for a quick draw contest. Dismay flickered upon his ravaged face as he assessed her situation. Then his professionalism took over.

"Let her go," came his icy demand. He drew his gun and braced it with his other hand, sighting down the barrel for what should have been a killing shot.

Alexander only laughed. "Your toys cannot harm me, mortal fool."

Cobb smiled narrowly. "They can when the bullets are cast in silver. You can only take me by surprise once, if you're lucky. You're luck's just run out. Stacy, walk toward me."

But Quinton's grip tightened as he ducked in closer behind her. Stacy whimpered as his cold breath blew with chill anticipation against her exposed throat. She tried to keep her focus on Cobb, clinging to the hope that he would somehow save her from this madman's grasp. But she didn't know how he could manage it. Perhaps this was how it was meant to end, with no happiness for her, no salvation for Louis.

No.

That couldn't be true. It couldn't. Not after all she'd gone through, all she'd survived already.

Louis! Are you there? Are you all right?

She couldn't feel him in her thoughts. She had only her own resources to rely upon.

She threw her elbow back with all her strength, feeling the thud of its impact with Alexander's ribs. He grunted in surprise then laughed at her attempt to escape him.

"You'll have to do better than that, my dear," he mocked her.

"How about this?"

Louis's question caught them both off guard. As Quinton turned with a snarl, Louis swung a car bumper like a baseball bat. The heavy gauge metal collided with the side of Alexander's head, bowling him over, Stacy tumbling with him. She rolled free, skinning hands and knees on the slick pavement. The vials spewed from her pocket, tinkling across the wet cement. Fumbling for them, she found one shattered and one other whole. She tucked it into the safety of her purse as she searched for the last two.

And then Louis was there, lifting her up, enveloping her in the security of his embrace.

Spread-eagle on the ground, Quinton snarled up at Cobb as the agent looked down the short barrel of his gun for a killing shot.

"This is not over, human," he hissed.

"You're wrong there." He steadied for a clean, conclusive end to Alexander. But the vampire had no intention of obliging him.

"We will meet again, meddler, and then I will have your soul."

And Quinton was gone.

After blinking in brief amazement, Cobb let the revolver drop to his side, shifting his attention to Stacy.

"Are you all right, Doc?"

Stacy grinned at him weakly. "You are one handy guy to have around, Cobb."

She caught the keys he tossed her.

"Go on. Take my car. Get out of here before the gates lock down. I told Forrester you were killed with Starke. He won't know the truth until they sift through that mess inside. By then, you can be far away and out of his reach."

"But what about you?"

"I already have a new job to do. One that won't strain my concepts of right and wrong. One I think I'll rather enjoy." He touched the raw gash on the side of his face and smiled rather grimly.

"Be careful."

She crossed to him in a rush and, knowing she'd never see him again, hugged him fiercely, pressing a quick, hard kiss to his uninjured cheek. When she stepped back, he was grinning wryly.

"See. Told you you'd come to like me. Now get. I'll handle things here."

After a nod toward the other man, Louis took hold of her arm, guiding her toward the car. By the time she slipped behind the wheel and glanced into the rearview, there was no sign of Frank Cobb in the puddled aisle. She slammed the vehicle into reverse and, with a squeal of tires and rubber track, sped out of the garage and away from Harper.

And she didn't look back.

If she had, she would have seen Frank Cobb glancing down at something he'd nudged with the toe of his boot. He bent to examine the blood-red vials then slipped them into his pocket. He flicked out a cigarette, lit it and sent a thick stream of smoke jetting toward the tubed lighting overhead.

"Good-bye, Doc. And good luck," he called after the final blink of taillights.

TWENTY-TWO

Stacy didn't share Cobb's optimism that someone from Harper wouldn't come looking right away. Beneath his shiny thousand dollar suits and smarmy smile, Greg Forrester was a street fighter. He wouldn't back down until he had what he wanted. So she would just have to see that they were well out of his greedy reach. They'd want Stacy back to reconstruct her notes now that Starke's foolishness had gotten her killed.

She wouldn't be Harper's prisoner again even if they gave her carte blanche in the research department.

Some things had no price tag. Integrity was one of them. Her father had taught her that.

Continually checking the rear view mirror, she directed the sleek sports car down the less congested midnight streets of Seattle.

"This isn't the way to your apartment," Louis commented as they sped past the turn off.

She thought of what those rooms contained—the evidence of her lonely life. Gaudy clothing made to seduce passion but not to submit to love. Trappings of a woman she no longer had to be. A broken computer that would give no secrets away. A collection from a child's dreams, remnants of a happy fairy tale she could never claim...until now. Her chance of happiness wasn't contained in those faded memories. It rode beside her.

"There's nothing there I need. I'm not that person any more."

Louis said nothing, but his small smile conveyed his understanding. They were both about to embark on an adventure, reaching for what had previously been frustratingly out of their grasp. No longer.

He hadn't asked, so she told him.

"I have everything you need with me. There's no time now. When we get where we're going."

"And where is that, Little One?"

It was her turn to smile and be mysterious. "I'm not without resources. I've got the means. The destination is up to you."

They stopped outside his building. Stacy was about to suggest she wait while he went up to retrieve his manservant when the aged Asian appeared at the front door. He walked briskly toward the car and nodded.

I've taken care of everything, Master.

His voice sounded within her head. Stacy could only stare, amazed.

"Very good, Takeo. We are leaving tonight. Have everything waiting at the airport as we discussed."

Yes, sir. And the lady?

"She's traveling with us. See all my accounts are transferred and everything is readied for shipping."

I will be ready.

With that assurance, he went back across the street and disappeared into the old hotel.

"Go," Louis told her.

As they resumed their journey, she asked, "He's been with you for a long time?" There was so much to learn about Louis and his life. So much she didn't know. In time, she would discover all. She looked forward to it.

"Takeo has served me well since I rescued him from poverty as a child. He has no power of speech, so our communication means all the more to him."

"He is your initiate."

"He is my friend." He was silent for a moment, unspoken concerns crowding his brow.

She glanced at him, feeling his distress. "What is it, Louis?"

"Our arrangement has slowed his aging. He is over two hundred years old."

She gasped but never disbelieved. Louis turned toward her, anxiousness lining his face.

"What will happen to him when I revert? Will he resume his natural age and fall into dust?"

"I don't know, Louis. I've had no experience in such things."

"How can I cut him off from the treasured communication we share? What kind of reward is that for his loyalty?"

She touched his knee. His hand found hers, their fingers lacing together in the dark.

"If he is your friend, he will understand your desire to return to a normal life."

"Another of those sacrifices I seem so eager to accept in order to save myself?"

She didn't respond to those once bitterly spoken words. She didn't know what to say to take the sting of moral conflict from his heart. She could have argued that he'd already given his friend a life expectancy well beyond his natural years. But that truth would give no comfort. So she said nothing as she wheeled the car into police headquarters.

Their destination shocked Louis from the morose turn of his thoughts.

"Why are we here, Stacy?"

"I'm here to go into incredibly deep debt to a friend."

***

Charlie Sisson eyed Louis as he stepped past him to offer a hearty hug for his former partner.

"So this is good-bye?"

"Don't get all misty-eyed on me, Charlie," she chided, contrarily blinking away the dampness rimming her own. She chafed the sleeves of his rumpled lab coat, frowning at the stains of his last autopsy and spaghetti sauce. "You need to find yourself another wife."

"No one would take as good care of me as you did, Stace." He moved back, nodding to himself, then reached into the huge pocket of his gruesomely patterned coat. He placed a packet of documents in her hand.

"Here's everything, including a passport to your new life as the widowed Mrs. Benthen. You'll be escorting the poor departed Mr. Benthen to his final resting place. All the paperwork is here, everything you need, with the exception of Mr. Benthen, whom I cremated earlier this evening. I assume you'll be supplying the deceased." His gaze touched pointedly upon Louis, but he kept his summations to himself.

"Charlie, you are the best friend a girl ever had."

He accepted her kiss with a difficult to maintain neutrality. "And don't you forget it," he murmured. "Now, can I also assume I'll be getting less night time business once you and your friend have left town?"

"I think that would be a safe assumption, though not completely under our control."

Charlie raised his brows at that reply, reassessing her companion's role in the about to end drama. "So, your friend here isn't the one—"

Stacy smiled. "No. Just an innocent bystander with an unfortunate past. But that's all about to change." She glanced at Louis, the glow in her eyes giving everything away.

Seeing it, Charlie grinned, pleased with that unexpected turn of events. "I hope you know what you're doing, Kiddo."

"I've never been more certain."

And the smoldering look she gave to her very alive-looking, albeit for the record recently deceased, 'husband' convinced Charlie that he had no cause for worry. Stacy Kimball had found happiness at last.

"You'd better get going," he said gruffly. "You've got a plane to catch. Someone's already booked you into first class, Stace, but your friend, unfortunately, will have to settle for cargo."

***

Early morning came with a lifting of the mists and an awe-inspiring view of the Cascades as the vehicle approached SeaTac Airport. Shades of pink and gray gradually climbed the distant peaks as sun rise reflected off the western range. Seattle was giving her a majestic send-off.

But strangely, though she'd lived in the Seattle-Tacoma area all her life, she felt no pang of separation. Instead, anticipation rose in steady measured degrees, just like the daybreak she hoped to soon share with the man she loved. Her future held the same promise as the crisp blue heavens waking in pristine layers above her. Soon she would be one with that cerulean sky, crossing an ocean, spanning the distance between old life and new, on a wing and a prayer.

Usually brusque baggage handlers greeted her with respectful murmurs as she and her gleaming cargo passed through Customs. The officer who took her papers expressed condolences, but his clearing stamp remained untouched.

"Is there a problem?" she asked at his hesitation.

"No, ma'am. Just a little extra governmental red tape this morning. It shouldn't take but a minute."

Dread twisted a tight knot in her belly as Stacy watched the customs officer turn to hand her forged passport to a uniformed military man on the other side of his station. She took a fateful step forward, craning to see a meticulously stitched cheek beneath impenetrable dark glasses. She didn't move, couldn't breathe as Cobb examined the fake documents and then looked at her. In his hands, he held her freedom, her future. And with a word, both would disappear.

Slowly, he handed the folder back to the Customs officer.

"Stamp it. Sorry for the delay, Mrs. Benthen. And sorry for your loss."

As she accepted the cleared document and her papers back, Stacy managed a faint, "Thank you, Captain."

But Cobb was already looking beyond her, toward the next exiting tourist. They passed silently, within inches of each other.

"Stop!"

The cry echoed from across the busy Customs area. A path appeared between the travelers and their stacks of luggage, opening the way for Greg Forrester and two armed guards.

"Stop the flight!"

Cobb stepped in front of Stacy, covertly pushing her on her way as he said to the Customs man, "Call airport security. And get these people on board as soon as possible. They'll only be in the way. I want this area cleared."

"All right, Captain. On your say so." He picked up the phone and began to dial.

Cobb went out to greet the breathless and angry Forrester.

"Didn't you hear me? That was Stacy Kimball. Why didn't you stop her?" Forrester hissed in a low, angry aside.

"Mr. Forrester, you're making a mistake."

But Cobb's calming tones couldn't reach through Forrester's rage. He took one last look at the woman hurrying up the companionway and at the casket gliding away on the cargo conveyor belt then turned to the guards behind him to order fiercely, "Stop her. Shoot her. She's getting away with everything that belongs to me."

Never making a conscious decision, Cobb acted, wrestling with the first guard for control of his weapon, but the second lifted his rifle without hesitation and took aim between Stacy's shoulder blades.

"No!"

Stacy heard Cobb's cry and turned toward him just as the guard fired. The rest happened like the slow fanning of motion cards, the discharge of the gun, the projection of the bullet, her recoil that could never be fast enough to get her out of harm's way.

And then a blur passed in front of her, and the danger was gone.

At her feet lay Takeo, the bullet meant to take her in the chest piercing his brave heart. Stunned and weeping, she knelt down, but one look at his rapidly glazing eyes told her he was beyond help.

Take care of him.

That final wish whispered through her head, and smiling softly, she squeezed his hand.

"I will."

Stacy responded vaguely to the tugging at her arm. It was the Customs official.

"Ma'am, there's nothing more you can do here. Your flight's about to leave. This is a government matter. Please, let them handle it."

Because she had to, because to linger would have the official wondering if she were more than just an innocent bystander, Stacy walked away without a backward glance, holding the memory of Takeo's sacrifice close to her heart where it would reside forever alongside her gratitude for Frank Cobb.

"We had her," Forrester was seething at the enigmatic Captain Cobb. "I watched the security tapes. She took samples from her lab before it was destroyed. She didn't die with Starke. I saw her leave the building. Don't you understand? You let her get away. I had her and the research she stole from me."

"You had nothing, Mr. Forrester," Cobb stated with chill certainty. "It wasn't her. I checked the lady through myself, right up close and personal. Don't you think I would have recognized Doctor Kimball?"

"It wasn't—" Forrester glanced at the fallen man and at his two gunmen, the seriousness of his situation sinking in at last. Shaken by his mistake, he took a stiff step back, already seeking a way to distance himself from the debacle. He could see the airport security team jogging down the corridor, hands on holsters. A hard glint of self-preservation glazed his eyes.

Let Cobb assume responsibility.

Apparently, his employee was of the same mind, insisting, "You need to go, sir. You need to get out of here before security arrives. I'll handle things."

"But that man—"

"Is the dangerous felon we were after. He's wanted for international espionage. He was our target all along. I'll make sure all the necessary warrants are drawn up." Cobb smiled grimly in the face of Forrester's horrified dismay. "Trust me, sir. I'll make it go away. Erasing problems is part of my job."

"Thank you, Cobb. I'll see you get a bonus for this."

Cobb glanced toward the companionway where anxious staff were busy closing it off and clearing the way for emergency personnel. "No need, sir. It's all in a day's work."

Fifteen minutes later, Stacy was in the air.

TWENTY-THREE

Warm air blew in from the open window to wrap lovingly about her, caressing her bare arms and teasing playfully through her unbound hair. Outside, torchlight created a crystal clear reflection of the sprawling, mosque-like structure in the still black waters of the *bassin*. She'd been gently informed upon arrival that it was not, as she'd assumed, a swimming pool lined by a fringe of graceful date palms, but instead a very practical way to collect precious irrigation waters from the mountains beyond. She admired the blend of seductive beauty and utility. And she knew she would love this place. It embraced her with a sense of permanence.

The ocher-colored walls reinforced with straw seemed to have stood for centuries with their thick, fortress-like stance, romantic towers and palatial arches. Jetting from the techno-steel of the twenty-first century into this exotic world where rich aromas and Moroccan leather spiced the air, and ancient mystery seemed to rise up from the desert sand like a mirage, left her faintly disoriented and yet willing to be tempted by the lure of a Sheharizade fairy tale. The tension of hours past finally surrendered to the cleansing winds.

Amanjena was not a Sultan's playground but rather a brand new resort catering to luxury and relaxation, its name meaning peaceful paradise. To Stacy, it was a haven, a well-spring from which she would arise, renewed.

She stepped back into the room, awed all over again by the soaring ceiling and whispering draperies, their pale tangerine color mixing like a tart splash of flavor with the orchid-tinged columns and sunken couches of the private *menzah* in their suite. A bricked floor circled a small, fountained pool strewn with rose petals. Elaborate tiling climbed half-way up the walls. Oranges from a nearby grove sat out beside a mint tea service in an inviting lantern glow. The sound of water was everywhere, cooling, hypnotic and restful. Closed behind the twenty-foot-high entry doors carved with Berber designs, it was a world apart from a world gone mad, and just what Stacy needed.

She crossed from the partially covered gazebo into the dressing area with its twenty-six-foot-high domed ceiling. Here the colors were soft and glowed against the lacquered wall and meticulous parquetry. And the only thing out of place was the long, rectangular box she'd brought with her. Her fingertips trailed across its smooth finish.

Soon.

She answered a modest tap at the door to see a traditionally garbed room service waiter bearing a tray.

"*A-salaam alaykum.* Peace be with you," came his greeting as he carried the fragrant Tandoori sea bass to a small private table. He bowed out of the room and, as the door closed softly, she heard a welcomed voice behind her.

"A kingdom befitting my princess."

She turned into his arms. "Oh, Louis, this place is a dream."

"It's a reality from which we may never wish to wake," he corrected as his lips brushed her brow.

They held one another for a long moment. Then she could tell the precise instant his thoughts focused on his martyred servant. His pain was a palpable emotion.

"I'm so sorry about your friend. He saved us both, though I know that is scant consolation."

Louis hugged her closer and sighed against her hair. "He is at peace, and for that I am grateful. And for you, I am more grateful still."

His kiss was as sweet and exotic as the night air, a light flickering hint of what would come later.

"What made you choose Marrakesh?" she asked, revolving in his embrace so that she rested back against the sturdy support of his chest. "When you said you'd arranged for our airfare, I had no idea this was the destination you had in mind. I was expecting something a little more...mundane. Have you been here before?"

"Long before it offered luxuries such as these. I thought it a lovely oasis in which to lose ourselves until we wish to be found. And eventually, when you are ready and if you are willing, we can have a private facility built, here or anywhere on the globe, where you can continue your research without interference, to be used only for the purposes intended. The choice is yours. Whatever will make you happy."

"But the money—"

He shrugged elegantly. "What is money if it can buy nothing worthwhile?"

She'd almost forgotten that she was with one of the wealthiest—and most generous—men in the world.

"So," he crooned, "how does this compare with your rainy Seattle?"

"I love it." She leaned her head back upon his shoulder, her eyes closing. "I love you."

His mouth touched briefly to her temple, tasting its warmth and pulse, drawn irresistibly to both. Defiantly, he turned so that his cheek rested against her hair.

She could feel his hunger rising.

"Stacy, I want this to be the start of our life together, as one and the same being. Use the serum so that I might join you in this celebration."

She stiffened slightly, not ready to face the harsh facts of what they'd escaped. "It hasn't been tested, Louis."

"Then test it now, my love. I have waited centuries and find I cannot wait another second longer."

She moved away from him, the beauty of the mood spoiled by her anxieties. Trying to summon up her clinical objectivity, she searched in her bag for the vial.

"There's only one. I lost the others in the parking garage at Harper. I just hope they broke. At least they're unmarked and will give nothing away."

He reached out to take the vial from her, handling it with the reverence due a religious artifact. "But will this be enough?"

"Yes."

"Then don't worry about the others."

She was distracting herself from what she didn't want to confront—the truth of whether or not she could cure him. Never before, not even with her own case, had she felt so pressured to succeed. Never would the outcome of her work be experienced so personally, so intimately.

"I thought you had unshakable faith in your ability, Doctor Kimball?"

His gentle chiding chafed up her pride. She regarded him through coolly professional eyes.

"I do."

"And I have faith in you. Just do it. There is no other way to know for sure."

Of course, he was right.

She prepared the injection as he stoically pushed up his sleeve.

"Should something happen to me, I want you to know that I've already signed all that I own over to you to use honorably as you see fit."

Stacy snapped the syringe and grinned at him. "Now that *is* faith."

The lightness of the moment wouldn't hold. Their gazes mingled for a last loving communion, then she became what she had to be—a scientist about to explore one of the greatest unknowns—life.

He didn't react as she swiftly injected the serum.

"There," she remarked tautly. "It's done. You should sit down."

Louis never made it as far as the low couches.

Terrible pain gripped his middle, doubling him over, then dropping him to the woven Berber rug. Excruciating agony twisted through his veins, alternately burning and freezing, leaving him gasping on hands and knees. Tremors quaked along limbs that could no longer hold him. Then the brick floor felt cool beneath the inferno blazing within him.

"Louis."

He heard Stacy's voice from far away, a pleading echo of what he couldn't hold or reach or even retain.

Light seared his eyes, his brain, his being.

He was dying. Or he was being reborn.

Bella, call me to you. Show me the way. Do not desert me now.

Then there was nothing.

Hours had passed.

Stacy paced the opulent suite, restless in her own helplessness. All she could do was wait. It was up to fate now as to whether or not her skills were adequate to save the man she loved.

She wanted a cigarette. Desperately.

Instead, she forced herself to eat the exotic meal alone and satisfy her cravings with mint tea. A poor substitute when her nerves were screaming for relief.

Louis lay unmoving upon one of the low cot-like benches next to the sunken pool. He was still, as still as when she'd first seen him at his preternatural rest. No trace of breathing moved his chest. There was no pulse, no heartbeat. But no damning signs of death, either. Just this maddening immobility that told her nothing of his condition.

She hated the waiting, the not knowing, the not being in control.

She continued to traverse the rooms, blocking out what was foremost on her heart and mind—the awful encroaching reality of how she might have to go on without him. Or continue to live in this split life of day and night to be with him.

As dawn's pastels began to tint the jagged mountains, Stacy had to face the possibility that she had failed him. Uncertain of what changes had occurred, if any, to his body chemistry, all she knew was she'd have to find someway to get him inside the safe surround of his casket before daylight reached them. She would have to drag him, lift him...

"How long have I been asleep?"

The sound of his voice shocked through her like the snap of an electric current, startling her into a brief paralysis of body and mind. She watched him sit up, as if rising from a nap, to regard her with a mild look of question.

"Louis... Are you all right?"

He thought a moment. "I don't know. Isn't that something you should be able to tell me?"

"How do you feel?"

He flexed his fingers, turned to place his feet upon the floor, as if both acts were new and strange to him. "Odd," he told her. "Curious."

Prompted to resume her professional mode, she quickly tested his heart rate, finding it fast and light, but steady.

Normal.

Frustrated, she looked about. "I have nothing here to tell me the results. No microscope, no way to draw a blood sample, not even a stethoscope. I feel like a surgeon asked to perform a heart transplant with a pocket knife."

He covered her hand with his surprisingly warm one. "And you could, if you had to."

"Let's not deify me just yet." Her tone was sharp with anxiety. How did he manage to remain so calm, so unconcerned? His detached attitude rattled more than it soothed.

"There is one way to know for sure."

Something in that casually spoken claim set off a flurry of panic inside her as she asked, "How?"

"The dawn is only moments away."

Then she understood.

"No!"

"If I survive—"

"No! It's an unnecessary risk. Tomorrow, when you awake, we'll go to the nearest clinic, or possibly I can located the equipment I need to be sure."

"But I feel awake now."

It was true. He felt none of the dragging lethargy that usually came with the approach of day. His senses were alive and tingling, yet when he tried to reach out mentally to Stacy, to reassure her along their sensory link, he found nothing. Perhaps her change had altered her ability to receive his telepathic messages.

Perhaps...

He stood, and she rose with him, her hands clutching anxiously at his sleeves. If only there were some way to calm her, to quiet the desperate anguish he saw in her lovely eyes. But this was a moment he'd prayed for and prepared for over the centuries, and he was ready.

"Let me go wash my face and then, my love, we will watch the sun rise together."

Her generous lips trembled then bowed into a faint yet amazingly brave smile. "I'll wait here for you."

He leaned forward to kiss her smooth brow, tasting the salty warmth of her skin and scenting her delightful perfume. But both seemed so faint, so far removed.

The bathroom was a hedonist's dream come true. A huge sunken tub set with corner pillars had a skylight that opened to the pale silver of the early sky. Potted palms lined the luxurious basin, making it appear like a maharaja's desert fantasy. And Louis couldn't wait to sink into scented waters with Stacy's supple form sliding against him. The impatient stirring in his loins was another surprise because there was no accompanying sense of hunger to ache along his jaw.

He was thirsty, but not for blood.

He neared the elaborately patterned sink and turned on its gold fixtures to let cool water fill his palms. The taste went down, quicksilver and curiously satisfying. Then slowly, feeling the first quivering of reluctance, he lifted his head to regard the oval mirror hanging above the basin.

"Stacy!"

She heard his cry and raced frantically to his side. She paused to see him standing before the bathroom mirror, lost in the study of his own reflection, his hand touched to his temple.

"Louis?"

His sudden laugh was an unexpected shock.

"Look," he said excitedly. "Look what I've found."

She drew closer, puzzled by his animation, just beginning to realize the significance of his reflection in the glass. "What is it?"

He pulled a strand away from the rumpled, dark auburn locks. "A gray hair. Stacy, I have a gray hair." And he turned to her with all the thrill of an adolescent discovering his first real whisker.

Louis Redman had just entered a new phase of life.

He was growing older. For the first time in nearly six centuries, time moved forward again.

"Oh, Louis."

Their embrace was long and fierce and when they parted, neither's cheeks were dry. He seized her hand.

"Come. There is something I must see."

Together, they ran into the adjoining room, out onto the airy *menzah*, where arm in arm they watched as a glorious sunrise changed the surrounding room into luscious shades of peach and lavender. Louis tipped his face toward the brightening sky, absorbing the light, the heat of the new day. The breath shuddered from him.

After a moment, he looked to the precious woman curled against his side.

"Thank you." Those two soft-spoken words throbbed with meaning.

"I love you," she replied.

He stroked his palms over her face, her hair and finally down her arms until their fingers met and mingled. His green eyes glittered, not from unnatural inner fire but from pure happiness.

"There is only one thing I would ask of you now, Stacy Kimball."

"You know I would give you anything."

"There is only one thing I desire. Just one simple thing that would have been impossible if not for you."

"What is that?"

He smiled.

"Grow old with me, my love."

Sinking into his kiss, Stacy whispered, "I will."

ABOUT THE AUTHOR

With 43 sales to her credit since her first publication in 1987, Nancy Gideon's writing career is as versatile as the romance genre, itself.

Under Nancy Gideon, her own name, this Southwestern Michigan author is a Top Ten Waldenbooks' best seller for Silhouette, has written an award-winning vampire romance series for Pinnacle earning a "Best Historical Fantasy" nomination from Romantic Times, and will have her first two original horror screen plays made into motion pictures in a collaboration with local independent film company, Katharsys Pictures.

Writing western historical romance for Zebra as Dana Ransom, she received a "Career Achievement award for Historical Adventure" and is a K.I.S.S. Hero Award winner. Best known for her family saga series; the Prescott family set in the Dakotas and the Bass family in Texas, her books published overseas in Romanian, Italian, Russian, Portuguese, Danish, Dutch, German, Icelandic and Chinese.

As Rosalyn West for Avon Books, her novels have been nominated for "Best North American Historical Romance" and "Best Historical Book in a Series." Her "Men of Pride County" series earned an Ingram Paperback Buyer's Choice Selection, a Barnes & Noble Top Romance Pick and won a HOLT Medallion.

Gideon attributes her love of history, a gift for storytelling, a background in journalism for keeping her focused and the discipline of writing since her youngest was in diapers. She begins her day at 5 a.m. while the rest of the family is still sleeping. While the pace is often hectic, Gideon enjoys working on diverse projects—probably because she's a Gemini. One month, it's researching the gritty existence of 1880s Texas Rangers only to jump to 1990s themes of intrigue and child abuse. Then it's back to the shadowy netherworlds of vampires and movie serial killers. In between, she's the award-winning newsletter editor and former vice president of the Mid-Michigan chapter of Romance Writers of America and is widely published in industry trade magazines.

A mother of two teenage sons, she recently discovered the Internet and has her own web pages at: http://www.tlt.com/authors/ngideon.htm and http://www.theromanceclub.com/nancygideon.htm.

She spends her 'spare time' taking care of a menagerie consisting of an ugly dog, a lazy cat, a tankful of pampered fish and three African clawed frogs (adopted after a Scouting badge!), plotting under the stars in her hot tub, cheering on her guys' hobbies of radio control airplanes and trucks, bowling and Explorer Scouting or indulging in her favorite vice—afternoon movies.

Don't Miss
Nancy Gideon's

Novelization of the Horror Movie

In The Woods

"Horror at its finest and most eerie!"—Midwest Book Review

In the woods a creature was buried centuries ago...a creature of unlimited power and capable of unspeakable terror. Unleashed upon the world during the Medieval ages, its rest has been undisturbed...until now.

Two firefighters entered the forest and found a grave. Not knowing whether they would find the remains from another victim of the serial killer stalking their town or simply someone's pet, they dug. The two men ran out of the forest that day, only to bring hell with them ...

"Horror and mystery combine to delight readers with a work reminiscent of early King." —The Mystery Zone

"Horror fans be on the look-out for this terrifyingly delicious novel!" —Vampyres

Coming Soon
From ImaJinn Books

Midnight Enchantment

ISBN 1-893896-04-8   Price: $9.95

After a 400 year existence as a vampire, Gerard Pasquale wants only to be left alone to shadow the midnight streets of turn of the century New Orleans . . . until blackmail binds him to a mortal bride who throws his dark world into an upheaval. Certain he can escape the unwanted bargain through the treacherous terms he makes, Gerard discovers his new wife may not be as helpless to resist his will as he at first believes!

Haunted by a whispered past of witchcraft and voodoo, Laure Cristobel became a bride out of necessity; to protect herself and the unborn child she carries. Though alarmed to find herself wed to a monster, she's dangerously close to falling in love with the man he once was . . . the man she hopes she can make him once again through her own magic skills.

Midnight Gamble

ISBN 1-893896-14-5   Price: $9.95

Against the uninhibited decadence of 1920's New York where bootleg liquor flowed until dawn to the sound of hot jazz and rolling dice, day-walking vampire, Frederica Lavoy is sent to bring her immortal love, the exotic and mysterious Eduard D'Arcy to meet her father's justice for crimes against humankind. But it it justice that waits, or vengeance, as an age-old enemy begins to manipulate both hunted and huntress? In this game of cat and mouse, the stakes are not just life and death, but the immortal soul.

ORDER FORM

Name:_____

Address:_____

City:_____

State___Zip_____ Phone*_____

Qty	Book	Cost	Amount

Total Paid by:		
☐ **Check or money order**	**SUBTOTAL**	
☐ **Credit Card (Circle one) Visa Mastercard Discover American Express**	**SHIPPING**	
	MI Residents add 6% sales tax	
_____ **Card Number**	**TOTAL**	

_____
Expiration Date

_____
Name on Card

Would you like your book(s) autographed? If so, please provide the name the author should use_____

***Phone number is required if you pay by Credit Card**

Shipping costs:
1 book $2.00
Each additonal book $.50
(Shipping prices for U.S. residents only. Foreign customers will be notified if we can ship to your country, and we'll get your approval of shipping charges prior to filling your order)

MAIL TO: ImaJinn Books, PO Box 162, Hickory Corners, MI 49060-0162

Visit our web site at: http://www.imajinnbooks.comQuestions? Call us toll free: 1-877-625-3592